The Music
of What Happens

John
Straley

BANTAM BOOKS / New York /

The Music of What Happens

Toronto / London / Sydney / Auckland

THE MUSIC OF WHAT HAPPENS
A Bantam Book / March 1996

BOOK DESIGN BY MARIA CARELLA

Library of Congress Cataloging-in-Publication Data
Straley, John, 1953–
The music of what happens / by John Straley.
p.   cm.
ISBN 0-553-09677-X
I. Title.
PS3569.T687M87   1996
813'.54—dc20   95-32036
CIP

Published simultaneously in the United States and Canada

Bantam Books are published by Bantam Books, a division of Bantam Doubleday
Dell Publishing Group, Inc. Its trademark, consisting of the words "Bantam
Books" and the portrayal of a rooster, is Registered in U.S. Patent and
Trademark Office and in other countries. Marca Registrada. Bantam Books,
1540 Broadway, New York, New York 10036.

PRINTED IN THE UNITED STATES OF AMERICA

BVG   0 9 8 7 6 5 4 3 2 1

FOR FINN STRÅLEY

who broke the silence

Once, as they rested on a chase, a debate arose among the Fianna-Finn as to what was the finest music in the world.

"Tell us that," said Fionn, turning to Oisin.

"The cuckoo calling from the tree that is highest in the hedge," cried his merry son.

"A good sound," said Fionn. "And you, Oscar," he said, "what is to your mind the finest of music?"

"The top of music is the ring of a spear on the shield," cried the stout lad.

"It is a good sound," said Fionn.

And the other champions told their delight: the belling of a stag across water, the baying of a tuneful pack heard in the distance, the song of a lark, the laugh of a gleeful girl, or the whisper of a moved one.

"They are good sounds all," said Fionn.

"Tell us, chief," one ventured, "what you think?"

"The music of what happens," said great Fionn, "that is the finest music in the world."

—James Stephens, *Irish Fairy Tales*

The Music
of What Happens

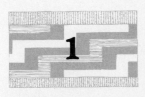 It was early spring when I was released from the psychiatric ward. In other parts of America the fruit trees were blossoming and the airborne seeds were letting go their pods, but here in Sitka, Alaska, the sticky leaves on the alder trees were curled like tight little fists into the limbs and were refusing to come out. A few gray whales had passed by the outer coast, and if I held my head just right out the window of the hospital's third floor I could hear the looping song of a varied thrush. But the shadows were long and the days still had that taste of winter, like the bitter iron filings that my medication seemed to leave in the back of my mouth.

My psychiatrist said, "Cecil, you've been through a lot. Maybe you'd better stay away from crime . . . as a lifestyle, I mean."

He stood in the window with the sun behind him. I was smiling as I looked at him, but I had no clue what he was saying. His lips were moving, the sun was shifting around his head and I could hear the soft rush of his voice, but I couldn't, for the life of me, turn it into anything meaningful.

People say I'm not a very good private investigator, but even so, I should have been able to understand the words coming out of his mouth. I'm a defense investigator, meaning I help people accused of crimes, so by the time I get involved—weeks, sometimes years after—all that's left of a crime is words. In my own defense, I'm cheap and I'm loyal, which I suppose is more than you can say about most investigators. But I'm not much good at putting clues together. A woman I knew once told me I would never amount to much because I had no regard for the truth and floundered helplessly in a world beyond the literal. She was wrong, sort of. I have a high regard for the truth, I just can't find much agreement about what it is. As for the "world beyond the literal," I don't know what she was talking about.

My doctor leaned forward and for some reason his voice snapped into a pattern of words I could recognize: "Cecil, it's called a transitory ischemic incident. Just try and say that, if you feel something coming on again. Your head injury, probably coupled with your past substance abuse, created a stroke-like seizure and it affected your memory, at least temporarily. You had a fluctuation in your neurological function that caused a deficit in the area of your brain that delineates cause and effect. You're not crazy . . . well, you're neurotic and a drug abuser, but that's not it . . . really it's . . . it's just . . . weird brain shit."

"Weird brain shit? That's your diagnosis?"

My doctor smiled at me and scratched the bridge of his

nose. "Most of the things we used to call insanity are neurologically based. I could coo over you and prescribe some drugs but it would still be . . . weird brain shit."

I liked this guy. He looked to be in his fifties but he seemed much younger. He was an anarchist, a salmon fisherman, and finally a psychiatrist. He wore a red T-shirt under his flannel jacket. He had a blood blister under his right thumbnail. The first good feeling I had once I started making sense to myself was that this guy was trying to tell me something he, at least, believed to be the truth.

My doctor looked down at me trying to make eye contact and his voice was soft. "Do you remember your head injury, Cecil? Do you remember the events surrounding it?"

I leaned back away from him. It had been a simple thing. Priscilla DeAngelo wanted me to follow her son, who was in the custody of his father. Priscilla was an old friend. I had a crush on her sister in high school. I had known Priscilla when she, her sister, and I were children. But that was thirty years ago and Priscilla was now locked into a custody dispute that was as bitter and heartless as a professional dogfight. Priscilla had hinted that she wanted me to bring her six-year-old boy back from Seattle where her ex-husband had taken him. I took the hint and her expense money but made her no promises. There has been so much of this kind of child surveillance and transportation lately they have made it a new felony: child stealing. I wasn't into adding anything new to my rap sheet but I needed to get off the island so I took her money and the two-hour jet ride south to Seattle.

I looked up at my doctor and didn't speak. But I did remember, and the memory ran past my mind like a filmstrip: I was in the parking lot of a large mall. I had been eating frozen yogurt. I watched an empty shopping cart roll across the lot and hit the open door of a minivan. The tiny boy in blue overalls and a T-shirt was standing beside the van door and when the cart hit him, his nose mysteriously, or so it seemed to me, started to bleed. I took four steps toward him, forgetting that I was not supposed to be seen. "Young Bob," I whispered, and stumbled forward. His father saw me, and the cart, then rushed at me carrying what looked like a wine bottle in a paper sack.

From there everything went from music to noise. I remembered the parking lot. I remembered lying on my back and staring into a field of sparkling bits, like dust caught in the light. These specks floated aimlessly, and I remembered an urge to wave my hand and circle them into some sensible form. When I did, the image coalesced into a large white man yelling, waving a wine bottle in a paper sack, and puffing his chest out at some teenage kid in a green apron. The cart was on its side, like a horse thrown down on the ground, the wheels spinning, as if kicking to get up. There was yelling and horns, the rattle of iron wheels bouncing on the pavement. The little boy had blue-black hair and white skin. The blood ran down his coveralls in dark spots like eighth notes. He looked down at me in that instant before he started to cry, and his blue eyes had that blank stare of recognition as if he knew I too was about to disappear.

He was scooped up in the arms of his father. The next I remember it was dark and a security guard was yelling at me as

I lay in the middle of a deserted parking lot. "Hey, you need a doctor? Hey, you need a doctor? If you don't, you gotta get out of here!"

"Yeah, I remember," I said to my doctor. Sitting in the hospital ward I had been nagged by the feeling that going crazy had been a disappointment. I had always expected a more dramatic purge, something along the lines of van Gogh at Arles, something full of passion and beauty rather than lying on my back in a mall parking lot with a boysenberry yogurt cone melting down my chest. The world was not an Impressionist painting but an ugly scramble of noise and dirty pavement.

My doctor looked at me with concern, glanced through his half glasses at his charts and then back at me. I watched his lips.

"Look, Cecil, you don't need the talking cure. Psychotherapy is a business that promotes the idea that your life is a story everybody knows, even before it happens to you." He looked around the ward. The kid with the shaved head and razor scars on his temples stopped spinning and stood still. The doctor leaned closer in to me and whispered: "But that's bullshit. This isn't a story. Your life isn't a story. No one knows how this is going to come out."

"Doesn't that bother you?" I asked.

"Me? Shit, no. I know it bothers you, but not me. I like talking to crazy people. But I don't really understand them . . . other than knowing that they are a little different."

He tugged his half glasses up to the bridge of his nose and looked down at my chart again. He had the stubble of two days' growth of beard and his skin was pink from one of the windy days out in his skiff. He said, "So, listen, you work as a private investigator, right?"

"I guess. I suppose I may have some business left."

"You shouldn't get anxious. Anxiety won't help you heal. I want you to do something light, Cecil. Reading would be good. Review some files. But try and stay in a stress-free space for a few weeks. Can you do that?"

Stress free. As my memory came back over the past weeks I had remembered some of my cases. I had one sex case for a private attorney, but he dumped me when I missed the hearing deadline. I had an insurance find . . . locating a witness for an insurance company out of Portland. But that wouldn't take long since the guy they were looking for lived just down my block and his number was plainly listed in the phone book. I was going to have a hard time milking that for hours. The best moneymaker was the child custody case from hell, but I thought I had blown that ride.

It had started six years before on the day the baby's father mentioned death in the delivery room. The baby was Robert Carl Sullivan III. Everyone called him Young Bob, even before he was born. Old Bob Sullivan was the grandfather and Robert Sullivan II ("Don't call me Bob") had married Priscilla just after they both dropped out of college. Priscilla and Robert Sullivan had the requisite fun as a married couple who enjoyed their status as honorary adults conferred upon them by their marriage certificate. But a few days after Young Bob's birth,

Priscilla left the maternity ward in the rain and came to my office wanting me to help her arrange a divorce.

She stood in the doorway, the rain sheeting down from the edge of my broken gutter. Young Bob was curled in his hospital blanket, his tiny coconut head cupped in a stocking hat. He was as red and angry as a scraped knee. I invited them in.

She stood by my stove holding him in her arms as she spoke. She would only look down at Young Bob. Her voice was low. Her fingers played at the edge of the blanket near her son's mouth. "I thought I might die," she started. "It hurt so much and they were talking about cutting me open to take him out. I couldn't let them knock me out. So I pushed. I worked hard. I never felt anything like it. Then all of a sudden he was there. He was so heavy, so beautiful, even when he was all gray and waxy. The nurse thought he might not be all right. But I knew he was. He smelled so fine."

I nodded my head stupidly and offered her something to drink but she waved me away as she sat in the straight-back chair next to the stove holding her son.

"The baby didn't cry for a long time. The doctor and nurse kept fussing with him. Robert was standing by my head, squeezing my hand. After a long time the baby started to cry and Robert said thank you to the doctor and that made me angry. I guess I could understand that—in the heat of the moment, you know—Robert would thank the male doctor and ignore me. But then Robert did something I can't make sense of. He leaned over me and he was crying, and he said, 'The baby looks dark, his skin, I mean, his features.' I asked him, 'Is there something wrong with that?' Then he said, 'This baby is going to die someday, isn't he?' Our baby was hardly breathing and he said that. Why would he say that? Why would he even think that?'' She looked at me for an answer. She looked across the distance of the small room and I could only shrug. Young Bob squealed, his tiny lips making a circle in his wrinkled face.

That was the beginning of Priscilla's need for a divorce. Something I could only guess at had happened in the delivery room, some boundary had been crossed on Young Bob's natal day and Priscilla wanted free of Robert because of it. At least that's what she said. She wanted sole custody with no visitation. That was the beginning of a marital jihad. There were lawyers and court dates. The judge tried compromises and efforts at reconciliation. Priscilla would have none of it. She fled the state with Young Bob the day after one judge had ordered supervised visitation and, worse, joint custody. Robert's hired detectives found her and the baby in a rented room above a Vietnamese grocery in Anchorage. This incensed Priscilla even more, so she had hired me to uncover the conspiracy in the Department of Social Services and the Legislature. She had lost her child. No simple explanation would do. In fact, after several years of fighting, no explanation would do. She really didn't want to know why the judge had given visitation to the father. She wanted revenge. After a point I think Priscilla wanted revenge more than she wanted Young Bob. I try to avoid kid cases but she paid my fees as I did the interviews and collected the documents. I read them to her over long luncheon meetings in a waterfront café. One guardian's report noted that Priscilla displayed "erratic boundary setting." This upset her so much she threw a cup through a window. She destroyed a tape machine after listening to one of my interviews, so I began to edit the tapes just so I could keep her calm. The truth of it was, I made up a lot of my reports. I know I shouldn't have, but Priscilla had been eighty-sixed by all the therapists and counselors in town so I was the only one left who would talk to her about "the case." The counselors were tired of "the case" and were waiting for her to start working on why she was so upset by her ex-husband's existence. But Priscilla never adopted the tone they were looking for. Therapy was only a strategy on her part to get Young Bob back. Priscilla had no intention of opening up. She spoke to the doctors only as a general might talk informally to the reporters in the war room: congenial but always formidable.

Robert Sullivan II had stayed in the Seattle area, working as the shop steward in the longshoremen's union. He had smart lawyers, so there was not much of his voice in the record. But the lawyers were eloquent. They characterized Priscilla in the code words for feminine excess. She was "shrill" and "unreasonable." The judges, the doctors, and all of the decision makers were, of course, "reasonable." They were also men. Priscilla began to see large-scale cultural prejudice in this. Eventually she saw a darkly shaded and labyrinthine conspiracy.

Whether Robert loved Young Bob I could never say. I had only seen them together briefly in the parking lot on that day of the bloody nose and the wine bottle on my head. They looked happy then.

My doctor spoke and my body jerked as if drifting off to sleep. "Anyway . . . stay away from trouble, Cecil. If you really want something, just come and see me. I'll give you one prescription and one refill. That's it. But don't get used to it. Once it's gone, it's gone." He stood and smiled down at me like a guy going fishing. "The drugs just make it so you're dopey and crazy. See ya."

He was out the door.

For some reason the psych ward didn't make you ride a wheelchair down to the front door. This was also a disappointment. I had been looking forward to the ritualized hospital departure where I could take my first emotionally oriented steps away from my wheelchair into a waiting taxi as if I were bringing a brand-new baby home. But that was not happening. The doors opened with a soft whoosh and I had about a two-mile walk home through a blustery spring day.

I wasn't depressed, which was also kind of a surprise for me. But my mind was relaxed and untethered like a lumbering zeppelin floating awkwardly in the fast-moving clouds. I reached into my pocket and took another Xanax, then another, just to be sure. I made it out to the road and up onto the bridge across the channel to town. Wind etched faint straight lines off the tops of the whitecaps, but the sun was out and clouds were light and hazy off the horizon. A group of oldsquaw ducks floated in the eddy behind the fuel dock. I began to reappraise my feelings about insanity. I was perfectly at home in this little island town: the fishing boats looked clean and well-painted, the cars were driving slowly without honking their horns. I could see down the street to the backdrop of the green mountain dropping to the sea, from the old post office to the Russian cathedral, from the retirement home to my favorite bar. The sunlight sparkled and seemed to bind the whole vision together, like a lively tune or the manic scattering of sun in van Gogh's paintings of the orchards. I had remembered being unhappy in the past, but here I was walking one step in front of the other, breathing in the salt air thinking, "What could I have ever been unhappy about? How could a person be sad in a world as lovely as this?" This was excellent medication.

Once off the bridge I walked the waterfront down the other side of the channel toward my house. I was humming a bouncy tune and waving to people I owed money to, for I now knew my insanity would be like Elwood P. Dowd's, in the movie *Harvey*, walking to his sister's house with a six-foot rabbit beside him and a pocketful of business cards and plans to have dinner with everyone he met.

When I opened the door Toddy was crying and Priscilla backed me up against the coat pegs. She held a broken-off dental probe to my nose and screamed: "I oughtta fucking kill you! I oughtta jam this thing up into the spongy part of your brain! You didn't bring him back and you let him get away!"

The veins in her throat were distended as if she were being held underwater. Saliva flecked off her lips as she screamed.

She jammed the dental probe into my nose so that I could feel it needling into my sinus. A thin line of blood snaked down the probe and around her knuckles.

The only thing I could think of to say was: "Priscilla, would you like to stay for dinner?"

Priscilla's family lived in downtown Juneau in a house under a totem pole. Her sister was in my grade and several times I had been invited to the DeAngelo home for dinner. This was 1968 and there was an aura of strangeness about Priscilla's family that clung to them like the smell of fuel oil from their leaky stove. Her father was a fisherman who tried to open a cannery business. When the cannery burned to the ground he salvaged enough to buy a large boat to haul fish for the other plants. Scandinavians dominated the commercial fishing business back then, so Mr. DeAngelo's Italian accent made him suspect. His skin was darker, and no amount of humor and friendliness would cut through the gloom of suspicion that seemed to follow him from the barrooms to the machine shops where the Norwegian fishermen would sit around the stove and make their spring plans. Mr. DeAngelo looked too much like an Indian. When his cannery burned there was talk of arson but when an Indian watchman dropped a cigarette into the rag bin of the competition's plant five days later, the Norwegians suspected DeAngelo must have been behind it.

The fire would have been enough to separate the De-

Angelo family from the community but there was more. Mr. DeAngelo had three children, one son and two daughters. The son was more handsome than anyone had the right to be. At least this was the opinion of the blond, blue-eyed daughters of the fleet. Ricky DeAngelo had a small gas boat and he ran supplies to Tenakee, a small village built around a hot spring some fifty miles from Juneau. He would load up his gas boat with cigarettes, groceries, gardening supplies, magazines, and chocolate bars, and haul them out to the retired miners and fishermen who had settled near the waters. At times Ricky would take passengers, and most often they would be girls just old enough to know what they were doing. Ricky was killed by one of their fathers.

He had been walking up the dock in Juneau with his arm around Dina Jorgenson. They were going to meet Priscilla and take her to the show. Priscilla was twelve years old and she was waiting behind the corner of the building to jump out and surprise them. She didn't think anything of the man hunched against the building with his hands tucked into his mackinaw. Ricky had a wild careless smile as Dina nuzzled in closer to him and he kissed the top of her sweet-smelling hair. He laughed ruefully when Dina's father stepped from behind the laundry building, with the shiny pistol pointing from the end of his arm, and Ricky was still grinning as he lay on the dock with a hole ripped in his chest, the gulls flying up in a screeching bluster. Dina ran up into the woods away from her father. Priscilla cradled her brother in her arms, wiping the dark hair out of his eyes, crying and speaking to him. Blood streaked his white cheeks from the tips of her fingers. Mr. DeAngelo found them there and tried to convince Priscilla to let her brother go, but she refused. When the doctor came with a black leather bag she only allowed him to put a dressing between her chest and the red faucet of Ricky's wound. The next day the headline in the local paper stated, "Italian Boy Killed in Waterfront Mishap."

Mr. DeAngelo ran his boat for a couple more years after that but he drank more red wine, earlier in the morning, until one fall some crabbers found his boat running in tight circles in Frederick Sound with no one on board. His body came ashore on Five Finger Light and the DeAngelos' house had black crepe over the front doorjamb ever after.

The DeAngelo house was peopled by women: mother, two sisters, and aunt. When I lived out the road during high school the older sister would invite me to dinner and the aunt had always offered to drive me home. I accepted partly because it gave me some more time unsupervised downtown before having to go back to my father's house.

My father was a judge and he ran a tight dinner table. He served the food that my mother cooked and carried to his place. My sister and I were expected to hold up our end of the dinner conversation. In my father's house, there would be no looking down anxiously into the food and avoiding the topics of the day. The Judge would quiz us on politics, sports, even the changes of the season. More often than not I would be stunned into silence when the Judge turned to me and asked if I thought the waterfowl were late in changing their plumage.

JOHN STRALEY

But dinner with the DeAngelos was always exhilarating. In our house the conversation flowed through the Judge presiding at the head. At their table, words sprayed around like a high-pressure hose let loose in the room: arguments, teasing, snips of gossip, and advice all came whirling around as the women reached across the table, standing up at their places. They would lash out in one breath with a barb that would have sent my sister and me to our room for a day, then laugh and ask for the vegetables in the next.

The DeAngelo women loved to talk about art and science. They worried their food onto the table in a procession of conversation starting at the store and continuing into the kitchen and culminating at the table. I remember garlic, butter, and red wine. The children were each allowed one glass of watered-down wine. One night the aunt and Priscilla got into a heated discussion on whether the fact that Einstein was a musician affected his opinion of quantum mechanics. Priscilla's argument ended with the premise that the violin was an irritating instrument and no one who played one could have a thought worth listening to. The aunt became agitated and spilled her wine as she was picking at a piece of potato that had landed on her lap. "But it's music, darling. It is music. You have to love God if you have been touched by music." I hadn't any clue as to what they were arguing about but I smiled at the mother sitting at the side of the table as she looked lovingly at her awkward and quiet older daughter.

This older daughter was Jane Marie. She was in my grade and she was the one who had invited me to share the meal.

THE MUSIC OF WHAT HAPPENS

Jane Marie DeAngelo had a powerful effect on me. At the time I thought it was just that she was beautiful: dark eyes and pale skin. It wasn't until years later that I realized I had been in love with her, but was too stupid and numbed by adolescence to recognize it. In the windstorm of talk at the DeAngelo table, Jane Marie always remained quiet. It didn't appear that she was shy or out of place, she just gave the impression that she had said what she needed to and would again, when the time came. As a teenage boy I was like a Great Dane puppy, awkward and constantly tripping over myself to please. I rarely had any conversations with her, but I remember clowning to try and make her laugh, trying desperately to imagine what I could say to engage her, so she would release me from her intractable power to make me act stupid.

After dinners Jane Marie would take me onto the side porch and show me pictures of her vacations out to Tenakee in the old gas boat. The side porch was glassed in and the siding was narrow tongue-and-groove fir painted with the thick lacquer they used to call "oil company green." On one wall of the porch was a picture of her father and brother standing on the dock smiling, their dark eyes glittering and sad, like ravens on the frosted winter rocks. Jane Marie did not speak much, but when she did, it was never sad or angry. She always looked me straight in the eye, which was something my family never did, so I couldn't hold her gaze. I remember once putting straws up my nose and shooting raisins out of them to impress her. This is not a pleasant memory.

It wasn't until years later, on the afternoon of my high school graduation, that I looked Jane Marie in the eyes and told her I was in love with her. But of course it was too late. She laughed, threw her hair back and told me to stop being dramatic. She walked toward the waterfront with her graduation bouquet of flowers and I never brought up love again.

Priscilla had the dental probe pointing directly at my eye. Toddy took one step forward from the corner. He was wringing the long tail of his shirt in both hands. Todd is my roommate and he's about my age in years. There is some debate as to what his mental age is. He put his hand on Priscilla's elbow and whispered to her, "I'll make us something that is exceptionally good. Would you like a cup of hot chocolate with some marshmallows? I could get that for you quickly. Then perhaps we could have some venison soup. Would you like venison soup?"

Priscilla relaxed slightly. Her features softened and the atmosphere seemed to brighten somewhat like the moon coming from behind a cloud on a stormy autumn night. She dropped the probe back on the table. I had tried to pick my own lock with it several weeks back and it had broken off in the key set so now our door stays unlocked all the time. That was fine because the key was lost anyway.

She said, "You don't know what it's like, Cecil. You just don't know what it's like."

That was true. I stood next to Priscilla and gave her a one-armed hug that touched her back and waist lightly. She didn't appear to have anything else tucked in her belt.

"Tell me what it's like," I said.

"It's all his fault. Him and his family. They never wanted me. They never wanted me in that crowd. They think because they've got so many connections they can do anything they want. They're gangsters. I hear now they want to make a deal. That means I'm beating them. I don't care what anyone else says. I'm not dealing with gangsters."

Here the shadow was starting to darken. I released Priscilla and walked closer to Todd out in the kitchen. He was pouring milk into a saucepan.

"Cilla, let's have some cocoa," I said. "We can't think of everything on an empty stomach."

She walked toward me and then right past. She stood in the window that overlooks the channel. My house is built out on pilings and the tide was high so you could hear the water lapping on the boat ramp underneath. She stood by the window and I saw her image reflected on the scene of the harbor: gulls swirling around the fish plant's outfall pipe, a seine skiff with a woman standing in its bow ready to jump to the dock of the marine supply store, the water rippling across the entire pane, highlighting the dark shadows that hung from Priscilla's eyes.

"What kind of deal do they want to make?" I asked her.

"Oh, I don't care. I'm not even going to find out about it. I'm not making any deal." Her fists were clenched. She spoke to the window. "It's just not right. It's just not right that he should have him and not me. My sister says I should compromise. She says I should be reasonable. Reasonable. *They* can be reasonable."

Priscilla never talked about love. She never used Young Bob's name, in front of me anyway. Priscilla always talked about justice. She was certain of the truth. She wanted rectitude and balance, but I never quite understood why. Or whether, if she got everything she wanted, she would have to invent a whole new personality just to keep her hatred moving.

Todd handed her a cup of chocolate that had marshmallows floating on top. Priscilla was offended by Toddy. Toddy didn't seem to fight against any label. Social workers had given up on the categories. He wasn't retarded, he wasn't classically autistic, and although he had an active and stilted vocabulary, he didn't really fit as an idiot savant. His file had his name on it. He was his own category. I think this is the real reason that Priscilla was uncomfortable with Toddy. He didn't fit into her multilayered conspiracy theories.

She also didn't like Toddy because he was on a vigilant search for the nature of Heaven. This seemed to Priscilla to be not only a waste of time but an irritating and threatening distraction. Todd's mother had died of hypothermia when Todd was a little boy but this didn't keep her from visiting him. She would appear in her old clothes if Todd hung them in a particular way above her shoes. On these visits his mother would tell Todd all about Heaven. Eventually she told him she was worried that he was becoming too concerned with Heaven and that she wanted him to live his life in order. On her last visit, Todd's mother told him always to tell the truth and not to worry. Then she was gone. Her clothes were empty for good, and Todd had no memory of any of the details of Heaven.

Todd took his dead mother's advice about telling the truth very seriously, but he had a struggle because nearly everyone he told his story to didn't believe him. They tried to talk him out of his beliefs. Sometimes he became agitated, but never violent. Todd had been in state custody for several months when I finally managed to become his guardian. Now his two passions were dogs and trying to read every volume of the *Encyclopaedia Britannica*. He felt certain these were the keys to his remembering Heaven.

But any talk of death seemed to anger Priscilla. She grabbed the hot chocolate and put her back to Todd, speaking to me rapidly.

"Cecil, I want you to bug Judge Gaffney's telephone."

"I'm not going to do that."

"Do you work for me or not?"

"I'm not going to bug the judge's telephone, Priscilla."

"The evidence is there, Cecil. Someone got to the judge. I know it was the Senator. I know it was. All we need is proof."

The shape of Priscilla's conspiracy theory was elegantly abstract. Almost like the recent theories of cosmology. The universe was bowl-shaped and the black holes were not eternal but emitted energy. For Priscilla, the courts, the Legislature, and the Department of Social Services were like black holes. She could never get information out of them and anything that went in funneled down to a secret that was abstract and infinitely dense.

State Senator Wilfred Taylor was such a black hole for her. Priscilla had peppered his office with Freedom of Information Act requests for his journals and his personal phone records. The fact that the records never were produced was proof positive to her they were critically important. I had spoken to Senator Taylor several times. He had been patient at first but later flatly refused to accommodate any request from Priscilla or me. Old Bob Sullivan, Priscilla's former father-in-law, was a friend of Senator Taylor's. Priscilla was convinced that the Senator had used his influence to corrupt Judge Gaffney, who had ruled in Young Bob's custody case. Wilfred Taylor was a state senator from Anchorage, a charming man who was routinely reelected largely on his strengths with big oil and the interior Native corporations. He was also a politically active Christian, who knew that free enterprise was the first of the "family values." I had stood in the hall of the state capitol and shaken his hand. He'd said, smiling, "There is nothing here. Tell Mrs. Sullivan or Miss DeAngelo, if that's who she is, that if this keeps up she will be making more trouble than any of this is worth." He shook my hand with a firm but fleshy grip. Then the elevator bell rang and the Senator moved into the crowd of suits reaching for his elbow.

Priscilla leaned against the top edge of my woodstove. She sipped her hot chocolate and looked thoughtfully down into its sweet steam. Her face changed once again from pleading to stony resolve. She set the cup down on the stove.

"Then I'll take care of this myself."

"Priscilla, you can't bug someone's office. If you end up in jail do you think you'll ever get Young Bob back?"

"Thank you for your concern, Cecil. But you and I are no longer associated in this matter." She was about four and a half feet tall but now she pulled herself up to every inch of it. "I will take care of this situation without your help, Cecil. I'll tell them what they can do with their deal. There's a plane to Juneau tonight. I will be on it."

She turned and walked down the stairs to the street-level boot room. Todd was standing with a cup of soup that he had held out in her wake.

The shadows lengthened on the bookshelves. It would be dark by five o'clock. But the sky was clear, so as the darkness came on the air above the channel seemed suffused with burgundy for a moment. It may have been officially spring, but I was still snoozing through winter. Todd put the pot of soup back on the stove and I lay on the couch. A Charlie Parker tape was playing and I had a book of poetry by Pattiann Rogers. I read a poem, then looked up to the shadows shifting down the walls, listening to the saxophone and the water on the rocks under my house. Toddy was using an awl and some dental floss to stitch reflective tape on a leather collar for his new puppy. The dog had simply appeared under our house one night. He had chewed up my plastic gas tank for the skiff and was retching some foul yellow substance onto the deck when Toddy found him. He appeared to be a very young Staffordshire terrier, maybe boxer mix. Todd had retrieved him and brought him into the house. They both looked at me with the same expression, and all of my resolve to live without canine company drifted away. Todd named him Wendell. As I drifted off to sleep on the couch the puppy knocked my bowl of soup over and started wildly licking the floor. I heard him start to chew on the spoon and I began to dream of flying across the Pacific in a hot-air balloon with Myrna Loy as she had looked in the Thin Man movies.

My lawyer showed up unannounced, just as I was swaying gently over a tropical waterfall with one hand on the wicker balloon basket and the other around a silver cocktail shaker. Dickie Stein stood over my couch and woke me up to my chilled living room where the fire had burned down.

Dickie Stein was a vision in his own right. His hair never lay flat and he always seemed to have his eyebrows arched in some comical expression. I know for a fact he didn't use drugs but he appeared always to be stoned. He was wearing a maroon Harvard sweatshirt, baggy shorts, and rubber boots that were rolled down midcalf. He had a sheaf of papers in his hand.

"How ya feeling, chief?" Dickie stared at me as if from a great distance. As the dream rose out of my mind he came more closely into focus. He had set a pan on the stove and Toddy was poking its contents with a wooden spoon. Then Toddy bent down and put some more wood in the firebox.

"I brought you some teriyaki moose. A client from Yakutat paid me off with what was in his freezer. It may have been a little old but I soaked it in sauce long enough that even an old boot would taste good."

"Thanks, counselor. Take a seat and we'll put on some rice."

"Yeah, well, that sounds pretty good but really I'm on the clock. I was looking for Priscilla."

"Gone. Maybe hours ago. I don't know. Catch her at the airport tonight. She's headed to Juneau to confront the Great Satan."

There was the low rumble of a jet aircraft rising above the water and the blues riffs. Dickie looked at his diving watch.

"Hell, man, you need a clock around here. It's late. That's the evening flight now. Why don't you have a clock in here anyway?"

"I'll put the rice on and we'll eat it when it's done. Don't need a clock." I reached for the mason jar full of rice above the cook stove. Toddy ran some water into a saucepan. Dickie flopped into a chair and thumped his boots up on the table.

"Christ, I wish I had got ahold of her. I just got this stuff and I think it will make her happy. Maybe it will even get her off my back for a little while."

I started the fire under the front burner. "That would make all of us happy. Whatta you got, her copy of the Zapruder film?"

"Wrong conspiracy, Younger. It's better . . . at least I think. Her ex, you know him, I believe—Robert Sullivan." Dickie looked up at me with a puzzled and condescending smile as if I were a sick bird in his hands. I rubbed my head where Mr. Sullivan had rattled my neurological cage with his wine bottle several months earlier.

JOHN STRALEY

Dickie picked his teeth with the corner of one of the legal papers. "Well, I've heard from his people finally. Maybe your encounter will do some good. His lawyers down in Seattle said that Sullivan is interested in talking about extended visitation with the kid, with the possibility of unspecified relaxed custody arrangements in the future. They will meet with Priscilla soon, if she will just calm down and try to be reasonable."

"Yeah, that could happen."

"Come on, help me with this. This is way more than she could ever hope for. We might be able to arrange supervised visitation at first, then get her into something more acceptable."

"Like her husband's head on a stick. I think that is her compromise position."

Dickie picked up the papers again and absentmindedly flipped through them. "The family suggested I contact her sister. Jane Marie. You used to know her, didn't you? She's some kind of scientist or something?"

"The last I heard she was a biologist. She has an old seine boat and does marine biology. She runs her own little mail-order business to fund her research," I told him, and flopped back on the couch.

"Christ," Dickie muttered, scratching his greasy hair with the end of a ballpoint pen. "Another eccentric. What is this, are there more eccentrics these days or just fewer normal people?"

"There never have been normal people. It's a myth," I said as I reached under the sofa cushions looking for an antidepressant I might have dropped while I was opening the bottle. "Listen, Dickie, there are just crazy people and statisticians. Of course, there is some overlap." I pulled up a greasy, lint-covered quarter. "But I haven't seen Jane Marie for years. I don't know where she fits in." I put the quarter in my pocket.

Of course I wasn't trying to ignore Jane Marie DeAngelo. Whenever her name came up I made a point of listening carefully. Jane Marie was working on humpback whales. She was documenting their feeding behavior and keeping track of their population numbers in the waters of southeastern Alaska. She wasn't working for any agency or university so she was funding her own work by writing a newsletter and selling games by mail. Recently she had been in the news. She wanted to establish a field camp at an old mining site and there had been some public controversy about her cleaning up the mining materials. Two weeks ago I had seen her picture in the paper. I had touched the photograph with my index finger, letting it rest there for a moment. She was still very beautiful, particularly for a crazy statistician.

Dickie had stopped flipping through the papers and was reading one. "This is weird. What do ya think? Robert Sullivan says we should deal with Harrison Teller as local counsel."

"Teller? He's out of Fairbanks." I poured the rice into a pan and Toddy moved to the refrigerator to root around for some vegetables. Wendell began chewing on the toe of Dickie's boot. Dickie grinned down at him, gently nudged him away once and then gave him my book of poetry to chew. I walked across and took it out of his jaws immediately. Wendell looked up at me with the cocked head and vacant eyes of a true poetry lover. I wiped the slobber off the cover and put the book back on the shelf.

"Christ, Dickie. Those nitwits in Seattle wouldn't possibly be aware that it's about as far to Fairbanks as it is to Russia. It would be like them having local counsel in Chicago. Besides, Teller isn't a member of the Bar anymore."

Dickie leaned back and put his boots up higher on a stack of magazines, trying to keep them out of chewing range. "Harrison Teller. This could be great. I'd love to meet him. I mean, the guy is a legend."

Dickie had just turned thirty-six. He had left Harvard Law almost eighteen years ago as the Young Turk who was disdaining Wall Street to make a name for himself in frontier justice. He made a point of not needing the cachet of the Ivy League. But now he was fast becoming a middle-aged boy in a backwater Alaskan town who was noticing that the eastern establishment was not exactly stinging from his rebuke. He had been wearing the Harvard sweatshirt more and more. Dickie hated himself for being so smart and yet still so vain, but that was part of why I liked him. I was about the only one. Dickie and I used to drink together, but now during the winter we eat together and watch movies on the VCR.

"They never reindicted Teller, but hell, that guy could make money just on phone calls to old friends."

Wendell was up on the couch now and audibly tearing at the maroon sweatshirt. Dickie set the papers down on the table and picked up the remote control and flicked on whatever movie Toddy had been watching on the VCR. The TV in the corner bookshelf flickered and the image of Cary Grant appeared running across a dark lawn after an unwilling leopard. Toddy sat down on the edge of the couch. His bulk sagged the springs of the Hide-A-Bed beneath it. His shoulders drooped and he cut up pieces of limp-looking broccoli into a metal bowl.

"*Bringing Up Baby*. I love this movie, don't you, Cecil?"

"Who doesn't?"

"Do you think we could ever get a leopard, Cecil? I know you don't really like large pets but I think I . . ."

"A leopard? Look at this dog. What do you want a jungle cat for?"

Wendell had torn a hole in the Harvard sweatshirt and Dickie stared down at him lovingly, patting his head as if Wendell had taken a great burden off his shoulders. He turned and patted Todd on the knee.

"There's nothing better than a story about rich people being chased by wild animals they thought were their pets."

I took another Xanax. On the screen the young and graceful Katharine Hepburn crawled out of a pond in her soaked evening gown. Water beaded like pearls off the tendrils of her hair as she talked lovingly to the flustered Cary Grant. The quiet settled into the channel and Bird's horn still sang in the background. Somewhere just past the point, the gray whales were burying their heads in the sand to feed on the thick mats of crustaceans underneath. The water offshore would be muddy, the air would be partitioned by the calling of gulls and the breathing of whales. If this life is only a dream, may I have kept on sleeping.

The phone rang and neither Toddy nor I could get up to answer it. The light of the television held us. After the third ring Dickie looked around. He picked up the receiver after he turned down the rice.

"It's Hannah." He held the receiver away from his face.

Hannah is a woman who was formerly in love with me. She unexpectedly developed a low tolerance for whiny narcissistic drunks. I started to rise but looked over at the couch and saw Wendell, tearing at a piece of the Harvard shirt, and then at the shimmering head of Hepburn. She was a few minutes away from the capture of the leopards in the jail. I knew Hannah was calling to see if I was still sober after my release from the hospital. She wouldn't ask directly but would be very breezy and commonsense about it. Katharine was stomping around the woods with one broken high-heel shoe in her hand.

"Say I'm building her a sailboat called the *True Love* and I'll call her when it's done."

"He's building you a sailboat called the *True Love* and he'll call you when it's done," Dickie said into the receiver. He winced as the line went dead, then walked back to the couch. "No message, I guess," he said, and sat down. Then he said, "You know he doesn't make her a sailboat in this one. That was another movie."

"I know that." And I waved at him to keep still.

We watched the movie through to the end, then started at the beginning. We ate the moose teriyaki with the rice and wilted broccoli. Wendell settled down after a bowl of dog food and table scraps. He lay on the couch belly-up as Toddy patted the warm almost hairless skin under his legs. Dickie drank a nonalcoholic beer and dozed off. I turned off the light and helped Toddy find his flannel pajamas and then I went to bed. I don't remember my dreams from that night other than something about a small dark-eyed boy petting a leopard, and a warm feeling that I was floating in a world bound by some sort of intelligent optimism.

I slept until the shadow of the gulls passed over my face and I received a phone call from the Juneau Public Defender Agency saying Priscilla had murdered Senator Wilfred Taylor.

"This is no game, Mr. Younger. In fact, right now I'd have to say that she is in a very tough situation. The Senator is dead in the stairwell of the capitol building with a crushed skull and Ms. DeAngelo is screaming to everyone within hearing that 'he was a' . . . let me look at this so I get it right . . . 'he was a gangster, a bastard, and goddamn right I killed him if nobody else would.' "

I was listening to the voice of the young man from the Public Defender's office in Juneau. "Was this taped?" I asked him.

"Yeah. Unfortunately the reporting patrolman had his microcassette running in his shirt pocket as he made the approach. Ms. DeAngelo's voice was booming out in the stairwell."

"Who was she talking to?"

"I don't know, but I got a short interview with the cop this morning and he got the impression she was either talking to herself or screaming at the dead guy. It was about ten-thirty at night. There were a few other people in the building. No one saw anything, but some of them heard an argument."

"Was there a weapon? Anything on the blood spatter?"

"Right now the scene looks consistent with him hitting his head against the banister post. There is hair and blood, there and on the floor. I don't see anything about any other spatter evidence. I'm sorry. I just don't know right now. My guess is the scene is consistent with an argument. That's why the statements are so bad. Also, her state of mind when she went there. My guess is they'll try and indict on murder one. If it really was just a slip on the stairs during an argument we may walk her out. Hell, they may offer manslaughter, depending on what her intentions were in coming to see the Senator. The more they make her out to be a violent person with a plan to hurt him, the worse it looks for pure accident, the better for homicide."

I held the phone away from my ear. Dickie had gone back to his office to start calling around and trying to figure out bail possibilities, and to see if Priscilla's family could come up with money to pay him. Even if he could get her out he would need to find a third-party custodian, someone who she could be with twenty-four hours a day and who could vouch for her behavior when; and if, she got out of jail. He was trying to find a phone number for her sister Jane Marie.

"Listen, I don't want to talk about it now," I told the Public Defender. I fumbled with the phone on my shoulder.

"We'll come over. You guys have got her at least through the arraignment. Dickie will come over and talk to her. We'll sort things out then." I paused and added, "Will that be okay with you?"

The kid was fresh out of law school and new to the Public Defender's office. He was trying to make a good impression. I didn't know him but I could sense that he was going to get bent out of joint if we swooped down and took this case away. A juicy murder with lots of press attention would be a relief from the sex cases and the drunk-driving cases.

"Yeah, that will be fine. I'll at least get an idea of what the discovery is and as soon as you get here we can have a meeting to see what's best for her."

I was right, his feelings were hurt already.

I put the phone down and looked out my window. Spring had disappeared. Although the water was flat in the channel the rain was starting to fall in large but well-spaced drops, making small bubbles and confused concentric rings. A crewman was wrapping a blue tarp over the pilothouse of his old wooden troller, where just yesterday he had started caulking and painting around the front windows. No matter what month it is in southeastern Alaska you're never far away from autumn. Fall hangs in the shadows even on the warmest summer days. It's like the background of gossip at a lively party—it's always there and you can't help listening to it.

I packed my canvas coat with the wool liner, my fishing rain gear, a change of socks and underwear, a flannel shirt, my shaving kit, my idiot-proof camera, a tape recorder, three waterproof notebooks, and some pencils. I was about to button up my bag when I went back to my desk and got the Gouker hunting knife, and my silver bracelet that Dave Galanin carved for me. It was a Tlingit design of a bear. Dave gave it to me to see if it would change my luck. I had a feeling this would be its best test.

Toddy and Wendell would be okay with the house. They could walk to the store. We had charge accounts set up there and Toddy didn't have to handle money. I didn't have to worry about a car since I didn't have one. I remember clearly the day they took away my license for the final time. The judge said, "Mr. Younger, we will all be seeing the return of Halley's Comet before we see you with a valid operator's license." So, no problems with a car. I called a cab to the airport. Dickie would ride his bike over and leave it locked to a tree in the bog behind the airport parking lot.

A few raindrops spattered down on a gust of wind as I got out of the cab, paid the fare, and pulled my bag over my shoulder. The clouds were low but there was plenty of visibility for a landing. The flight up from Ketchikan was in and a few of the passengers were milling around. These are short commercial jet hops from Ketchikan north to Sitka and then inland to Juneau.

I think part of the reason I hate flying so much is I have such a vivid imagination and very little understanding of how planes really work. I took a couple of flying lessons but that didn't really help. Modern jet airliners are held together with rivets in much the same way the old aluminum canoes at summer camp were constructed. Except planes have thinner skins. Once, I was carrying a canoe across the tidewater to the camp bunkhouse with a friend when he slipped and we fell. A jagged rock gutted our canoe. I heard the explanations that the little boat had been sitting too long in the water at the dock and the aluminum had been eaten by electrolysis, but this did not help as years later I fly at six hundred miles per hour above the coastal range of Alaska imagining the hollow aluminum tube I am riding in exploding into a blizzard of shredded aluminum and sheared rivets. With each pitch of the engine I imagine a severed hydraulic hose flippering around in the inner guts of the plane, the captain lazily tapping the gauge with his index finger just instants before the silent implosion of atmosphere, flame, and sharp rocks. I am not fun on airplanes. I've had people request to sit next to parents with screaming babies rather than sit next to me.

I took a handful of pills as Dickie and I passed through the metal detector. By the time we found our seats, the experience of flying in an airliner had a weird ironic atmosphere, like an experimental production of Gilbert and Sullivan. I looked at Dickie sitting by the window just as the flight attendant walked past checking our belts. Her makeup was thick, her eyebrows dramatic as a geisha's. Past Dickie's shoulder I caught a glimpse of a raven diving on the remains of an airline dinner roll that had somehow ended up on the runway. The raven hopped up on the rail of the baggage truck. He tore the roll with the tip of his bill, then looked straight ahead.

"Man, these are bad facts." Dickie was looking at his

notes from his telephone conversation with the police investigator in Juneau. He had drawn a little sketch as best he could to help him understand how the Senator's body had fallen.

I smiled as the jet pushed back. "The facts are always bad," I said. "It's best not to let that worry you." The shadow of the jet's wing darkened across the black bird. Its feathers ruffled in the wind and confusion of jet engines. It grabbed the roll and lurched into the air.

These were indeed bad facts for Priscilla. She had a motive to hate the Senator and she didn't offer any defense when asked about her participation in his death. His skull was crushed. There would be crime-scene photographs and bloody clothes. It would be worse still because she couldn't afford much in the way of attorneys.

Priscilla had come to Sitka to distance herself from family memories in Juneau. She survived the way many island people do by working lots of jobs and doing short trips as a deckhand on commercial fishing boats whenever she could. She had fished while she was pregnant but after Young Bob was born she looked for other day jobs where she at least had the hope of covering the cost of day care. She waited tables and processed fish, and even sold popcorn in the movie theater. All of this was enough to pay the rent of her basement apartment near the waterfront but not enough to pay for Gerry Spence to fly to Alaska to defend her against a homicide charge.

The flight attendants were going through their takeoff speech and I watched their gestures as if it were a ballet. For some reason their performance seemed fresh and sincere even though I couldn't really understand what they were telling me. Dickie was nosing through his papers and shaking his head. The plane rumbled to the end of the runway and from the window I could see waves breaking a few feet away on the edge of the causeway. The engines throbbed and the plane lumbered forward. I closed my eyes.

After dinner and his second martini the Judge used to like to hold forth. "The lawyer's job is principally one of a storyteller," he'd like to say as he introduced almost any subject. "And the storyteller is bound only by internal contradiction, and solipsism. The story has to be internally consistent and its reference points have to be commonly held and not unique."

"And the truth?" some unwitting listener would ask.

"The lawyer doesn't have to establish every common reference point. The truth exists only onstage, only in court. At the edge of the courtroom, beyond the evidence, there is no truth worth considering."

"And the judge?" continued the questioner.

Here he would smile at this and lean forward rattling the ice in his empty glass. "Since the law is not a game, the judge is not an umpire." He would pause for dramatic effect. Then, after his words had sunk in, he would continue. "The judge is the conductor of an orchestra. He is no mere storyteller. He shapes the proceedings, the pace, and the tempo." He would stretch his smile over his teeth and lean back with an aura of self-assurance that I remember would drive me to my feet and out of the room away from the sound of his voice. "The judge balances the sound of all the players. His judgment, his decisions, his insight shape the verdict," I can still hear him saying.

My sister used to be a great trial lawyer but now teaches at Yale Law School. She doesn't do trial work anymore but lectures students as if they were her jury. I have heard the Judge's tone in her voice sometimes when she speaks. I left home after high school graduation, having no interest in my father's orchestrations.

But even his death could not distance me from him. I was broke and a drunk while my sister was trying every major case in Alaska. She hired me as an investigator to carry her briefcase and run down witnesses, and she brushed me up on the rules of court we both had learned from the dinner-table lectures.

Now, of course, I hardly drink at all and the memories of my father have dissolved down into silly anecdotes or sentimental slush, but surprisingly, I am good to have around after a murder. Because as Dickie and I hurled down the runway in Sitka we knew we weren't going to get paid in full and neither of us cared one bit if Priscilla had murdered Senator Wilfred Taylor, at least not in any profoundly moral sense. Priscilla didn't need a judge to come to her cell. She needed help. Or as my father would say, she needed someone to tell her story, and if she didn't have a story she needed us to help her create one.

JOHN STRALEY

The facts were always bad but there were always more facts, and with those we would create a story that would need to be bound by more than internal contradiction and solipsism. The story would have to have some music.

The tires thumped on the tarmac and then the nose lifted and the weight of the plane broke free from the ground. The bridge, the cathedral, my favorite bar—for some reason all seemed like they were in different towns. I could imagine the salmonberry bramble where the raven must have been finishing the dinner roll but I couldn't think of where it was, or even if it was a real bush at all. The lifting of the plane forced me down into my seat and even though I could see the curtain of green mountain down to the sea, I had lost the thread of what it was, or where. The mountain had become a tiny artifact in my jumbled memory. Then everything lifted up into the rain clouds and disappeared.

The flight attendants came down the aisle with juice and honeyed nuts. The cart rattled like it wanted to hop up and down the aisle on its own. The flight attendants were standing facing one another and one was walking backward but I couldn't for the life of me understand why. They were smiling and unintelligible noise was coming from their lips. It was as if I had woken up in a foreign movie theater.

"Transitory ischemic event," I managed to say, and I smiled at Dickie.

"Of course," he said. "Of course."

The plane broke into the sun and I turned to look at the

islands of snow and frozen granite floating in the clouds. Dickie was digging in his briefcase.

"Hold on. Christ, Cecil, you should always have something to read even if it's just a short flight. You know it takes your mind off things." He jammed some papers with writing on them into my hands, which were folded neatly in my lap.

The plane banked and he turned toward me: the sun came over his shoulder and into my eyes. "What's your doctor's name, Cecil? I bet it's on that pill bottle you've got there." He reached over and took the bottle out of my jacket pocket. He read the label, then picked up one of the telephones mounted on the back of the seat in front of us and dialed a number. The plane rumbled and dipped into a lurching powered-down turn, falling back into the clouds for the approach into Juneau. I wasn't frightened any longer. In fact I was suddenly disinterested. The plane lurched and the seats creaked and I shut my eyes until the engines went dead.

When the plane stopped rolling I knew that I had to walk off the plane but I didn't understand how or why. My doctor appeared to be standing at the end of the gateway. I was concentrating on walking and only kept going forward because that was the momentum of the movement around me, and every time I stopped it seemed to cause unspecified eddies and confusion. My doctor was wearing his halibut jacket open and a gray flannel fishing shirt. He slapped me on the back. "Hey, buddy, looks like you're dancing *way* behind the beat. Just lucky I'm taking the next plane back and my service caught up with me here. Still got those pills? Let me see 'em.'' Then Dickie walked up behind me and handed the bottle to the doctor. Dickie was sucked into the wake of people and my doctor emptied out the last three pills into his palm.

"You aren't crazy, Cecil. You're just messed up. This prescription was supposed to last you ten days. It's been one day and it's almost gone. I'm cutting you off, pal.'' My doctor put the pills into his coat pocket. "It's for your own good,'' he said, and grabbed me around my shoulder. "After the effects of those pills wear off you're going to be a little irritable. Stay out of trouble and avoid confrontation because you're going to be coming down for a while yet.'' I must have looked sad or disappointed but his expression was gay. "It's a brave new world, but not for you, buddy.''

He sat me down in a chair in the baggage area. Dickie was arguing with someone near the baggage belt. The doctor was talking to Dickie at the same time. I looked down at the papers that Dickie had given me on the plane. At first they were black-and-white patterns, abstract and symmetrical on the page as if I were studying the inside of a hive, but the longer I stared at the markings the more rhythm I recognized until finally I recognized pattern and then the writing snapped into focus.

It was a nicely printed newsletter, with bold headline type across the top. THE PLAYING AROUND REVIEW: *A journal of the games people should be playing. Serving the arctic villages and the world.* This was a catalogue and newsletter of games: board games, party games, card games, and word games. It listed Jane

Marie DeAngelo as director and founder of the newsletter, and V. A. Meegles as administrative assistant. On the second page was a column headed:

Kissing Games: What to watch for in the nineties. I couldn't help reading, *We here on the editorial staff of the* PLAYING AROUND REVIEW *believe—indeed, hold as one of our guiding principles—the assertion that children's games are primarily about accepting the rules and adult games are about beating them. With this in mind, we approach the area of adult kissing games with a great deal of caution.*

Dickie came charging back out of the crowd and flopped down beside me. Apparently my doctor had turned me over to his care for I saw the back of his halibut jacket floating out the door. For a moment, it had that mysterious swirl of an apparition, but I finally understood its relation to the fact that the doctor was wearing the coat and he was walking away. Dickie looked at me, speaking straight into my face.

"Goddammit, Cecil. He said you probably had a little problem but you ate too many pills and made it worse. He said you'll come down soon enough. Christ, I don't need this. I need to talk to Jane Marie but I have no idea where she is. I haven't entered an appearance in Priscilla's case and the Public Defender is out for a fucking jog. To top all this off, you are sitting here in a vegetative state playing the Woodstock sound track in your head while I've got the first good murder case to come along in years."

I must have been feeling better because I understood everything Dickie was saying except the stuff about Woodstock.

"Here . . ." was all I said, and I gave him the copy of the *Playing Around Review.* "It has the phone number and address of Jane Marie's business. It's a street address downtown."

Dickie took the sheet of paper and stared at it with a quizzical, almost panicked look, as if I had pulled it out of his ear. I couldn't resist adding, "I'm damaged but I'm still a detective." Dickie crushed the newsletter into his pocket and walked toward the cabstand.

It may have been the drugs, but Juneau was a sparkling jewel of a city. There was no rain but there were traces of old snow in the shadows and in piles around the parking lots. The Juneau airport sits on the flat plain of the glacial till, and as we got into the cab I could look over to the face of the glacier grinning blue and white up the valley. I could imagine the Mendenhall River snaking down the muddy cobbles where it dumps into the estuary near pastures and storage pads and a rubber-boots-only, sand-green golf course. Some days eagles crowd the red alder trees. Porcupines and black bears nip and snuffle garbage that is left out on back stoops. Driving into town we'd pass helipads, national chain stores, a multimillion-dollar hatchery, and a health center. We were in the isolated capital of Alaska where the government comes to drink and make our dreams come true.

My luck was running good because Henry was driving a cab this day. Today he was wearing baggy sweatpants and a flannel shirt under a torn canvas vest. His insulated coffee mug swung in its gimbaled carrier as he moved the cab away from the curb. Henry has Russian Orthodox medals hanging on the dashboard and across the cab's ceiling. I knew Henry in jail. He had become very religious there and in fact had shown me a manuscript of his interviews with God.

"Cecil, you hear about the Senator getting his egg cracked?" He turned around toward the backseat to shake my hand.

I shook my head. Henry's cab smelled like a vinyl ashtray. Dickie was sitting in the front seat and rolling his eyes. Dickie grew up in a large town and I don't think he believes in the primacy of gossip, but being a trial lawyer he appreciates the power of myth so he listened quietly.

"Well, I heard Taylor was having, you know . . . carnal relations with some gal. He had a problem with temptation, Cecil. I know some of the guys from his church. All the time people in his waiting room would hear stuff falling off the desk. You know what I'm saying? I mean, he's doing it in his office during the middle of the day. This I know for a fact. You know it too, Cecil. These legislators come down here, away from their wives and all, and the temptation is just too much. I heard his wife was mad as heck. Anyway I guess someone caught him this time and the Senator gets his head smacked on the stairs. The cops got the girl but they're still looking for the second one. That's what I hear. Like I say, I know these guys, friends of his wife from church. They know this stuff."

Dickie turned back to the papers in his briefcase and Henry started fiddling with the radio. What Henry really knew about the Senator's death was the instant lore that hovers around a public murder. He didn't know any of the facts, he just knew the lessons that we talk about after a killing. Most of the lessons about murder concern the dangers of Sex, Greed, or Insanity. Henry was telling me to start with Sex.

"Drop me at the jail," I told Dickie. "I'll meet up with you at the Public Defender's office."

Dickie didn't look up from his papers. He half turned to Henry and mumbled, "Take him out to the jail at Lemon Creek, please."

There was frost on the jail's chain-link fencing. The frost had a nice effect on the razor wire glinting in the sun. A small crow sat on top of the guard tower. From there it could see the gardens and the basketball games, the fields where men in blue uniforms walked the fence line day after day with high-powered rifles. He could also see the estuary down to the muddy plain of the channel, the shoulder of the mountain, spruce, hemlock, stone, and ice. As I came closer, the crow tipped forward and flew over the concrete bunkers, over the green houses, over the walls, over the fences, where it began to ride the cushion of cold air down the surface of the creek. Unfamiliar guards asked my name at each of the locked gates and I made it into the attorneys' room without a problem.

When the door on the prison side opened, Priscilla stood quietly with her head down. The guard touched her on the elbow and she looked up as if out of a dream. Her hair was wet and stringy, hanging to the shoulders of her bright red jumpsuit, her hands manacled to a heavy leather band around her belly. She shuffled in, sat down, and did not look up. The heavy door slammed behind her and she startled. The interview room was now silent.

She looked up. Her lower lip was quivering and she had a small bruise above her eye that was dark blue, and sickly yellow on the edges. Her bottom lip was split slightly and she was sucking on it as she started to cry.

"Are you okay, Cilla?"

She tried to reach her hands to the glass that separated us but the manacles pulled her short. The chains rattled. She rocked forward in her chair, pressing her face against the glass, and began to breathe out low heaving sobs. Her face was flattened and distorted against the glass. Her nose was running and her eyes were shut hard and tight.

"Cecil . . . get me out of here."

I could see my own reflection on the glass, my face a mask over her contorted features. I put my palm on the window as if I could feel her cheek and she curled toward it, flattening her face even more against the cold glass.

"I found the proof, Cecil. But he destroyed it. I'm sure."

"Listen, Cilla, don't tell me what happened. Don't talk to anybody. No one. You understand? No matter who tells you how much it's going to help your case. Don't talk to anyone about what happened. Okay?"

She sat back in the chair, sniffling hard, her mouth turned down and quaking. She sat so low in the chair she seemed like a child. Except for the chains.

"Cecil . . . it's not fair. He admitted to everything. He had the list, the records . . . he . . ."

There was a commotion on the prison side: yelling and radios squawking. The door sucked open. The guard yelled into the room, "Okay, let's go! This is over. Out. Out. Out."

I slapped my hands against the glass. "Wait a minute. This is an attorney visit. Shut that fucking door, right now!" The door on my side of the room opened; two hands wrenched my arms behind my back, and pulled me from the room. I saw Priscilla being pulled from her side. Our reflections twined on the glass. Her eyes and mine were wide and startled. Then the doors slammed.

The shift sergeant's face was in mine. "You ain't *anybody's* attorney, Cecil. You can come back when you work for the lawyer that represents her, but you're not seeing her now. You got it?"

"This have anything to do with the bruising on her face?" I pulled hard against the two guards who held me. The sergeant nodded to them and they let me go.

"You don't need to worry about Ms. DeAngelo, Cecil. She is getting on fine. No questions. No photographs. You get out of here. Now."

"This has never happened before. You know I work for her."

"Well, it's happening now. You give me some court paper that shows you work for her and maybe I'll think about letting you back in. But a lot depends on how fast and how nice you get the fuck out of here." Again the sergeant nodded and the hands clamped down on my wrists and I was lifted toward the door.

This was the first time I had ever been thrown out of a jail. It went counter to my intuition but I struggled with the guards as they pulled me through the gates in the cyclone fencing. One of them knew me from my visits in the past. He whispered, "Christ, cut it out, Cecil. You're not a tough guy. I got a bad back. I don't want to tweak it just showing you the gate. Besides, you got someone waiting for you here."

When we got to the last gate the guards released me again but I pretended I shook free. I stood watching the guards' giant blue shirts disappear through the fence, adjusting my coat and posturing as if I had gotten the best of them. I felt a hand on my shoulder and turned.

A big man in a heavy wool coat that could have been a buffalo robe enfolded my hand in the palm of his.

"You're Cecil Younger, is that right?"

I stared up at the man's bushy beard and under the wide brim of his felt hat and nodded stupidly.

"I'm Harrison Teller," the big man said. "Why don't you get in the car so we can get out of here."

Teller put his hand behind my back and moved me toward a car with the unarguable force of the tide.

3

Like a lot of men who are larger than life, Harrison Teller had a symbiotic relationship with his reputation. He fed it, and it fed him. He had grown up in Jackson Hole, Wyoming, and had gone to Harvard undergraduate, then to Stanford for a degree in chemistry, then back to Harvard for his law degree. It was said that in graduate school he had been involved in a lab creating the early and highly expressive forms of LSD. I had heard his interest in criminal law had been spurred by the drug bust at the lab. He moved to Fairbanks during the pipeline boom and lived in a tepee, practicing criminal law and selling pot to the pipeline workers at prices that have never since rebounded. Eventually, he moved indoors and squared away his practice in a log cabin two blocks from the courthouse. There had always been colorful and dynamic lawyers in the territory, but Teller was the first of the new breed who had grown up outside of the tight musical-chairs network of attorneys, legislators, and judges. Almost all defense attorneys love to make a show of fighting authority, but Harrison Teller genuinely hated it. It didn't matter what you had done, he would represent you with a depth of passion and vitriol that would garner thousands of dollars in contempt citations with each trial. Teller didn't contribute to the Bar. He considered his fines his Bar dues. He hated to lose and he never made deals. His posture would be the same with his client and the DA: They drop the charges and publicly apologize or we go to trial. This always sounds good to a client early on in a criminal proceeding. Only once did the State drop the charges and they never apologized, so more than once Teller's clients found themselves on a faster and wilder ride than they wanted. Marshals routinely had to escort Teller out of the courtroom. In one trial the judge ordered him to be manacled to his chair by the ankles, the defense table skirted with green cloth so the jurors could not see the chains. Over the years several of his clients had cut deals behind his back so they could go quietly to jail and avoid having to stand in front of the bulging-veined judge on the day of sentencing. But generally Teller had developed a tough and loyal clientele. He was in-house counsel for the Hell's Angels, and somewhere in his riding kit every biker who wore colors in Alaska or the Northwest Territories carried a plastic bag with a quarter, a pencil, and Teller's business card. Teller defended Eskimo men who had killed members of their own family in drunken blackouts. He represented the white supremacists when the government raided their compound near McLear. He represented Alaska's fledgling Nation of Islam sect in a prison riot case. He drove a one-of-a-kind, four-wheel-drive

Mercedes-Benz that had been shipped from Medellín, Colombia. He wore two-thousand-dollar suits that he never pressed. After fifteen years of litigation his old tepee was set up in the backyard of his office, in the triangle between the wading pool, the swing set, and the cottonwood tree. He used it as a sweat lodge.

Teller had married a Yupik woman from the Kuskoquim Delta and they had a son named Ky. The week before his wife went into labor, Teller sat in his sweat lodge fasting and meditating to bring on visions. His wife's relatives attended the birth and after he cut the umbilical cord with his Swiss Army knife scissors, Teller rolled in the snow. Parenthood was the one thing Teller was not skeptical of. He showered Ky with gifts and luck tokens. He carried the baby on his back on the first moose hunt of the year and he read to him from Marcus Aurelius that first winter in the cabin. He even started taking on fewer and fewer cases because of the time he needed to be with his son. He bought a float plane and a cabin on a river a hundred miles northeast of Fairbanks where he and his family would hunt, pick berries, and sing together late into the endless summer days.

This was all before the killings started. In 1989 Teller was pressed by a family to take on a murder case. He defended a young white soldier who had strangled three Filipino girls, and had weighed their bodies down with old snow-machine parts and sunk them in the Tanana River. The military police had gotten a confession based mostly on luck and guesswork, because they really didn't have any evidence linking the boy to the crimes. So when Teller got the confession suppressed, their case fell apart. They went ahead with a circumstantial case at trial and he was found not guilty. Harrison walked out ahead of his client with his head bowed away from the cameras. The young soldier flashed the peace sign and went drinking with his buddies from the motor pool. The next week he was transferred to Germany.

Six months after that someone broke into the back of Teller's house and murdered his wife and baby: four .22 caliber slugs in each, two to the head and two to the heart. The baby had been wrapped in a blanket made from the hoods of twenty-seven arctic loons. Even in death Ky held his blanket to his ear, his thumb near his mouth. The father of one of the soldier's young victims, a man named Adolfo Camise, turned himself in to the troopers and he ended up pleading to two manslaughters with twenty-year sentences each, to be served concurrently. This was a deal so good even Teller wouldn't have turned it down.

After the deaths of his wife and baby son, Harrison Teller moved out to his river cabin. He drank and took drugs and shot automatic weapons off the porch so that most people were afraid to travel that section of river in the daylight. He might have just died there if the momentum of his bad luck hadn't kept rolling down the cliff.

A year after Camise was sentenced for the murders he was strangled in prison by an old biker named Lucky Day. Day had been a client of Teller's and was due to get out in fourteen months. He was seen wrapping a towel around Camise's throat in the laundry by a couple of guys who had worn snitch jackets so long they were comfortable with the fit. When the loop dropped around Lucky he gave up Teller, looking to cut a deal, which he eventually got. Two years after the young soldier was acquitted of three murders the authorities charged Teller with solicitation of murder and he stood trial in Anchorage.

The trial was held midwinter in Anchorage. It took on many aspects of the carnivals before Lent. Every day there were news stories and front-page profiles. To defend him, Teller hired a young Harvard graduate who looked to be about fifteen years old. The young lawyer was soft-spoken and awkward around the jurors. But he had the gift of taking his thick glasses off just at the right time during cross-examination and staring at a witness until, unable to remember the pat answer, the witness would start to babble. Lucky Day was on the stand for a week. Teller sat mute. He never spoke to the press. He never looked at the cameras. He carried the young lawyer's briefcase in and out of the courthouse. He never pulled on his lawyer's sleeve once during the trial. The jury was out for an hour and a half, then came back and acquitted Teller. Eight of the jurors offered to help the young lawyer with a civil suit against the state.

But Harrison Teller didn't sue. He moved back to the river. The DA in Fairbanks, who had for so many years been belittled by Teller, worked night and day to indict him on new charges. And from time to time he would. That DA eventually managed to have Teller suspended from the Bar for some tampering with his trust account. By that time Teller didn't answer his mail. He was out on the river, taking a daily sweat, and singing up to the moon during the nights that all seemed to be part of an endless winter.

Once when I was working in Fairbanks I met a woman who had been Teller's lover during this period of his wildest grief. She was an exotic dark-eyed Mormon girl from Utah. She always dressed up. Always. She correctly felt it set her apart from other women in Fairbanks. She wore heavy gold earrings and dramatic clothes that seemed to snap in the wind like banners. She had been asked by Teller's in-laws to check on him. We flew together one late summer day in August. The clouds were heavy and dark in the blue sky above the interior. The float plane rolled and dipped until we landed on the river near the sandy beach by Teller's cabin. We had been drinking for two days and she was wearing an evening dress that dipped down to the small of her back, with dark blue scarves lifting off her shoulders in the wind pushing ahead of the storm. She lifted her knees high as she walked up the beach in the soft sand. I could see her tanned legs as she moved ahead with an awkward cranelike gait. With one hand she held her hair away from her eyes, with the other she carried her expensive backless evening slippers. She walked up the bank into the thicket of willows downstream of his dock, where the pilot wouldn't go for fear of drawing gunfire from the cabin.

The pilot and I waited. I lay in the sand and watched the dark armada of clouds drifting in the immense sky. A camp robber lit in the willow near the end of the prop. We heard nothing but the river riffling against the floats until the girl came back and sat beside me. The scent of cottonwood drifted with her perfume. She kissed me very hard, putting her tongue in my mouth and cupping my thigh in her left hand. She leaned back. All she said was, "Let's leave this unhappy place."

This was my first good look at Harrison Teller in the flesh as he opened the door to his rental car outside the prison and motioned me in. His eyes were a piercing blue beneath the brim of his felt hat and above the wild growth of his beard. He had a stare that seemed to snap into focus when he looked at you and then softened once you started talking. It was a disarming glance, like the flash of a chrome pistol under a suit coat. The steel gate in the prison fence behind us clicked shut and I sat in the front of the rental car. Teller folded himself into the seat opposite me and turned awkwardly. He held out a bag of sunflower seeds:

"Seed?"

"No, thanks. Did you fix it so I couldn't talk to Priscilla?"

"Fucking bureaucrats. I can't believe it. Listen, if it were up to me you could have her all to yourself. I'm just looking out for her. I'm just trying to arrange some things. I couldn't let you talk to her. You understand it's nothing personal."

He started the car and we lurched down Lemon Creek to town.

"She's still represented by the Public Defender. Is that right?" I asked him.

"That's right. As of now, anyway."

"And you're not her lawyer?"

"I'm not anyone's lawyer."

"Where are we going?"

"Don't worry, son. You'll get your billable hours in this thing. But you're not on the clock right now, so don't ask so many questions."

The car was pulling out onto the only four-lane highway in southeastern Alaska. Teller accelerated with a force that threw me back into my seat. I wedged my shoulder against the door post, reached my leg over the carpeted hump, and tromped down on the brake. The car skidded and fishtailed into the side rail. Teller was pulled up hard against his chest belt but his head bumped into the visor, knocking his hat off. He showed a wild mass of brown and gray mottled hair. His eyes looked like welding torches as he reached a large hand over to my shirtfront and grabbed me by the scruff. I took the two fingers of my right hand and darted them into his windpipe just hard enough so he started to sputter, releasing my shirt. I grabbed the top of his hair and very gently tapped his forehead against the steering wheel. In cadence with the rhythm I was tapping with his head I said softly:

"I'm . . . not . . . your . . . son." Then I let go of his hair.

Teller sat over the steering wheel not really hurt but trembling with all the possibilities of what he wanted to do to me next. I undid my seat belt and unlatched the door.

"You don't know me, Mr. Teller, so I apologize for my reaction. But there is a long, long list of people that I have to take shit from. You are not on that list."

I grabbed his bag of seeds and got out of the car.

Being the only thing resembling a freeway in the capital city, this road is heavily patrolled. The flashers were on and the trooper was bringing his notebook out of the car as I walked up to him.

"I tried to tell him he shouldn't drive, officer. He's been drinking ever since he lost his job. There was nothing I could do about it."

I gave the trooper my card. He nodded and walked toward Teller, still humped over the steering wheel like a sulking bear. I didn't hang around. I stuck my thumb out and caught a ride with one of the guards from the jail who happened to be slowing down to check out the action. As we pulled away, the officer was asking Teller to get out of the car and was about to have him go through the field sobriety test. I imagined I was listening to the roadside litany of excuses. The "It wasn't my fault, you had no reason to stop me, I wasn't even driving and even if I was I've only had a couple of beers, because your machine doesn't really work, and even if it did you don't know how to work it" defense. The sun broke momentarily from a dark cloud. Teller was touching the tip of his nose with his index fingers as we changed lanes into the traffic.

"Cecil, what's up, man?" the guard asked me, looking into the rearview mirror.

"Fucking lawyer," I mumbled, and my breath steamed the side window. The guard rolled his eyes and leaned back into his seat as if I had said it all. He flipped down the visor against the sun, which was between clouds. I watched my own face in the frosted glass and suddenly mumbled something half remembered from school: "How I hate thy beams that bring to my remembrance from what state I fell."

The guard looked over at me, now confused, but still in basic agreement. I shoveled some seeds into my mouth, crunching up the shells and all, cursing my doctor, and wishing these seeds were my pretty Xanax.

To this day I can't remember the Associate Public Defender's name but I can recall clearly that on the morning I first met him he needed to wash his hair. His hair had those dirty hair horns from where he had been pulling at it all day in court. He was wearing a Blackhawks hockey jersey and baggy black shorts. His tennis shoes were unlaced and he was standing face-to-face with Dickie as I entered the room. I was out of breath because it had taken me forty minutes to walk from where the guard had dropped me to the hillside downtown where the capitol building and the courthouse stood across the street from each other.

"I'm telling you she doesn't want another lawyer." The Associate Public Defender was standing and addressing Dickie as if this were a mock trial. "She's bailing out first thing in the morning."

I could tell Dickie was feeling good about the fact that at least he was better dressed than this guy but angry because he didn't understand what was going on. "What the fuck do you mean, she's bailing out tomorrow? Bail's two hundred thousand dollars. Her family is coming up with two hundred thousand dollars and she is still qualifying for the Public Defender?"

The PD tugged nervously at his hair, twisting the ends

into little spikes. "First, I never said anything about who put up the bail. That was your assumption that it was family. Second, it's only her personal finances that are assessed for her appointment to the Public Defender. You know her situation. You know she could never afford a murder defense."

"Tell me who posted her bail."

"I can't. Attorney-client privilege."

I sat on one of the flea-market overstuffed chairs that were positioned opposite the gray metal government-issue desk. I pulled out the jockstrap and wet swimming suit that were under the cushion. The Public Defender looked a little nonplussed but took them from me. I offered him a seed and he shook his head. "What's Harrison Teller got to do with this?" I asked.

"Listen . . . fellas . . ." The PD sat behind the desk, which was about two feet under stacks of files. He precariously placed his feet up on an outer stack. He was obviously relishing the scene. A public defender's day is largely made up of humiliation and pettiness so he was going to glory in the small bits of degradation he could pass out. "If you want to know about Mr. Harrison Teller then you'd better ask Mr. Teller. But I'm not going to discuss my client's business with you. Without her permission, of course."

"What about it, Cecil?" Dickie demanded. "You were out at the jail. What does she want?"

"She wants out of jail."

"Don't fuck with me, Cecil. What did she *say*?" Dickie was hissing now as if he was about to suck a valve.

"Hey, she acted like she wanted to talk to me, but that was before I got bounced out of jail for not having permission to talk to her." I tried to give a hard-guy stare to the Public Defender.

He spread his hands in a practiced manner to protest his innocence. "I didn't do that, Cecil. I swear. If Ms. DeAngelo wanted to see you, that was her decision. I'm not playing games here. Look, you get her okay to have you guys represent her and that's fine. I'll turn over everything but not until."

I turned to Dickie, who was gathering up his yellow pads and files without speaking, but with short noisy jerks of his hands. "I got a ride partway back with Mr. Teller himself," I said with a mouth full of seeds.

Dickie fell completely out of character. "Teller! You met Teller? What was he like? You sure it was him?"

My stomach felt like I had ball bearings rolling around in it. I reached in my coat pocket for the missing bottle of Xanax. "Oh, yeah. It was him. I think I made a very good impression on him."

Dickie stepped closer to me. He squinted into my eyes. "Cecil—the doctor took those pills away from you, right?"

I copied the Public Defender's hand gesture of innocence, palms up, eyes wide. "No pills, okay? Really, I think in a couple of years Mr. Teller will look back on our little interaction and laugh."

Dickie slammed down his briefcase. "Great! I don't have a client. I can't get a straight answer out of pencil dick here . . ." He gestured to the smiling young barrister who was now fussing with his hair by looking at his reflection in the window. "But to compensate for this lack of information I get to work with a brain-damaged investigator." He glared at me as if I were a dog turd on the carpet that he was refusing to clean up.

I held my hands prayerfully before my chin. "Don't you love this job?"

Dickie snatched up his case and whirled to get the attention of the man at the desk. "What time did you say the bail hearing was?"

The Public Defender kept staring at his own image reflected on the window. "Uh, I'm not really sure. I'm pretty sure it's first thing in the morning." He deigned to glance at one of the files under his feet. "Yeah, that's it. Tomorrow, eight-thirty."

"Who's it in front of?" Dickie had one foot out the door. I was still sitting back chewing the shells. One of an investigator's important duties is not to step on the dramatic exits of the attorney he works for.

"Judge Gaffney." The kid looked flatly up at Dickie, like a bad poker player trying to conceal his glee after he looks at his draw.

Dickie slammed the door and we sat in the silence of its rebuke.

The Young Turk kept looking at the window. I looked out past it to see that the weather had changed. A woman carrying a sheaf of papers across the street to the capitol building was bracing herself against the wind. She tried to keep her hat on and at the same time hold the stack of loose papers. She stumbled on the curb and the entire mess flew away like cottonwood leaves fluttering down the pavement. A raven sat in the parking lot across from her, squawking wildly with its hackles up.

I looked at the young lawyer. He was now trying to make his hair lie flat. I said: "Ah, life. The older I get, the more I like it."

He gaped at me as if he had just woken up. "Huh? . . . Yeah." Then he focused on me for the first time and leaned forward. "Hey, Cecil, looks like you've been lifting weights. What's your max?"

The woman across the street was down on her knees grabbing at one piece of paper with her hand while teetering on one knee to keep her foot on another. Her blue hat had rolled down the street and the raven was sitting on top of it. I got up and walked outside.

"Let me help you with this," I called out to her. I worked downwind from her, grabbing her hat and then scooping pieces of paper as I went upwind. She was muttering under her breath, trying unsuccessfully to balance the pile of papers and pick up the single page under her foot.

"Goddammit to hell," she muttered between clenched teeth. Then she looked up at me, embarrassed, relieved. "Can you believe it? I almost had it made. Then I tripped and the wind came up. They said to get these papers over to the other office quickly . . . I . . . I . . ." Her voice was starting to make the turn from anger to panic.

I stood on the corner of the paper under her foot and put my hand on her biceps. With my free hand I offered to help her up.

"Thank you." She stood and I held out the papers to her. The wind blustered down the canyon of the street between the courthouse and capitol. The clouds were darkening to granite, sweeping from the south up Gastineau Channel. The raven hopped twice off the curb and then flew down Fifth Street out toward the docks. As the woman straightened up, she tried to dust off her knees where her stockings were torn and sagging. Her hair whipped above her head as I handed her the blue hat. Her eyes were red and tired. She looked at the rumpled papers and started to cry.

"Oh, Christ. Oh, Christ almighty. They'll say I can't do anything right. They'll say I should take time off. They'll say I'm too emotional. And you know what?" she sputtered out as she wiped her nose with the tips of her gloves. "They're right. I shouldn't be doing this stuff. I should be . . . somewhere else. But . . . but . . . everything has been in such chaos with the police and the reporters . . ."

"I can only imagine." I heaved my elbows up and tried to offload the papers into her arms. Another gust of wind hit, blowing grit into our eyes, and we stumbled against each other. "Let's get out of the weather and I'll help you sort this out."

"Oh . . . oh . . . really that's quite all right. They told me to just move these from the Senator's office." She was starting to cry again as we crossed over to the capitol steps. "They told me just to move them. But I guess it would be okay. We can go back to the office and sort them. I'll be late with it but then they should have had someone help me in the first place."

She stopped talking and looked embarrassed again, aware she had been caught speaking her internal dialogue. Someone else held the doors open and together we backed into the foyer of the capitol building and out of the wind.

I handed her the papers. "Your name is Rachel, isn't it?"

She looked a little startled, then wiped her nose again, making the extra effort to pull herself together. Her skin was flushed pink, her lips red. She seemed younger now than I remembered. "Why, yes. You know, you look familiar to me, but I'm sorry . . ." Her voice trailed off.

"That's okay. My name's Cecil. We met long ago at a party, I think. Don't worry, I'm forgettable."

Juneau's capitol building is not very prepossessing. In most American cities it would be mistaken for a public library. Rachel and I walked up the marble stairwell. As we came to the third landing, she backed away, startled, like a high-strung horse seeing something in the shadows. She gestured forward to the corner post of the stairs. Softly she said, "This is where it happened."

The post was a carved stone column. The cap was rounded but at the very top was a one-inch dimple the thickness of a pencil. The post had been thoroughly cleaned but up on the banister traces of fingerprint powder still clung. At the landing was a faint chalk line near a rubber mark that could have been made by a shoe heel. I looked around and saw nothing more that looked like a crime scene, but as we mounted the next stair I saw in the far corner, under the iron radiator, the faint brownish-red smear of the Senator's blood that had been missed by the janitor's sponge.

At the office, a large white man with folded arms stood beside the door. He was wearing a blue suit his mother bought him for confirmation some thirty years ago. Next to him, taped to the wall, was a hand-lettered sign reading *Out of respect to the Family all inquiries and business will be handled in our Annex Office. No members of the Press are allowed on these premises.* Rachel nodded to the living doorjamb and said, "I'm okay, Tom. He's just helping me with these papers." She spoke very slowly. Tom looked at me as if I were the spare part for the copier and then shook his head.

Inside were several young men in white shirts with their ties loosened, looking over notebooks. In the corner was a paper shredder that was quiet but had a box overflowing with tiny ribbons of documents. On the window seat watching the storm move up the channel sat an attractive older woman. Her gray-blond hair was pulled back. She wore a dark business suit with a plum-colored blouse. Rachel moved to a small desk in the corner and dumped the array of papers. The woman on the window seat looked away from the storm with little interest. Rachel studied her carefully before she spoke. "Hi, Barb. The wind scattered these papers. I brought them back to straighten them up." The blond woman turned back to the window without speaking. She reached absently for a lit cigarette in an ashtray near her knee. Rachel moved close to my ear and whispered, "That's Ms. Taylor, the Senator's wife . . . er . . . widow."

The door to the inner office that had been Senator Taylor's private room opened. Three older white men in black suits stood huddled together near the computer terminal. Harrison Teller sat in the chair opposite the big mahogany desk. He had his heavy coat on and his hat was hung on the tip of his foot. He was leafing through two or three papers. He glanced up and his eyes met mine through the open door. As he lowered his hands I could see that the papers were lists that could have been names and addresses. Teller looked at the woman sitting on the window seat who was now watching him; she nodded her head and then looked back out the window. With his index finger Harrison Teller made a beckoning gesture to the aide who had opened the door to ask a question. The aide stepped in and closed the door.

I knew I was about to be tossed out but I needed to figure out what I was going to take with me. I put my hand on Rachel's elbow. "I can't believe you have to move out of the office so quickly!" I said.

Her attention stayed on the papers. "Well, nobody's kicking us out. They just want to get Senator Taylor's affairs in order."

"Just get him out of here!"

The voice blurted out from behind the closed door. Everyone except the Senator's widow looked up, wondering what storm was coming. I had a few seconds left.

"Is that really a paper shredder?" I asked Rachel. "I don't think I've ever seen one."

Rachel was trying to flatten out one of the rumpled papers. "Yeah," she said with some exasperation. "Some men brought it in the night that Senator Taylor was . . . the night of the accident. They use it. I don't have anything to do with it." She looked up at me and smiled sweetly.

The door opened and one of the older men stood in the doorway. He spoke with a thick, stern tone. "Rachel, will you come in here a moment, please?" He stood back from the doorway and the young aide came out toward me. Behind them both I could see Harrison Teller's hat bobbing up and down on the toe of his boot. Rachel went into the office. Teller did not look up at her as she walked in but was watching me as the door shut softly without a sound.

The aide came forward. "I'm sorry, but we're very busy here," he told me. "I'm going to have to ask you to leave. If you have any business with the office you can come over to our annex headquarters. We should be open next week sometime. So, please. I . . . need to ask you to leave."

The kid was scared. He was obviously not the one paid to be the tough guy. He got his check for kissing ass, not kicking it. I walked to the door and smiled. "Please say good-bye to Rachel," I told him. The kid nodded and followed me out the door. I walked to the stairs and looked back. I saw him talking to the buffalo named Tom at the door. As our eyes met Tom stretched his suit front tight, not missing the chance for an aggressive display, even if it was too late.

Intermittent rain was falling on the windy street. The drops spattered on the dry sidewalk with a muffled ticking that seemed to build in rhythm, until the clouds smothered the sun and the wind whipped the entire street with water.

In some parts of the world a spring shower is a soft exhilarating experience, but here it feels like ball bearings falling from the sky. I took a deep breath and walked down the capitol steps toward the courthouse. In the glass-enclosed entryway I saw Jane Marie DeAngelo.

She was reading the notices on the bulletin board, eating a candy bar, wearing a black linen shirt and brown canvas painter's pants. I could never have predicted my reaction when I saw her again. There was nothing extraordinary when I first saw her but I shivered as I walked down the steps. I started to walk past but I looked back. She was chewing thoughtfully, not looking out the window but staring up at the wall where the ragged ends of flyers waved in the air from the heating ducts. She nodded, her expression engaged with something beyond what she was reading as if she were imagining a pleasant future or trying to discern something on the horizon.

She had close-cropped black hair that was longer on top so there were dark strands pushed slightly in front of her eyes. The eyes were a dark blue and they drooped in a way that gave her the look of a sad-eyed angel. She wore gold earrings with blue stones set in the center. As she stood chewing and smiling, looking off past the wall of hand-drawn advertisements, I couldn't help thinking about how beautiful she had looked on that afternoon years ago when she had laughed at me and walked away. I stood in the rain without feeling the small stream of water start to go down my neck.

When I was a young narcissist I had an almost overwhelming faith in the power of ardent love. I would re-create myself into almost any role in order to breathe in the atmosphere of romance and sexual promise. I was at times a clown, a sulking bully, an aesthete, and a jock, and today I'm a detective. I will say anything, and become anyone, in order to ingratiate myself with a beautiful woman. But here I was with this storm coming on, having re-created myself into this tired shell, and you might have thought I had learned something from experience. I didn't want to, but I walked across the rain-drenched street to the courthouse and knocked on the glass.

 I stood in the entryway with my wet hair plastered to my head. She looked at me without recognition. Then concentration broke away as if she were waking up. I held her gaze for a moment, then my eyes flickered down.

"I'm sorry. Did I interrupt you?" I said to my feet.

"No . . . no." She shook her head, looking down slightly to see who I might be speaking to. She looked embarrassed and I panicked for a moment, worried I had brought her unwillingly out of her thoughts. She shifted on her feet and her profile changed its curvature.

"Hey! You look like somebody I used to flirt with," she said in astonishment. "Are you?"

I honestly couldn't think of the right answer.

"I think so," I said with conviction.

"Cecil! I was just thinking about you. What has it been, twenty-five years?"

"I don't know," I replied in another dazzling display of wit.

Once, after my mother finished reading a John Updike novel, she asked me if it's true that men are always thinking about sexual intercourse. She was sixty-two when she asked me, forty years into her marriage with my father. I was twenty-six, and I had probably been thinking about sexual intercourse when she asked, so I'm sure I ducked the question. But her question sticks with me. For the truth is, I used to think about having sex all the time and because now I don't, I'm beginning to worry. Where once I always walked in a fog of sexual urgency, now I just get moments that feel like the flu coming on and I'm more likely to be relieved when they pass. But there are still moments when I meet someone, or even just pass them in the street, when my intellect unplugs and all of my reason is encoded on the surface of my skin, as if my brain were dusting my genitals with a feather. Whenever this happens I have a hard time talking.

"No. I was just, you know, I just didn't really recognize you. But now, of course, I do. Because . . . you're Jane Marie, right? You're Jane Marie DeAngelo. Of course you know who you . . . are. . . ." My voice drifted away into the sound of the rain striking the glass.

Jane Marie stepped forward and said, "That's weird because, you know, I've thought of you a lot over the years but you never . . . just appeared before."

She smiled at me. Silence. My mind was blank. She looked slightly panicked as if she didn't know what to do with me standing like a stunned animal in front of her. My sexual urgency began to turn to awkwardness, crawling up my leg as if I were sinking into a pool of asphalt. I knew if I just thought hard enough I could think of something sensitive, and at the same time witty, that would turn the momentum back around and break the silence with some gay, knowing laughter. Instead I said, "Your sister is in jail for killing a state senator."

This is not exactly what I could have hoped for in an icebreaker. Jane Marie's eyebrows arched and her sad Elvis eyes narrowed at me, trying, I think, to determine if this was just a very badly executed attempt at humor.

"She's getting out tonight," she said through a confused smile.

"Tonight? Are you sure?"

"I just spoke with a man named Harrison Teller. He said Priscilla would be at my house for dinner. In fact, I was going to go shopping for dinner. In fact, I've got to go. I'm supposed to meet my Aunt Edith and . . . I'm supposed to meet Edith." The raven who had harassed Rachel was finished with the bread. It waddled back and forth in front of the glass door, with its comic poking gait. It chortled with that oddly echoing sound we could hear through the glass. We both stood still and watched it, unable to turn away. This is the creature who created the world: the thief and the trickster. Raven is like a boardwalk fortune-teller—he always tells the truth, only in his own way. I knew what his advice would be. Go for food. Stay with the pretty woman.

"Great," I said. "I'll help you shop."

THE MUSIC OF WHAT HAPPENS

"No. Really. I don't need any . . ."

I held the door for her, then feeling that might be incorrect, I tried to go through the door ahead of her and we bumped under the door frame. I felt her breath on my face. She was laughing.

"Well . . . well, I guess I could use your help," Jane Marie DeAngelo said through her laughter. "But we'll have to be quick. I want everything nice for when Priscilla gets there."

Aunt Edith had a fierce grip on the shopping cart. Jane Marie and I walked on each side of her as she wheeled past the meat case toward produce. Edith was picking through green and yellow peppers and Jane Marie was trying to tell me about the arrest of her sister for murder.

"My God, I can't believe the price they want for these peppers!" Aunt Edith exclaimed.

"They wouldn't let me see her, Cecil. They wouldn't tell me anything. At the jail they said she couldn't have visitors."

"How many will there be for dinner?" Aunt Edith looked at me suspiciously as she asked.

"I don't know, Edith. Five or six, I suppose. You . . . have other plans, I'm sure?" Jane Marie looked at me and I shook my head, stupidly thinking I was declining an invitation.

In my family we heard more than what was being said. In Priscilla and Jane Marie's family everyone was used to being ignored, at least part of the time, so a conversation had the characteristic of concurrent monologues. The DeAngelos always appeared to communicate through a code of non sequiturs.

"Six for dinner, I think," Jane Marie told her aunt, still looking at me.

"Well, I'm not paying what they want for these peppers. I'd have to draw on retirement. Beets. No. I suppose we could have broccoli?"

"Yes."

I waited and Edith turned the cart like a barge toward the head lettuce and bunched vegetables. I waited to see if there was any more discussion of dinner. Edith was grimacing at the limp-looking broccoli. Then I asked Jane Marie, "Did the police talk to you?"

Jane Marie squinted at me, drifting a moment in memory. "Last night . . . last night?"

"Outrageous!" Edith wheeled away. She had left a yellow pepper in the broccoli pile. Absentmindedly, Jane Marie picked the pepper up.

"They asked me questions. What did I know about Priscilla and her feelings about the Senator? What did Priscilla tell me about what she was planning to do? But I got the impression they were mostly interested in what she knew about the Senator."

"Could you tell them anything?"

"Tell me this," Edith piped up from the fish case behind us, "what do you think of fresh halibut? That is, if it's fresh."

Jane Marie looked straight at me. "Halibut is fine. No. I wish I could have told them something. But really . . . Cecil, I don't know a thing. I know Priscilla thinks the Senator was responsible for Young Bob being taken away. She believes the

Senator was at the heart of some kind of conspiracy or something. To tell the truth, I don't listen all that well when Priscilla
starts in on her theories.''

"All right. Five pounds. Five pounds of *fresh*.'' Edith was
poking her nose at the glass case. Jane Marie held up three
fingers to the man behind the counter. He nodded and took a
piece of halibut off the scales.

"Did they ask you anything that seemed odd?''

Jane Marie took the yellow pepper to the others. "They
asked a lot of questions about Priscilla's husband . . . Robert.
They wanted to know if I had seen him recently.''

"Have you?''

"Robert? Robert? You don't mean he is coming to dinner
too!!'' Edith was between us now.

Jane Marie backed up. "No. No. I haven't seen Robert. I
don't know . . .'' She walked hastily down the aisle around
the corner formed by the cases of bottled salad dressing. Edith
turned the firehose of her stare on me.

"Now I remember you. You're the young man who always
sulked at the dinner table, then acted silly whenever you
thought we wouldn't notice. Whatever happened to you? Did
you ever have a thought worth having?''

Edith smelled of a fragrant powder I could dimly remember. I thought of the damp smell of their house and of windows
open on a rainy day. Her head had a slight tremor; her expression was both stern and comical.

"She's lying, you know,'' Edith said firmly.

"What?''

"Just how many people do you think will be at dinner?"

Jane Marie came back around the corner almost bustling with her concentration on the floor. She stopped close to me and made an effort to look up. Edith was silent and was smiling at both of us.

"You know. There was this one policeman. . . ." Jane Marie shifted from one foot to the other. "He had a dark suit and an expensive haircut. He looked like he was from out of town. He insisted that my interview not be taped and this caused a problem for the policemen. Do you think that means anything, Cecil?"

"He could have been a federal officer, FBI or something. They don't like to tape. Did they?"

"Did they what?" Edith stood between us with her bird-like head swiveling back and forth.

"Did they tape you, Jane Marie?"

"Yes." Jane Marie was now more nervous. The clatter of the store arched up around us like the night sky and it seemed uncomfortably silent. Finally, Edith turned. "Lemons. I don't see how they could screw up a lemon." She stalked away from us.

Jane Marie's shoulders sagged and her arms hung limply as if she had been ambushed by an inexplicable grief. I touched the tips of her fingers and she took my hand. She looked up. Her dark eyes were brimming with tears.

"Cecil, I think you should really get going. I don't want to keep you here. Please, I can handle this."

She hugged me and I felt the curve of her back through

her sweater. I looked down the aisle and I saw Young Bob running up to Edith's cart.

Priscilla's son was carrying a huge box of cereal. "Can I get this?" He held it up and Edith squinted at it as if he were holding up a dead cat.

"That's not food, angel. I said you could get some food. Your mother would never—"

Young Bob looked up at me. At first he was puzzled and then he laughed, pointing. "Hey! You're the guy Daddy bonked on the head!"

Jane Marie took me by the elbow and turned me toward the checkout counter. "We'd better get going. Ah . . . you and I should clean up the house before dinner."

I looked over my shoulder and saw Young Bob slam-dunk the cereal into the shopping cart and heard Edith whispering something about "just between the two of us."

Jane Marie DeAngelo's house was up a long flight of stairs that runs up the side of the mountain. It was the same house her parents had lived in and the same house of my uncomfortable teenage dinners. It was the last house on an iron staircase that had landings for a half-dozen other houses. Behind the house was a narrow lane that cars could drive in all seasons except when there was slick winter ice. Jane Marie had cut up the house into apartments after her mother had died. She rented out two apartments on the top floor but kept a small apartment and office for herself on the bottom. The old glassed-in porch where we had sat as kids was now the common entry for all the apartments. We walked in and I recognized the smell: candle wax and faint mildew. The walls were still oil-company green. The memory was coming back so strongly I felt I might be shrinking. I looked around for differences. On the interior wall photographs showed humpback whales, their tails rising up out of the water. There was a sign on the outside door that read *Playing Around Review*.

Jane Marie took her coat off and hung it on a peg. I followed her down the narrow staircase into her apartment. Her space was in the bottom floor with windows out to the channel and the mountains of Douglas Island. She had three small rooms: an office and sitting area, a kitchen and a bedroom with a tiny bath. Back in against the hillside were some storage spaces and blocked-off staircases. When I walked into the room I felt that strange swirl of displaced memory. It was Jane Marie's old childhood home but it had shrunk. Across the small room an old man was putting the cover on a computer monitor. He stopped and looked at us momentarily, then directly at me with what was either surprise or suspicion. Jane Marie put her hand on his shoulder and spoke to me.

"Cecil Younger, this is Mr. Meegles. He's my right arm."

Mr. Meegles had a friendly barroom smile from deep-set eyes behind a brow that had been scarred over the years. I could see he didn't have his upper plate in, and it looked like he had gravy stains on the front of his T-shirt under his tweed jacket. He stuck out his hand, and moved around the desk.

"She means her right-hand man. But she's embarrassed to say it."

"No. No . . ." She added quickly, "You're too important to be just a hand."

The old man rubbed his fingers through the thin gray hair on top of his head, then looked nervously at his hands with sudden interest. "Awww . . . I don't know about that. Hey! Your sister called." He looked up at Jane Marie.

Jane Marie flickered a glance at me. "Priscilla called?"

"Yeah, she did. I'm sorry I didn't pick up in time. I was working away on getting the last of this edition on birthday games out. I wasn't answering the phone. I would have, but I didn't recognize her voice. She sounded so small and squeaky-like I didn't think it was her until she hung up. She left a message on the machine though."

"Well, darn it."

"I'm sorry, Jane Marie." Mr. Meegles fumbled with his jacket. "I just didn't recognize her voice."

"Don't worry. If anybody is at fault, it's me. I left you with the deadline and went chasing around. I should have been here when she called." Jane Marie looked at her watch. "You'd better get going. You can make the next bus if you hurry. But I was wondering, Mr. Meegles, if you would like to come to dinner tonight with me and my sister. We are having a few friends in. Nothing formal, you understand."

Mr. Meegles smiled as if she were the sun on his face. "I wouldn't have to wear a tie?"

"No, of course not, just a few friends. Very informal."

He put on his slicker and studied the two of us standing next to each other. "That would be fine. I would like to come.

I'll just hump these bones down the stairs then, go feed the cat and take care of some chores and be back in a bit. I'll bring something sweet." He winked and was up the stairs and gone before I could get my hand out of my pocket to say good-bye.

"Mr. Meegles was sleeping at the bus stop when I met him a couple of years ago," Jane Marie told me. "He'd been the bookkeeper for a logging company down in Forks, Washington, before the business went gunnysack. His wife left him and the bank got his house. He works for me as long as he's sober, which is almost all the time now."

She reached down and touched the button on the answering machine. Mr. Meegles had been right. Priscilla sounded thin and shaky. She had called from a phone in maximum segregation. On the tape, her voice echoed off the concrete walls around her.

"Jane Marie . . . please pick up if you're there. Jane Marie . . ." There was a long pause. Priscilla sighed several times. In the background you could hear a woman coughing steadily and a distant buzzer releasing a heavy metal lock. "I told them I was calling my lawyer. I gave them this number. They won't let me call anybody else. My lawyer says I have some kind of hearing coming right up. He won't tell me what it is. Where is Cecil? Where are you, goddammit . . ." There was another pause, and then some metallic clatter in the background. "This is Priscilla," she said in a weak voice. Then the sound of the receiver dropping and we could hear her breathing hard and sniffling, and the sound of a heavy footfall and rattling keys coming up from the background. The line went dead.

Jane Marie took the tape out of the machine. "Well, I'm saving this," she said. "What kind of hearing is coming up?"

I sat down in a sagging director's chair that faced the window. "The Public Defender says she has a bail hearing tomorrow. But Teller tells you she will be here for dinner?"

"How much is her bail?" Jane Marie instinctively fished in her pocket for her checkbook to look at the final balance.

"Your sister's bail is two hundred thousand dollars. Cash only."

"Stop!" she cried, and flopped down in the office chair opposite mine. She looked at her checkbook again as if she didn't recognize what it was, then slapped it shut.

I put my foot up on the arm of her chair. "I take it you don't have the cash?"

Her smile was crooked. "No."

"Where did Young Bob come from and where is his father?"

She spread her hands in front of her in a way that reminded me of the Public Defender. "A man brought him here to my house last night."

"What man?"

"He didn't introduce himself. Young Bob called him Gunk."

"Gunk? What did he look like?"

Jane Marie ran her fingertip over the surface of her desk absentmindedly. "He was a rough one. Leather vest, tattoos, wallet chained to his belt loops. Big guy."

"Biker?"

"We didn't talk sports, but that would be a good guess." She bent down and picked up some papers next to the trash can and put them on her desk with an air of disinterest. I started for the door. She moved out from behind the desk and blocked me at the narrow doorjamb. "What are you doing?"

"I'm leaving."

"Why?"

"I'm angry."

"Why?"

"I'm running the risk of being dramatic."

She narrowed her eyes on me and smiled with recognition. "You can be a little dramatic."

I tried to edge out through the door. "I'll help you but . . . if you don't want me to, let me get out of here because—"

She walked up behind me and put her hand over my mouth. "Stay," she said. "Only let's not talk."

Jane Marie turned me around and pulled in close to me so that the top of her head brushed against my mouth. It had a warm pull against my lips.

We looked out the windows across to the mountains on Douglas Island. A strange afterlight seemed to be lifting off the surface of the snow above the timberline. The wind lifted a haze of ice in a horsetail off the sharpest ridge. A sudden blast battered the windows and rattled the glass in the frames. We could hear heavy footfalls coming up the outside stairs. I tried to formulate my next words as the steps came closer and the cold wind billowed into the upstairs hallway. I started to speak but she had pulled away.

Edith and Young Bob came clattering down the stairs. Young Bob was dancing and carrying the cereal box over his head as if it were a trophy of war. Edith dropped her canvas bag on the desk. She took a long breath, brushed a strand of gray hair from her eyes, then looked at us steadily, one to the other, as if she were expecting us to confess.

"Well. I'll open the wine," she huffed. "Janie, put on some music. Bach, I should think. Can you chop, Mr. Younger?"

Jane Marie moved ahead of me through the sitting area and into the narrow kitchen. She picked up her Aunt Edith's satchel of groceries and set them on the counter. In the kitchen there were birthday decorations on the wall. I noticed that many of the balloons had deflated so they looked like dried fruit; others were covered with dust. When she turned on the overhead light I could see these were years and years of decorations, the new taped or pinned over the old. Banners with names overlapped on the ceiling, covered the walls, dusty sagging crepe paper ribbons hung loosely in their curls, meeting in the center of the room on the overhead light fixture. The effect created a web of shadows on the floor.

Jane Marie's face was half in shadow. She lit the stove with a wooden match and reached for a box of instant macaroni and cheese from the spice shelf. "I hate to take down decorations, don't you?"

Young Bob rustled in behind me and sat beside the chopping block. He started drinking juice out of a dinosaur cup. His dark eyelashes fanned against his cheeks as he sucked on the twisted plastic straw. Edith reached across and pinched his jowls.

"Look at this boy. I love this boy. He's one of Botticelli's angels."

Young Bob squirmed, then giggled, and when he broke free of his aunt his cheeks were red. His smile could have made even the worst thug light-headed. Jane Marie put her arms around him. She kissed him on the ear. He burbled and grimaced.

"Don't." He squirmed but he gripped her hands around his stomach.

Jane Marie held him and spoke softly. "You can take that juice into the office and watch the VCR. You remember how to turn it on?"

The six-year-old looked suspicious. "Do I have to watch nature stuff?"

Jane Marie feigned looking hurt and stroked his hair. "No, I got you good stuff—ninjas and killer robots."

"Yes!" The boy made fists with both hands and held them over his head like a boxer. He left his dinosaur cup, jumped off the stool and ran out the door banging into the wall.

"Come back for your juice!" Edith screeched after him.

The boy came rushing back and grabbed his cup. Then he set it back on the counter. He hugged Jane Marie around the waist.

"Thank you," he said, and his voice was muffled against her thigh.

Jane Marie curled her fingers through his black curls. When the boy looked up his face was open, betraying nothing but gratitude. Then he whipped out the door.

"And don't spill!" Edith called out after him. Then she looked accusingly over her wineglass at Jane Marie who was still smiling at the empty doorway. "Ninjas and killer robots?"

"It's what he likes. Why should I get him something he doesn't like?"

"The reasoning of a spinster aunt," Edith muttered, and took a long drink out of her glass.

"What do you know about the Sullivans?" I started chopping carrots but nodded up to Jane Marie, who was rinsing the lettuce.

"They were old friends of our family. They came from the Midwest around the same time my family moved here. I guess they had Italian ancestry. Our families did things together. Priscilla knew Robert, that's Young Bob's dad, when they were both kids. She had a crush on him early on. Our fathers joked they would arrange the marriage. After my father died, Robert's dad kind of looked out for us. He helped my mom out with money."

"Would he have put up the bail money?" I asked.

Jane Marie put the lettuce down on a clean cloth. "It's possible, but . . . after the divorce and all the squabbling over Young Bob, the Sullivans and Priscilla aren't exactly on the best of terms."

The sounds of a Bach partita drifted around the room like dry snow, blending with the thumping soundtrack of the ninja movie in the next room.

"Priscilla always insisted that the Sullivans used their influence to have Young Bob taken away. Could that be true?" I put the carrots in a large salad bowl.

Jane Marie shrugged. "Mr. Sullivan—that's Old Bob—he had been some kind of lobbyist for the labor unions. I don't really know how he got established. He became a powerful man during the construction of the oil pipeline. He knew all the politicians. My dad used to say Mr. Sullivan must have been the smartest or the luckiest man in the state. I'm sure Priscilla is right that there was a connection between him and the Senator. But there really wasn't anything the Senator could have done about taking Young Bob away from her. Priscilla likes to dwell on conspiracies only because she doesn't want to think about her own mistakes. She can't face the reasons why the judge and the social workers didn't think she was a good parent. Instead of working on that, and they gave her lots of chances, she always looked to new conspiracies."

"Was it the Sullivans who arranged to have him brought up here and delivered on your doorstep?" I asked. Jane Marie was looking at nothing but her cutting hand. Edith stopped slicing halibut and looked at her for the answer to my question.

"I don't know, for sure." Jane Marie did not look up.

"All right then, what do you know about the Senator?" I reached into my pocket and found the old bag of sunflower seeds and offered them to Edith. She looked at me with a crazed expression as if I were offering to set her on fire, then she snorted, "No."

"I didn't know the Senator well," Jane Marie said. "I just heard the same capital gossip everyone heard. Even though he was a big man in his church, he was a womanizer. He had secrets that kept him from running for governor, but you know, Cecil, that wouldn't distinguish him in this town."

The door to the outer office banged open and I heard Priscilla's voice over the swirl of music.

"Hey baby boy!"

We filed out of the narrow kitchen and saw Priscilla on her knees hugging Young Bob tightly. Her eyes were closed and she rocked him back and forth, murmuring, "My baby boy, my angel boy."

Young Bob broke the embrace first. He pushed back, grinning. "Hi, Momma. Janie got me a ninja movie!" Priscilla was stroking his hair. Her eyes were wet with tears. She spoke in a high-pitched voice. "Oh, we're going to turn that off now. I want to see you."

The boy's shoulders drooped and he looked deeply disappointed. Priscilla hugged him and flashed a dark look at Jane Marie. Priscilla smiled through clenched teeth.

"All right," Priscilla said.

Young Bob hugged her and said, "Thank you." Priscilla let her fingers linger in his hair as he sat back in front of the TV. Then she walked past us into the kitchen, turned, and held her index finger in Jane Marie's face.

"You intentionally did that. You intentionally ruined my

homecoming with him. I can't believe you did that." She
hissed in a furious whisper. Her finger was shaking.

"Oh Cilla, I just . . . I'm sorry, I didn't mean to inter-
fere."

Behind us, Edith was hiding the box of cereal.

"And you—" Priscilla turned to me. "You did *nothing* to
help me. If it wasn't for Mr. Teller I'd still be in jail."

"Teller put up your bail?" I eased into the kitchen to
block Priscilla's view of Edith and the cereal box. Edith
straightened up quickly and shot me a look of thanks.

"I've been told not to talk to you," Priscilla said with an
official air.

"By Teller?"

"I think we better change the subject. Cecil, you are no
longer part of my legal team."

We were at an impasse. I could tell from her expression
that Priscilla was not going to budge on this issue. She stood as
flatfooted as a pyramid, and I knew she could stand that way for
as long as one.

Edith squeezed past me with some wineglasses in her
right hand and a bottle of French white wine in her left.

"We should toast Priscilla's freedom!" she chirped, and
handed around the glasses.

I toasted with Young Bob's dinosaur cup of leftover juice.
Priscilla glared at me through narrowed lizard eyes while the
others raised their glasses gaily. The Bach ended and the silence
sat like wet snow.

Eventually, Mr. Meegles reappeared with a bag of sugar

doughnuts that he had bought at the liquor-store deli near the bus stop. He had a small flask in his back pocket and his breath was sweet with cheap whiskey. Jane Marie scowled at him at first but ushered him in graciously and gave him tea all evening.

Jane Marie lowered her drafting table and placed it in the sitting area. She covered it with a bright yellow tablecloth and Edith set the food there. The dinner conversation swirled around opera and theater, and then why television was bad for children. Young Bob sat politely eating his macaroni and cheese for a time, but eventually he started stacking his silverware on top of his glass and tried to launch bits of carrots with a spoon catapult. Priscilla hissed at him. Mr. Meegles, who was sitting across the table from them, constructed goalposts from his knife and fork, encouraging Young Bob to shoot field goals. Jane Marie kept score, while Priscilla continued to glare and rant about the influence of television.

Finally, Young Bob blurted out, "Why do people in the movies kiss all the time?"

"Because they love each other, sweetie." Jane Marie reached over and returned a carrot missile to his stockpile.

Priscilla snorted, "Love!" She looked around the table challengingly. "Love is the inflated currency of television. They have sold it so much it has no value anymore."

"Tristan and Isolde." Edith closed her eyes and sat back in her chair. She had put an opera on the stereo and a soprano voice looped around the room. Her eyes closed, the old woman held her hand out in front of her as if her skin could feel the music.

"Why do people on TV love each other, Momma?" Young Bob looked up at Priscilla. She twisted away from him.

"They don't, baby. It's all make-believe. Stories. Let's change the subject."

I had seen Mr. Meegles hold his teacup under the table and sneak shots of whiskey into it. Now he reared back in his seat and spoke to Young Bob.

"People love one another, buddy boy, because it's way less complicated than hating them."

Young Bob laughed and his hand absently reached over and rested on top of mine.

Priscilla shoved her chair back and got to her feet, disgusted with the drunken aphorism. Jane Marie leaned close to Young Bob and lifted his chin up with her finger.

"You know, we had a brother." She spoke to the small boy and Priscilla sat down again, listening. "He would have been your uncle. I suppose he was like people on TV." Jane Marie looked across at Priscilla and Priscilla nodded in agreement. Her eyes glistened. "He was handsome like those boys on TV. He was handsome like you're going to be someday, sweetie. And he loved girls. Oh my, he did love girls." Young Bob crinkled up his nose at the thought of loving girls. Jane Marie continued, "It got your uncle in trouble, the way he loved those girls. I want you to listen to this, baby, 'cause maybe he did some things wrong. . . ." Tears ran down Priscilla's cheeks and Edith reached over to hold her hand. ". . . But it wasn't bad what he did, being handsome and loving those girls that way. You'll do the same thing."

THE MUSIC OF WHAT HAPPENS

The boy kept wrinkling his nose. "Did you ever love anybody?" Young Bob demanded of his aunt.

Jane Marie wiped her eyes. "You know, buddy, you have to be very brave to love somebody. You have to be very brave and have lots of patience. I wasn't like your uncle. I always had a lot of patience but maybe I wasn't brave enough."

"Did anybody ever love you?"

"I think one boy did." She looked at me and then quickly back to the dark-eyed child. "He was brave but not very patient."

"Who was it?"

Jane Marie got up to clear the table. "*Now* it's time to change the subject," she told Young Bob.

We listened to the entire opera. By the end of it, Mr. Meegles was asleep on the couch with a powdered sugar mustache above his upper lip and a wool blanket thrown over him. Edith had driven home. Priscilla and Young Bob were asleep in Jane Marie's bedroom.

The storm outside caused the old house to creak. Jane Marie and I were lying in her childhood hideaway, the small space under the old blocked-off stairway. She stretched her arm above me and her skin was pale as a birch limb. Her fingers played overhead in the small cubbyhole. I could see scrawled writing and creased photographs taped above our heads. Lying on a flannel quilt with a candle and a flashlight, Jane Marie's hands ran across the narrow fir boards as if she were taking an inventory: old handwriting with hearts and loops, boys' names written over and over, pictures of the Beatles, scientific illustrations of salmon and shore birds, party invitations taped beside school photos, love poems, sketches of fishing boats, a map of the Arctic, and in the corner shelf by the door, the fading photograph of her father and brother, propped next to it a snapshot of Young Bob as a baby. There was barely enough room for the two of us side by side. The air was close with our breath and the scent of the wax puddling at the base of the candle.

I was reading my name, which was caught there in her teenage writing. It said, *Cecil Younger is a jerk. He doesn't even know I'm alive.* Then underneath I read, *Priscilla is a big fat snoop.*

Jane Marie turned to me and our faces were inches apart. "You know, Cecil, you should have come back after that last time I talked to you."

"You were so mean to me," I said, realizing I was starting to whine. "I said that I loved you and you told me to get lost."

"How did I know you were serious? You were such a clown. I mean that thing with the straws and everything." She spoke to the ceiling.

"Hey, I didn't mean that," I protested.

"What? Blowing raisins out your nose is something that happens by accident?"

"Yeah . . . well, sometimes," I said. I was clearly beyond all help.

She turned and smiled at me and there was something in her face and eyes that suggested a knowing and intelligent forgiveness. I touched her cheek and felt a thrill in my heart as if I were walking out of nerd prison. I turned away from her quickly before I said something that would put me right back in.

"How did Young Bob get here? He is supposed to be with his father," I said in my new steady voice.

She reached up and traced the photograph of Young Bob. "I told you the truth, Cecil. A man brought him here unexpectedly. He just . . . came to me out of the blue. Before I heard about the Senator, before I heard about Priscilla being arrested. He just came here and gave Bob to me."

I tried to lift my arm to put it around her shoulders but we were too cramped for that. So I put my arm down and held her hand, which was wedged tightly between our hips. I could see a tear tracking down from her eye, across her temple. It came to rest in the hollow of her ear.

"All I want to do is help Priscilla take care of her son." She reached her hand up to where Priscilla's name was written. "If he is hurt, I won't be able to make sense of anything. Do you understand what I mean?"

I didn't. Then. The best I could do was try to form a question by keeping my silence and running my finger next to hers where she kept tracing her sister's name. She shivered suddenly and blew out the candle. "I wanted you to see this place," she said softly and squirmed against me to get out. Then she stopped. Her face was down by my feet near the mouth of the cubbyhole.

"I always had a crush on you, Cecil. Always."

"Yeah, well . . ." I said, my new calm voice dissolving.

"You were funny. That thing with the raisins and all. That was funny."

"I was a sophisticate, even for Alaska." I was beginning to sweat.

"No, I mean, it was silly and dumb but that was the effect you were looking for. You were just trying to get me to break out of my shell, weren't you?"

"Oh yeah, that was it. Definitely." My head was light. I needed to get some air. Jane Marie pinched my toe and disappeared out the cubbyhole door.

"I thought so." I could hear her voice chuckle.

I crawled out from under the stairs. We went into her kitchen and ate the leftover macaroni and cheese. Jane Marie gave me a sleeping bag and a foam pad that I was to lay out on the floor by her coffee table. She set up a cot for herself in the kitchen. As I walked with my bedding past the door of Jane Marie's bedroom I heard Young Bob saying to Priscilla, "Please. Please just read the part where Templeton goes out and eats all the stuff on the fairgrounds. Please."

I peeked in. Priscilla was lying under the covers of the double bed. Young Bob was next to her. He was on top of the covers draped sideways across the bed. His pajamas were hiked up his legs as he gently kicked against the mattress. Priscilla had the book folded across her chest and one hand stroked his dark hair. "We'll get to that part. Charlotte and Wilbur haven't gotten to the fair. We're almost there. I don't want to skip ahead." She looked up at me standing in the seam of the open door.

This was one of the only times I had ever seen her so relaxed and content. She didn't even scowl at me but waved her hand absently with a dreamy smile and I stepped back away from their room.

I lay on top of the sleeping bag in the darkness listening to the storm and the sounds of Jane Marie settling into her cot in the kitchen. The wind swept the alder and spruce trees on the north side of the house. I could hear rain running in the iron culvert up the hill. Sometimes rocks would clatter through the pipe and I could count the brief silence before I heard them clicking down the streambed. The storm sprayed against the windowpanes and a few of the gusts worked around the casings, flickering the candle.

I lay staring at the shadows on the ceiling, trying to make sense of why Priscilla was out of jail. It wasn't all that easy to get out of jail after killing a politician, even in a strongly libertarian state like Alaska, but Priscilla had seemed to do just that. The candle wavered its light on the ceiling slats and I made lists of people who could have come up with the bail.

I heard a thump in the room close to me. I jumped up and immediately cracked my shin into the coffee table. Then I heard a moan. I picked up the candle and walked toward the couch near the tiny office area. I held the candle down to the dark form until I recognized Mr. Meegles, who had flipped on his back and in doing so had knocked a book and two videotapes off the couch onto the floor. He was snoring lightly. I covered him with his jacket and went toward the bathroom for a drink of water.

The door to Jane Marie's room was still open and the light was on. I looked in. Young Bob was asleep, sprawled on the bed with his head on the pillow. I could hear his breathing, even and untroubled. His eyelids flickered and he looked happy. Priscilla was sitting up with her back propped against the wall, the book folded on her lap. She stroked the boy's cheek and kept murmuring something. At first I couldn't hear what she was saying but by looking at her lips I could understand. "Radiant . . . radiant . . . radiant . . . ," she said. I backed away and got the drink of water, then went back to bed.

Sleeping without drugs has a way of flattening my dreams out. I either don't remember them or they are dull and predictable like old TV commercials that come in fuzzy black and white. But on this night, I was dreaming of green whales drifting in the sky like the aurora borealis. I must have smelled the candle when it snuffed out because the whales were at a birthday party with horns and hats but they gradually became more and more tangled in the dusty crepe paper that started to cling to them like steel cables, cutting into their skin. There was a whale on the table, his flukes wrapped in a tangle of rusty cables. He was slapping the floor, banging his body, and sawing himself in half against the steel cables. The birthday candles were blown out. All the whales were sinking underwater, the one on the table still banging and banging.

I woke up and a man in a ski mask was standing over me.

It looked like his eyes were unusually wide apart but as I held my hand over my face I realized he was shining a light in my eyes. I heard him cough out one word.

"Shit!"

I sat up quickly and past the legs of the man in the ski mask I got a glimpse of another. This one had two small flash-lights above each ear attached to some type of headband. He was going through the papers on Jane Marie's desk. He had been pounding on one of the locked drawers. Mr. Meegles was not moving on the couch.

"Go! Go! *Go!*" I heard the man at the desk hiss. Now I could see the man standing over me had lights on his forehead that made it impossible to see his face. He was lifting some-thing that looked like a crowbar over his head. "Go!" the man at the desk hissed again. The form standing above me calmly said to me, "I can kill you if you want." I lay back down.

The man standing over me tucked the crowbar in his belt and shouldered into Jane Marie's bedroom. I scrambled to my feet and ran for the front door. As I approached the man rifling the desk, he lashed out with an iron bar. It snagged on my T-shirt. I toppled against the couch and my hands felt a damp, sticky pad.

The darkness atomized into screams and breaking glass. The bearlike shadow of the first man came from the bedroom. He had Young Bob in his arms. Priscilla was shrieking some-where in the darkness. In the dim light, I saw my hand covered with blood. The man carrying Young Bob banged into me like a football player. I grabbed his knees but he broke free. Jane

Marie's naked body arched out of the doorway, swinging something in her hand. The man still going through the desk turned so fast he threw the crowbar at the window, which shattered. He spread his hands above his head, protecting himself as he ducked and ran. I heard the sound of wood smacking bone. The storm filled the room, lifting the blinds and scattering papers into the weird, swirling air.

"You get out of here. Now!" Jane Marie's voice lifted above the wind and the crunching glass.

The headlamps careened around the room. I saw shadows tripping over each other in the doorway. Papers like leaves falling. I saw her white skin, breasts, buttocks, her arm working what looked like a shortened baseball bat again and again against his forearms, against his thighs. She was speaking to him now, punctuating each word with a slap of the club. "You . . . bring . . . him . . . back," she said. I had fallen at the foot of the couch and only then realized my pants were half up. I jerked my pants on and as I crawled up on top of the couch I felt the dampness again and I could see Mr. Meegles's mouth open. Blood streamed down his forehead. Bubbles of blood and mucus came from the flattened stump of his nose so I knew he was breathing. The two men taking Young Bob clattered up the stairs. I followed the sound. I stepped out from the doorway and looked around. The streetlight defined the pool on the landing where Jane Marie stood naked holding what I could now see was a fish club. The men in stocking caps and dark clothes were bounding down the stairs, their flashlights flung away or in their pockets. Above one of their shoulders I could see Young Bob's pale face, his mouth open in a scream like the breath escaping from a drowning man. The trees on each side of us arched and whipped in the darkness. I heard the men stumble down the iron steps at the bottom of the hill. The wind sizzled off the ridge above us. Dogs started to bark. Lights in the nearby houses came on. Jane Marie hung her head, started to walk toward me into the house but she turned suddenly in a violent afterthought and flung the club down the stairs. I could see the muscles in her arms, her shoulders articulated under the milky light as the club disappeared into the dark, clanging down the iron steps. She lightly bounced up the grating on her bleeding feet to stand beside me in her doorway. Her feet left bloody prints.

"We'd better get inside," she said.

Down in the office I taped a piece of cardboard over the broken window as she put on her robe and picked the broken glass out of her soles. She then turned her attention to Mr. Meegles. She gingerly dabbed at his face with a paper towel. He was moaning and could make a fist when she asked him to. Priscilla cowered in the corner of the office wrapped in a quilt, with her head buried in her hands.

I moved over to the desk and looked at the locked drawer whose top lip was bent but unbroken.

"What's in here?"

"Stuff . . . Nothing." Jane Marie was kneeling by the couch and grimacing as she lightly dabbed around Mr. Meegles's crushed nose. Her robe was open, exposing a curve of leg that made her seem more naked now than she had outside on the stairs.

"It looks like they wanted whatever was in here."

"Papers, bankbooks, nothing. They tried to open it because it was locked. That's all."

I reached over to the phone and started to dial.

"Who are you calling?" Jane Marie sat up, covering herself.

"I'm calling the police."

She stood and walked over to me. She took the phone out of my hands and put it down. Then she leaned in close to me and cradled my head in her arms. Her robe was open and my cheek was flat against her stomach. I could smell the soap in the terry-cloth robe and the spring storm on her skin. She was trembling.

"If we call the police they will keep us up the rest of the night. They'll ask a lot of questions and won't answer a thing. Please, Cecil, let's just get some sleep. We just need to take care of each other right now. We will take care of the police tomorrow."

I stared up at her dumbly. I rubbed the small of her back through her robe feeling the tension in her body. She scratched her fingers through my hair and lifted my head.

"Cecil, don't call the police."

Then she walked away from me through the destroyed room, leaving small flecks of blood on the scattered papers.

I looked over to Priscilla in the corner of the room. She

leaned against the wall of the apartment, her arms resting on her knees, a blanket over her head. She stared into space without expression but her body trembled, making the blanket quake. She could have been in a roadside ditch somewhere, deserted for days. Watching her, I was overwhelmed by a memory that both illuminated and darkened my understanding of what was going on.

After the murder of her brother Ricky and the squalls of memorial services and criminal proceedings, Priscilla began to shrink away from the world. No one who loved her really knew where she had gone. The girls' mother wept and swore and stayed up all night talking to the photographs of her son while her husband worked on fishing gear in the back of the house. Jane Marie made the meals and took over her mother's duties. But Priscilla walked through the routines of her life like a ghost, never talking about what had happened, never alluding to the past at all.

One day, almost a year after Ricky's death and only several months before her father would be lost, Priscilla did not come home from junior-high band practice. Jane Marie didn't want to worry her parents so she told them Priscilla was spending the night with a girlfriend. Then she asked me to help her find her sister. We were seventeen then and in my goofiness I was honored, and even thought of this as some kind of "date." I remember picking out the right clothes to fit with a heroic rescue mission.

None of Priscilla's friends and teachers had seen her. A friend of mine who had a job washing dishes at the café said he'd seen her by the liquor store stopping people and talking to them. She still carried her trombone case. He never saw her go in the store. He said that later in the evening he might have heard her talking in the back alley behind the café. The three of us went back there and found a circle of cigarette butts and a broken bottle of apple wine. Jane Marie pushed the glass with her toe and put on her warm gloves, then said, "I think I know where to look."

There are old mine shafts in the hills surrounding Juneau. Many of these shafts were inadequately sealed. There are miles of underground passages in the mountain. Every lost dog in town was presumed to be at the bottom of one of the many shafts. In our childhood imaginations the shafts were slowly filling up with the bones of animals and lost children.

At the mouth of one of the shafts was a shack that sat under the massive eaves of rock. I had been there a few times. There were mattresses on the floor and a barrel stove to keep the place warm. There were bottles piled up from drinking parties and dirty blankets to spend the night if you didn't want to go home with wine on your breath. We got flashlights from Jane Marie's garage and started up the mountain road to where there was a steep trail to the shaft site. About three hundred yards from the end of the trial we were met by two drunken men running down the hill. One had a cut across his forehead and all he would say was, "Don't go up there, man. She fucking tried to kill me." Then he turned and stumbled down the trail. We heard the sound of breaking glass from up near the cabin.

It was a calm night; none of the trees moved. When we walked through the front door we stepped on broken glass. I remember being grateful for my thick-soled shoes. The cabin smelled like urine in the corners and sweet wine on the dusty mattresses. The fire in the barrel stove pumped like a blast furnace, the stovepipe glowing red. All of the windows were broken out. The shards of glass were like teeth in the window frames. All of the chairs and the one table were in splinters. On the floor squatted Priscilla with a blanket over her shoulders, her face a grotesque mask with tears tracking down her face. Her hands were cut and she had yellow vomit stained down her blouse. The trombone was bent around one of the window frames, the slide resting on the floor and the bell poking into the room like a lily. When we walked in Priscilla did not look up but kept repeating: "I didn't mean it. I didn't mean it. I didn't mean it." She tapped her bleeding palms on the plank floor.

In the years afterward, Priscilla never mentioned that night. We took her to a friend's and she slept all the next day. When I was seventeen I didn't understand what was going on, I was so wrapped up in myself and in this strange world I both did and didn't want to emerge into. So I suppose I simply forgot about what had happened that night. But seeing her on this night in Jane Marie's apartment with the storm raging through the broken windows and her son missing I wished I had asked her then what it was she didn't mean, and why she needed to be forgiven for it.

I started to move toward Priscilla to help her stand up; she slapped my hands away. Jane Marie turned away from Mr. Meegles, who was holding a compress on his own nose, and she turned to Priscilla and took her into the bedroom, where they settled for the night without saying another word to me.

The next morning the sky was blue above the islands. The snow line looked like smeared chalk down into the trees on the mountains across the way. Thick fog lay just below the house so the view showed islands of granite and snow. Jane Marie was gone. In her office some of the papers had been picked up and placed in a cardboard box. There was a note taped to the computer screen: *Took Meegles to doctor. Meeting police there. Back soon . . . JM.*

I went around the desk and tried the locked drawer. It opened easily. It was empty. I finished getting dressed, grabbed my knapsack, and went down into the fog for coffee.

The coffee shop on South Franklin had a few regulars hunched over their papers. I placed my order and sat at a table near the back. Some early-morning runners in spandex and synthetic fur were rewarding themselves with decaf lattés. Two old public-defender clients without coats, but with three shirts on, were trying to sober up so the shelter would feed them breakfast. And in a chair near the window was Rachel, who looked like she had been crying.

I walked over to her and she looked up from her newspaper with a sudden start. There was a photograph of Wilfred

Taylor in a black border on the front page of the newspaper.
Rachel's reddened eyes narrowed and she pulled away.

"They fired me, you know."

"I'm sorry."

"They said you work for . . . her. The woman
who . . ." She put her head down over the coffee, moving her
fingers lightly around the rim of her cup. She bit her lower lip
but the corners of her mouth twitched as if she might break
down. But she went on talking.

"I worked in the Senator's office two years. I handled everything for him. I worked late when no one else would. I
drafted legislation. He asked my opinions. I was useful, you
know." She stared up at me. I shook my head. I didn't really
know.

"Did you ever have a good job?" She didn't wait for me to
answer. "Well, I did. Now I lost it."

The waiter with a nose ring and a triangle shaved on the
side of his head brought me my double espresso. I sat down
without being asked but Rachel pulled her gloves back from
the center of the table giving me the cue that I could sit.

I said, "I didn't mean for you to get fired. And about my
working for Priscilla . . . well . . . there are two schools of
thought about that. It appears I don't really work for her."

"Then why did you use me to snoop around in the office?"

I sipped the bitter coffee. "I saw you from the office
across the street dropping papers. I wanted to help you. It
wasn't until I got inside the capitol that I remembered you. It

was a complete accident that you turned out to work in that office. I'm not that good an investigator to plan that all out. Accidents are more common than plans."

I lifted my hands palms up. If I were a dog I would have lain on my back and shown her my belly. If I know anything about getting witnesses to talk it's that almost everyone wants to unload but they have one thing they have to say before they'll ever be able to move on to what they really know. My job is to help them say that one thing.

"Well, you still cost me my job," Rachel said, shaking her head.

"I know. This wouldn't have happened if he were still alive."

"You're right. Wilfred Taylor was . . . a good man. . . . He took a lot of heat, but that was because he had principles. People didn't understand him like that. He wouldn't have fired me. He wouldn't have stood for it." Her voice broke.

"I heard he was a very complex man. Kind, and very complex. He tried to make everyone else happy. He never took care of himself."

She was shaking her head and now tears started to run.

"Rachel . . . now that he's gone, the gossip will start and you won't be able to help him. You understood the Senator better than most people, didn't you?"

She nodded her head, agreeing with me. I waited out a long pause, letting her listen to her own labored breathing, letting the pressure of that one thing build.

Finally, I dangled it down there. "Tell me about Wilfred Taylor. What was he really like?"

"I loved him," she said with a long exhalation of air. "I know what everyone says about him. But he wasn't like that at all. He cared for me. He respected me. Maybe he's the only one that ever really did." Her mascara smeared down her smooth cheeks and her nose ran so she wiped it with her knotted napkin.

I suppose this is the real work of a private detective. I can't drive a car, I don't carry a gun, and I've never broken into a house in my life. I just get people to talk to me. As I watched Rachel crying I wished it had been true. I wished the Senator had loved her and they'd had long evenings together talking of building governments based on service and commitment. I wished they had gone to the library together and kissed in the outer doorway where they would drop their books and everyone who looked up from their reading would see them and smile. But mostly I just hated my job, and was tired of not believing anything.

She wiped her eyes, smearing her mascara. "So, do you work for the woman who killed him?"

"I really don't know. I mean, I don't know both ways. I don't know if she killed him and I don't know if I work for her. Do you think she killed him?" Witnesses love to be asked to solve a murder. Even the most tight-lipped family members will loosen up if you ask them their final opinion of your client.

"She sure was scary and she was a pain in the butt." Rachel almost smiled. She was still twisting her napkin in her hands. "But I don't know if she really pushed him down those stairs or not. She sounded mean. She was crazy. She really thought we were out to keep her from her baby. I mean, Cecil, we had other concerns besides that woman's divorce but she called more than anyone else."

"Were you there that night?"

"When it happened? No. I did work late that night, though. I was there until about eight-thirty. The Senator was working late, too. He had been very concerned about the Freedom of Information Act requests that Miss DeAngelo kept filing. He had been getting advice from the Attorney General's office and they kept giving him opinions saying he had to turn the stuff she wanted over to her. But the Senator figured in this administration they were just trying to discredit him. So the Senator got local counsel and they told him to send part of the requested material and they could find an exemption for the rest. The Senator was upset. That woman had asked for everything in his personal files. He didn't want to give up anything. He said she was on a fishing expedition and he wasn't going to succumb to this kind of pressure from a kook."

I checked my watch, then signaled the man with the abstract haircut and ordered two more drinks.

"What did he have to hide?"

"The Senator? Nothing . . . nothing, really. I think he was trying to protect other people more than he was concerned about himself. You know, his supporters over the years. Many of them are important people, highly placed in oil, labor, and such. He didn't want them harassed by a madwoman like Priscilla DeAngelo. You can understand that?"

I nodded, agreeing, always agreeing. "When did Harrison Teller arrive?"

"Mr. Teller came a few days before . . . it happened."

"Before? Are you sure?"

"I'm positive."

"Why was Teller around?"

Rachel smiled weakly. Reacting to the urgency in my voice, she was starting to retreat. "I'm sorry. I really don't know for sure. Mr. Teller was friends with the Senator and his wife. Years and years ago the Senator had been a federal prosecutor in Anchorage. He said many times if he was ever in trouble, real trouble, he'd get Harrison Teller."

"Was the Senator in real trouble?"

She reared back in her seat, flattening her palms against the Senator's obituary photo on the table. Her napkin dropped to the floor. "Listen, this has gone far enough. I didn't want to talk to you anyway. This is too much like an interrogation."

I had crowded her, now I had to let her run. "I'm sorry. I'm sorry," I murmured, looking down for a place to lie on my back. The coffee came, thankfully. Witnesses rarely walk out on good coffee.

"Rachel, you don't have to talk to me. I just want to know the truth. It's the same truth that you can tell the police. If it's bad for Priscilla it can be used to convict her. But I need to know it all: the good and the bad. If you don't want to talk to me I understand, but I need to find out how the Senator died."

She squinted into her coffee. "I don't know."

"Then I'll have to listen to the gossip from people who don't really know," I added.

"There's plenty of that in this town," Rachel blurted out, her young face trying to look worldly with a runny nose and smeared makeup. "You're probably after those documents that were shredded too." She said this almost petulantly.

"I don't know anything about those papers. Tell me."

She slumped in her chair. "I don't know anything, either. I just know that the morning after he died . . ." Out on the street a couple of kids were standing in the fog sharing a smoke. Rachel watched them for a moment and then turned back to me. "That very morning before anything else happened, the men I told you about came and sealed the Senator's private office. Then the police came and they did the investigation, but the other men in the suits wouldn't let them go through the Senator's papers. I talked to the police. I got the impression the men in suits were from the federal government. They acted in charge. The next day we were told to move out of the office and the men in suits brought in the shredder. They said they didn't want to archive drafts of personal correspondence and junk mail but they didn't want to put the stuff in the garbage so the reporters"—her eyes met mine and did not flinch away—"so the defense investigators could find them in the Dumpsters."

"What was Teller doing in the office yesterday?"

"I'm not sure. I don't think Mr. Teller talks to . . . underlings." Here she smiled. "I think he was talking to the senior staff to see if they wanted him to keep on working on what he started for the Senator. And don't ask me. I don't know what it was. Teller only talks to senior staff and to Barb, the Senator's wife . . . widow."

"But you think it was some legal problem?"

"I'm just assuming."

"But Teller can't even practice law. He isn't a member of the Bar," I said more to myself than to Rachel.

"The only thing I can tell you is the Senator used to say that Teller was like an expensive weapon that everyone wants even if they weren't going to use it."

"And he never told you what he meant by that?"

"He never got a chance."

The shop was filling up with men in Burberry coats and tortoiseshell glasses, women with soft wool overcoats and expensive leather handbags. There were a couple of students in torn jeans and still some of my old clients busing the tables and picking through the best of the leftovers. It was seven-thirty. The business day of the State of Alaska was going to start in half an hour.

Rachel finished her coffee, stood up, and put on her worn-looking cardigan sweater. She was wearing sweatpants and running shoes. She wiped her nose and eyes one last time. "I don't even know why I put on makeup today. I forgot that I don't have to go to work."

I folded the newspaper so that the photo of Taylor was safely on the inside and I handed it to her. "Do you really miss your job?" I asked.

She thought about it, shook her head slowly. Then, "No. No, I really don't." She started to back away. "But I guess I miss having a place to go to and someone to talk to."

I stood up, but as I walked toward her she turned quickly and was out the door, shouldering between two men next to the pastry case with newspapers under their arms.

I walked around the corner past the bus stop and past several of the bars where most of the small and least offensive crimes in Juneau are discussed and plotted out. The door to one was open and the barmaid lugged a garbage can full of bottles out onto the sidewalk. The can rolled and crackled on its rim as I walked past. The barmaid picked up her broom to give the sidewalk a cursory swipe. I stopped and peered in. I could barely see the trophies and the animal heads mounted on the walls. Here on the outside I could smell the rush of last night's storm easing down the mountain: the taste of ice, rock, and sodden moss carried on the air. But peering inside the dark bar I could recognize some of the regulars sitting like humps over their mixed drinks. They had been fallers out at the logging camps or deckhands off the seine boats. I knew that smell of vinyl, stale beer, and smoke as it rode out the door and hit my face. I knew the fear of the daylight creeping in as the regulars lit another smoke and felt the curl of vodka ease up their stomach and around their brain. Just a few more drinks and they'd remember that they were the lucky ones, that only assholes and bureaucrats had to go to work in Juneau during the wintertime. They could sit in the dark and have another drink because real work means waiting for your season.

I thought about Jane Marie, the two men who broke into her house last night, and those papers missing from her desk. I thought about Young Bob. I thought about Rachel and her broken heart. I thought "Fuck it," and started to walk inside the bar when Dickie Stein grabbed me by the elbow.

"Jesus Christ, Cecil. Where are you going?"

"Hey, man, it's my job."

Dickie looked in and smiled back at me. "Not today it ain't. Listen, I'm getting this thing figured out."

"Okay," I said, as if I had just settled a very difficult problem.

"I've been on the phone to the East Coast since the middle of the night. I tracked down an old law school buddy of mine. He works for Justice."

"Don't we all," I said, as Dickie jerked me around and walked me quickly down the street and away from the bar.

"Funny," Dickie said. "My buddy works for the *Department* of Justice. He asked around and gave me some poop you are not going to believe."

"That won't be hard. Tell me quick before I faint."

"Priscilla's father-in-law, Old Bob Sullivan, is in the witness protection program."

"Your friend told you that?"

"Well, not in so many words."

"What kind of words did he use?"

"I gave him the names of all the principals in our case and asked him if he could give us backgrounds. He called back in twenty minutes and told me not to fool around with anyone in this case. All he would say was that Bob Sullivan did in fact have a criminal history under a different name and that he would tell me nothing more. I asked him if Sullivan was in the witness protection program and he said, I quote, 'If I knew that information I wouldn't tell you. But I'm telling you, Dickie, as a friend, Sullivan is *not* in the witness protection program.' ''

"That is your confirmation?"

"He's lying. It's obvious. If he wasn't in the program this guy would tell me flat out."

"He did."

"Christ, Cecil, he's a fed now. He's futzing around with the jargon. He would have told me straight out. I'm telling you, Bob Sullivan is in the witness protection program. It all fits. It's why they're trying to keep me out. They've got something big to hide and this is it. I'm going to stay right here and work on this. What are you going to do?"

"Well, I'm walking over to the hospital. Jane Marie's house got broken into and—"

Dickie grabbed me by the shoulder as if I had just announced our engagement. "What?! That's great! That proves it. I tell you the guy's a gangster. This proves it. What did they take?"

"Young Bob."

He glared at me. He looked like a caricature of a man working the angles. "This is great. This is great. I mean . . . it's too bad about the kid but still . . ." Dickie was grinning and clenching his fists. I've seen defense attorneys get like this before. When they think they know something the DAs don't, it acts like a powerful hallucinogenic drug. I didn't want to tell him about my conversation with Rachel that morning because I was worried he would start foaming at the mouth and try to bring Oliver Stone in on the case.

I tried to ease around him back toward the bar. As I nudged him close to its door I said, "By the way, your client is out of jail. But maybe she's Teller's client."

"No. No. She's mine." He grabbed me back out of the doorway. "Of course, I haven't really talked to her yet." We were standing on the sidewalk, people flowing around us like logs in a river. Dickie was standing, biting his thumbnail, lost in thought.

I waved him off and started walking toward the channel and the highway to the hospital. I left him muttering, "I'd better find Priscilla. I'd better find Teller. Teller knows. I'm sure he knows."

When I looked over my shoulder, Dickie was already storming up the street toward the capitol building. In four steps I saw him disappear into the fog.

I walked to the highway along the channel and turned north past the Coast Guard dock and the small boat harbor. The wind blustered around me and on it I caught the scent of bacon cooking. I heard the faint tinkling of Irish dance music. I closed my eyes to take it all in.

I caught myself slipping into a dream. A dream about going home and forgetting about this whole mess. Priscilla didn't want me. I was of no use to her. I thought of Young Bob disappearing down the stairs into the darkness and I despaired at the thought of ever being able to find him. My doctor said I was supposed to take it easy. I could stay in the bar. I remembered drinking in Juneau on those summer evenings, with cottonwood bloom in the air, waking up on a tarp in the woods behind Franklin Street, the foxgloves leaning over my head whispering to me as I woke up. I should be drinking and listening to flowers, not working a case that kept running away from me.

I almost stumbled over a raven feeding on a torn package of pretzels lying in the gutter. The raven hopped on the signpost that was a couple of feet to my left. It stayed silent for a moment and then started yelling at me for being so clumsy. Its hackles were up, its beak was wide, blaring in that weird angry voice. "I'm sorry. I'm sorry," I said, as I tried to move around it. It hopped back down by the pretzels but kept scolding me.

"Pay attention to the important things, dummy!" I heard it say.

"Okay, so what's important?" I asked.

The raven picked up one of the pretzels in its beak and waved it at me, then crunched it on the sidewalk and swallowed the pieces.

"Okay, okay." I hunched my shoulders and looked up. There, tied at the gas dock, was an old wooden seine boat called the *Winning Hand*. The door from its wheelhouse to the back deck was open. Someone was standing in the doorway of the wheelhouse and dance music issued from a speaker on the back deck. Jane Marie DeAngelo was on the flying bridge adjusting the throttle, and Harrison Teller was standing on the float preparing to cast off the stern line.

I ran to jump on the boat before it pulled away. I heard the raven crunching and muttering. Before I got to the ramp of the dock it spattered out a final screech at me and I felt it on the back of my coat like someone was throwing gravel.

I jumped for the stern of the *Winning Hand*. I heard the diesel engine blaring as Jane Marie applied more throttle. For a brief moment my body hung in the air above the widening gap between boat and dock. Then I hit the bulwarks with my chest. As I climbed onto the deck I saw Harrison Teller's face in mine. We stood up together. There was some ferocity in his eyes, set back in the underbrush of his hair and beard. They were a cold blue, as unexpected as finding an opal while digging for worms. I was about to say hello when he hit me on the head with something heavy and I fell into the water off the port side and started to sink in the swirl of the prop wash.

A long time ago I worked on a murder case with my sister. Our client shot his wife and child and dumped their bodies in deep water. Then he called the Coast Guard and told them,

"You've got to help me, I just killed myself." The bodies were never found and our client has since died in prison, but during the trial the prosecuting attorney criticized my work on the case saying, "You private eyes never really find anything, do you?" At the time I must have smiled and said something self-deprecating. But over the last ten years or so I've been working on my snappy reply. The truth is I didn't find much. Like the molecular physicist who finally was afraid to set foot on the floor fearing he would fall between the gaps in the wood itself, in my investigations I see more doubt than certainty. I never find the smoking gun or the lead pipe with the bloody finger-prints on it, because everyone is looking for those. I find every-thing else, everything that has been left in the overturned rooms: the surface that wasn't blood-splattered, the dust on the knickknacks and family photo albums, but not on the excep-tionally clean retirement plaque; the music on the radio in the empty hallway after everyone has been taken to jail or the morgue. I do this because there is always trace evidence of innocence, and innocence is largely overlooked, even by a man oiling a gun with a child crying in the background on the day before a killing.

I thought of this as I was sinking below the hull of the *Winning Hand* because I knew I was dying and I was pissed off about it. I was already mad at the whole investigation surround-ing my death. I thought of the kids from the rescue squad running around the dock getting a thrill as they laid out the green rubber bag they would put me in. I thought of the bored detectives and their cynical expressions as they watched my drowned body being pulled out of the harbor. One would pour out his coffee as he recognized me but the other would carefully put his cup on the railing so he could get back to it later.

I fought against the water at first but as I watched the bubbles from my lungs arch up above me like a kite string, I was suddenly comforted. At least this time I would be first on the scene and I would know more than the cops, even if I was dead.

The boat hook snaked down and snagged my shirt. Then I was on the deck of the boat. Jane Marie was yelling and pounding on my chest.

"You didn't have to hit him! We don't have time to take him to the hospital! We've got to be in the bay in seven hours!" she yelled at Teller, who was standing over me. Beyond him I could see Priscilla standing at the controls of the flying bridge. She nervously fussed with her hair.

Harrison Teller looked down at me. He was still holding a canvas bag with what sounded like nuts and washers in it. He shifted it from one big hand to another. He bent over so that his mouth was close to my ear.

"You are a pest. I'd like that, normally. But I don't need you on this case, Mr. Younger." He let out a slow breath, then straightened and looked out over the flat water of the channel. "It's too complicated to let you drown, and we can't let you make a fuss if we put you ashore. So I guess you've just signed on this cruise." He smiled at me with a wild grin, then walked away.

"Thank you," was all I could manage to say. The boat pitched slightly on the swell, and as we passed under the bridge I saw the raven on its handrail. The bird was glittering black, strutting back and forth like a bowlegged admiral. Jane Marie squatted beside me on the deck. She put her hand on the side of my head.

"He shouldn't have hit you. I'm sorry." She spoke softly.

"That's okay." I looked up and I thought I saw the raven chattering in her dark eyes. The wind blew her collar against her neck. I was starting to shiver.

"Let's get you below. I've got some dry clothes for you, I think. At least some underwear and rain gear." She pulled on my hand and I stood and walked unsteadily to the passageway into the wheelhouse.

I guessed the *Winning Hand* was fifty feet overall. She had an open flying bridge on top of the wheelhouse that you could only get to by the ladder on the back deck. From the flying bridge the skipper could navigate and steer in good seas. The *Winning Hand* had been a seine boat in her commercial fishing days but a boom and winch over the back deck was all that was left of her commercial gear. There was a thirteen-foot Mexican-style skiff called a panga strapped across the back deck with a Japanese outboard on the stern. The outboard had a tiller extension made out of plastic pipe, so whoever was driving the panga could stand forward and look over the bow. Below the panga were two small yellow kayaks. We made our way around the gear and inside.

The inside of the seine boat was really one small room on

two levels. The levels were connected by a wide ladder of four steps. Below was the galley and two pairs of bunks. Off the galley was also the access to the engine room and on this particular boat, an access passageway to the wet lab that had been built in the old fish hold. Above on the deck level was the main wheelhouse with a table that could be used for meals or for laying out charts. The wheel was positioned on the port side. The radar and radios were mounted above the forward ports where the helmsman could look out over the front deck. Just behind where the helmsman would stand was the table and on the port side and the stern were padded benches where the crew could sit around the table during meals. Even for a relatively large boat the quarters were cramped. Think of living and driving a house around from the kitchen and pantry.

As I walked into the wheelhouse I had to duck my head. The diesel stove in the galley warmed the entire area and the smell of its fuel mingled with the scents of bleach, coffee, and mildew. Charts cluttered the table in the wheelhouse. I moved over to look at them but Jane Marie cut me off, quickly rolling up the charts. She stuffed them in a webbing above the steering station. She spoke to me as she ducked below: "Take off your wet things."

"How long are we going to be gone?" I asked her.

"I don't know," she said, then reached under one of the benches and found a small duffel bag. Rummaging through it she pulled out a pair of red long-handled underwear.

"You can wear these and some old rain gear. Maybe Teller has some extra stuff he can give you."

"Where are we going?" My teeth were starting to chatter as I peeled off my wet shirt.

She handed me a small bath towel. "We'll talk about it later." She would not look at me.

"Am I being kidnapped?" I asked in a cheery voice.

"Listen, Cecil—do you want to go back to the dock?"

"No," I said, while drying my hair. "I just wanted to clarify the situation, I mean, about being abducted."

"You're not being abducted, for chrissakes." She tossed a pair of rubber boots at me and I caught them in my towel.

"I missed you this morning. Your desk drawer was empty. You must have had another break-in?" I kept my voice cheerful.

She gritted her teeth. "I'm sorry I asked you for dinner, Cecil. I'm not sure why I did. But I can't undo it." Jane Marie broke into a faint smile. I watched her. I liked watching her. She had on her rubber boots, folded down, brown canvas pants, and a dark blue flannel shirt. When she pulled her billed cap out of the back pocket of her jeans, something sparked in her eyes, like a thought she wasn't ready to express. I could hear Teller's heavy footsteps on the deck of the flying bridge above us. I took off my wet underwear and she walked past me.

"I'll let you get dressed. Maybe we'll talk later. But"—she stopped close to me and tapped her index finger on my naked chest—"I am not answering questions." She walked out and left me naked with the feeling I had been dismissed.

I put on the long-handles and the bibbed pants of heavy rubber storm gear. I went down the narrow steps into the galley. On the galley counter were some papers and a notebook. I picked up a manila folder and opened it. Inside was a proof copy of the *Playing Around Review*. This was a different edition from the one I had seen before. I opened to the letters section and read the first one:

Dear Jane Marie,

Thanks for the ideas for the stacking dice game. You're right, being more of a luck-based game I was hopeful it would be less stressful to play with the man I'm interested in. He acts as if he is so groovy and not competitive at all, but when he gets going on a game look out!!! All that male stuff comes out. He all but *pees* on the dice!!!

Jane Marie, he is really cute. But I don't know. If he gets tense playing a stupid dice game that is mostly luck anyway, how could we have a life together? I'm thinking of dumping him. What do you think?

Willa in McGrath

And the response:

Dear Willa,

I'm at my wits' end with this guy too. We've tried lots of games with him and it seems he just wants you to get used to losing. (Or he wants you to win only on his terms, which is the same as losing.) As we have discussed many times in these pages, we all accept losing but nobody (especially you, Willa) should get used to it. It's time to fish or cut bait for this guy. If I remember, you are particularly good at the five-letter word game and the Hollywood trivia game. I'd insist on playing either one of those when he comes over, and I'd kick his butt each and every time. (Only at the games, remember.) If he keeps coming back he might be trainable. If not, blow him off. There are bigger fish in the sea.

Yours,
Jane Marie

The rest of the newsletter was a catalogue listing of board games with brief descriptions and recommendations on what kinds of games worked in different social settings. It was fun reading but not worth jimmying a drawer open for. I set the file back on the table and started looking in the cupboards. I found a bag of macaroni, a dusty can of baking powder, a tin of hot-chocolate powder. I shut the lower cabinet. Above the sink was a storage bin and when I opened it a bag fell out onto the counter. Inside were two boxes of dry cereal, kids' cereal, color-ful and sweet. The grocery bag was fresh and white. The boxes of cereal were brand new. Jammed between the boxes was a box of candy with a giveaway offer for a ninja doll. I put every-thing back in the storage bin.

JOHN STRALEY

"Hungry?"

I looked above me in the opening to the wheelhouse. Harrison Teller filled the small space. He had one foot on the top stair and his hat pulled low over his eyes. His hair spilled out over the shoulders of his wool coat and he was stroking his beard. His gaze flickered down on me.

"Mr. Younger, have you ever been seasick a day in your life?"

"Not yet."

"You have breakfast yet?"

"No," I said, and as I did I realized I was very hungry.

"Let's see if we can take care of that." He came down the steps. "It's hell to be puking on an empty stomach. I'll make us something." He took off his coat and laid it on a narrow padded bunk that ran parallel to the hull line. He noticed the papers on the table and without looking at them placed them up into the cupboard. I had to brush right next to him to make my way to the ladder up and out.

We were moving toward the southern end of Douglas Island. I was trying to figure out where we were going but there were few clues because so far, we were headed the only way to anywhere. All boats leaving the southern end of the channel would head this way. The channel is narrow and shallow near the old mining camps of Juneau but then opens out. Gradually we would move into the swells curling in from the southern ocean entrances. Several miles ahead, the fog came down to the water. The horizon was subsumed in gray. I stepped out of the wheelhouse onto the back deck. I climbed the ladder to the flying bridge. Jane Marie and Priscilla were standing braced against the wind with their collars up.

"Look here." Jane Marie pointed to the east. Gulls were diving and the water riffled silver on the surface. A gull dove and snatched a silvery fish and silently an eagle dove out of the west bearing down on the gull, stealing its fish.

"The herring are moving in. I heard the sac roe fishery is standing by in Sitka. There'll be some parties there tonight," Jane Marie commented to her sister. Priscilla said nothing.

Priscilla might have been thinking about how she was missing the chance to crew on one of the herring boats. The herring fleet goes after herring roe for the Japanese market. The boats can turn huge profits for their crews in a half-day opening. Crew shares have been twenty or thirty thousand dollars in the past. This would have gone a long way toward buying her a decent defense lawyer. Maybe she was thinking of that.

Priscilla, Jane Marie, and I watched the water and the gulls cutting the air. The boat rolled gently. Even though the wind had the iron bite of winter, occasionally we eased into a pool of warm air.

"Why don't you just have them bring the boy back to you?" I floated my words out on the wind.

Priscilla scowled at Jane Marie. Jane Marie bit her lip but did not take her eyes off the course in front of her.

Jane Marie cleared her throat and said, "It's complicated, Cecil. Besides, I said no questions."

Priscilla squinted at me. "You're not covered by the privilege." She looked smugly at me, assuming that I didn't know she was talking about the attorney-client privilege for confidential communication.

Teller heaved himself up onto the flying bridge. He had changed into a sweater and an old waxed-cotton raincoat. He carried a thermos and three plastic mugs.

"I'll make us something hot tonight. Maybe you want a cup of tea?" He held the mugs out to us and then continued to haul himself up on the deck. The *Winning Hand* rolled on the throb of her own engine. Jane Marie reached across and took the thermos and mugs as Teller moved across to the port side of the bridge. There was not room enough for all of us to stand forward so I stood behind Jane Marie. Teller pulled a red apple out of his pocket.

"Here," was all he said. His hand with the apple hung between us and he asked me, "How is your head?"

"Just where it should be," I said, and took the apple from him.

Teller watched the eagle sitting in the snag on the near shore eating his stolen fish. "That bastard." He smiled at me. "The gulls should organize."

Jane Marie moved her cup of tea to her mouth and left it there, letting the warmth ease up onto her face. She never stopped scanning the waterway. I kept looking at her, for she seemed to change in each weather. I looked at the two sisters standing together. It had been a long time since I had been able to do that. Jane Marie's hair was short now and Priscilla's was down past her shoulders. This morning it was tucked up inside a rain hat. She squinted her eyes and the creases on her face showed the years of being out in the weather. The sisters had similar features: straight narrow noses, full lips. And even though Jane Marie was older and had been out in the weather more, her face seemed less worn than her sister's.

If you have to be kidnapped, being abducted in a diesel-powered boat is very restful. Juneau faded over our left shoulders. Along the shore I saw the end of the road and even though I had questions needling inside my head, I felt something quiet settling over the water. The thrum of the engine seemed less like mechanical noise and more like the breath of the old wooden boat. Traveling by boat gives the mind more time to look around; forward, backward, and maybe even inward.

Even Teller seemed to brighten, as if he were coming out of himself and was less heavy with his own plans. "You ever make this trip, Cecil?" he asked, and he looked at me with eyes that were softer and not cross-examining.

Jane Marie blurted out, "Yeah, he made this trip with me and my brother once. Do you remember?"

I hadn't, but the second she said the words, a dim memory began to surface, something about card games, hot dogs, and a fire.

"Right there . . ." Jane Marie pointed to the shore of the mainland. "You came with us on a short trip. It was the first time I ever shot the moon in hearts. I remember we were passing that point. I shot the moon and I threw the cards up in the air. You were so cute, Cecil." Teller was grinning like a dog, and Priscilla moved in closer to Teller, trying to keep away from me.

Priscilla's scowling could have warmed the air between us. But Jane Marie went on, "You tried to act like it didn't matter but you pouted the whole way home."

"I was your guest. You were supposed to let me win," I offered lamely.

"Fat chance." She was shaking her head.

"Were you playing for money?" Teller asked.

"No. My folks played for money. Even now I don't. Mostly I just wanted to play 'knee-sies' under the table with Cecil here. If we had been playing for money he might never have forgiven me."

Teller smiled at us. "Yeah, money screws up good games. I used to have a cabin on a river. We used to play some games for buttons. If you had enough buttons you . . ." His voice drifted off and he turned his head to watch a gull glide the air cresting above the boat. The gull disappeared down by the wake and then off past the curve of the island. Teller was watching some distant thing and he didn't speak anymore.

We finished the tea. Teller took the thermos down. Jane Marie stepped to the side of the wheel and toward her sister. She stood close to her sister and spoke softly to her. "Look. There is Shoot-the-Moon Point. A couple of miles on is where I cut Poppa's hair. Were you with us, Cilla? We sat at anchor after fishing and he wanted me to cut his hair." She and Priscilla watched the water slip under the bow. Priscilla put her hand on Jane Marie's shoulder in a gesture that may have been asking for support or for distance.

Suddenly Priscilla pointed south to the fog bank that lay

like a chalk cliff ahead of us. "That's where he was supposed to be fishing his last time out . . . when he didn't come home. He was supposed to be right there, but he wasn't." Her voice had the bite of anger. A flight of six old squaw ducks beat their short wings into the fog and disappeared.

Jane Marie stood at the wheel with her eyes closed for a moment. When she opened them I touched her shoulder. "If Young Bob's been kidnapped, the police will help you," I said to them. Then I turned to look directly at Priscilla and added, "No matter what."

Priscilla pulled away from us and walked to the ladder to go below. She looked with intensity at Jane Marie and shook her head. Jane Marie nodded. Priscilla went down the ladder.

Jane Marie and I stood without talking. She started to reach her palm to my face but stopped, then ran her fingers through her hair. Her eyes glimmered but this time with sadness and the weight of fatigue. I stood close to her and it struck me that what I smelled last night wasn't the rain or the storm on her skin but her skin's own smell.

"Yes. You can help me. In time," she said, even though I hadn't offered.

I started to reach out. She pulled away and turned back to steering her course. It appeared to be the end of our conversation. I still had the apple in my hand, so I took a bite. Then I climbed down onto the back deck.

Priscilla was sitting on the hatch cover in the stern. I walked around the lines that tied the skiff onto the deck and stood above her. The gulls followed above the wake of the prop. I could hear the hiss of the whitewater above the engine noise. I took another bite of the apple. I was chewing it as I watched Priscilla staring down at her gnawed fingernails in her lap. The apple was sweet and firm and I held it out to her to see if she wanted some. She shook her head.

"Do you know where Young Bob is right now?" I asked her.

"No," she said, not taking her eyes off the water.

"Are you really trying to get him back?"

She looked up at me as if I were about to pour gas on her. She stared and I could hear all of the threats and recriminations she was spewing in her imagination. But she kept silent. She grabbed the apple out of my hand and threw it overboard.

"Yeah, I'm trying to get him back," she said.

The apple disappeared in the rush of white water from the prop. It bobbed up and a gull dove but could not lift the fruit. The boat moved away from the apple with the white crescents bitten out of it. In just seconds, I could just barely see it, tiny in the gray-green water. The wind cut around me and I could smell the diesel exhaust from the stack. I was suddenly cold and feeling exposed to the weather. Priscilla lightly tapped her palms on the surface of the hatch and watched as the apple floated into the currents that churned with the force of the earth and the moon up and down this coast. We both watched it until it became as distant as the pinprick of Mars in a summer sky. Then it was gone. Priscilla stood up and went to the cabin without saying a word to me. The *Winning Hand* moved into the fog that had been ahead of us all morning long.

When I opened the door of the cabin I was met by the smells of garlic and tomatoes. I walked across the wheelhouse and looked down into the galley. Teller was making spaghetti sauce. He had his T-shirt on and had set up a portable radio in the galley. He was tapping a wooden spoon on the lip of the cast-iron pot in time to a broken transmission of "Ornithology" by Charlie Parker. He saw me and said, "Hey, I'm going to let this cook all day. Is that okay?"

"Fine," I said to him as I stood back from the galley steps and watched our new heading. Teller started humming along with the radio as Jane Marie came in the wheelhouse and turned on the radar to locate our position in the fog.

We ran until late in the afternoon heading gradually back to the north, then a brief tack south, picking our way past the many rocks on the edges of the channels and at the entrances of bays. Jane Marie steered and navigated from the wheelhouse, Teller fussed with his radio in the galley and Priscilla lay on a bottom bunk with her hands folded over her chest not sleeping but staring up into the planking above her.

Just an hour before dark we arrived in a tight anchorage between two smaller islands. While Teller put on a sweater and opened the wine, I went on deck to let the anchor chain run. Jane Marie reversed the boat until the anchor grabbed, then turned off the engine. Silence poured down on us like a warm rain. The presence of the small wooded islands moved in all around. A blue heron landed on the narrow beach unhinging itself like a marionette being let down. Back in the woods a raven made that strange sound like someone plucking a damped piano string. We sat around the table in the wheelhouse. Jane Marie and I were shoulder to shoulder and Priscilla came in moving to the corner and avoiding any eye contact with me. She would start to speak, look at me, then check herself. Time and again she jumped up and worked the knob of the VHF radio that was used for communicating. Jane Marie grimaced at her sister and motioned for her to sit down.

I felt a slight tickle in my head and then a pain like a shard of glass caught inside my temple. Jane Marie saw my expression. She pointed to a drawer to the left of the wheel. "There's aspirin in there." I didn't move. I had the stupid feeling I was about to dislodge something in my head. Both Teller and Priscilla watched me and from their expressions I imagined they were hoping I would pass out and die. Long minutes passed. Teller drummed his fingers on the table and Jane Marie watched me. Priscilla jumped up and again adjusted the VHF radio. She checked the squelch and kept looking at the numbers that indicated the frequency. Finally she blurted out, "I told you we couldn't trust them, for God's sake."

Jane Marie chose her words carefully. "We are here now. We can wait and monitor the channel on the radio they are supposed to call on. If that doesn't help, we will . . . change plans."

"Hell. Let's talk about something else." Reaching underneath his seat Teller pulled out a bottle of whiskey. He poured into three mugs, gave one to Jane Marie then held another out to me. I shook my head and he poured my mug into his own.

Jane Marie drank a sip and took a deep breath. She put

her mug down and knelt under the automatic pilot unit where there was a small office safe. She worked the combination and opened the safe, then stood up.

"Thanks for the drink." She spoke politely to Teller. "Earlier I saw you had a holster under your coat, and I saw a pistol down in the galley. . . ."

"Yep, that's right. Is there a problem?" Teller tried to work a winning smile on Jane Marie but she did not change her expression.

She continued in the same polite tone. "If there is an open bottle of whiskey I've got to lock the gun up. That's my practice."

Teller smiled ruefully and wedged himself back farther into his seat. He shook his great bushy head. "I'll be fine. You don't have to worry. The gun won't come out."

She moved past me quickly and reached across the cramped table. Her arm went inside his sweater before he could clear his hands from under the table. She pulled out a nine-millimeter automatic pistol with plastic grips. Priscilla shrieked, "Janie, cut it out. We need the gun. Just lock up the whiskey, for God's sake."

Teller made a sudden move. I stood up and he looked at me coldly. Later, I realized he thought I was positioning myself for a fight, when in truth I was looking for a place to duck. Jane Marie calmly held the pistol in front of his face. She slipped the clip out of the bottom of the grips and worked the action. The shell clattered down the steps.

JOHN STRALEY

"No guns and whiskey on this boat. If it's important enough, you and your pistol can sleep on shore."

Teller looked back and forth between us. Then he smiled and pulled the bottle up between his legs. "You're the skipper." He poured himself another drink.

Priscilla motioned again toward the radio. "We may need that gun, Janie." Her expression was growing frantic.

"No, we won't," Jane Marie told her flatly. Then she turned and handed the gun and clip to me. "Cecil, could you lock this up? Just put it in there and spin the dial."

I bent down and placed the pistol and clip in the safe on top of a brown accordion file folder. I gently closed the safe. When I straightened, a white light flashed. I felt the ice pick far inside my head as if it were sparking across hot wires. I sat down limply on the table.

Teller stared up at me. "You okay?"

I shook my head, which may have been a mistake. "It's only a headache."

"You want drugs?"

I looked at him eagerly. I thought of the bubbles of my breath arching up to the surface. I knew the pain would pass . . . or not, but either way pills weren't going to help. I didn't really know what was going to happen next, but if my mind was going to explode I guess I wanted to be there when it did.

"No . . . but thanks."

"Well, as long as we are guaranteed against getting in a

gunfight I might as well get serious." He fished into the pockets of his sweater and took out three prescription pill bottles. He shook out several pills and held them across the table in his leathery palm. "Painkillers and antidepressants. I get them by the caseload."

I forced my head to keep shaking no. Teller looked down at the pills and shrugged his shoulders. "What the hell," he mumbled. He washed them down with whiskey. I could smell the liquor and imagined the slow burn and the chemical haze moving in. I sat in the helmsman's chair near the starboard corner of the wheelhouse and considered changing my mind about the drugs.

Teller and Jane Marie moved down into the galley to prepare dinner. Priscilla kept fidgeting with the radio and watching the anchorage for the boat we were apparently scheduled to meet.

There were three radios in the wheelhouse: one old single sideband that was kept off, a citizen's band that was tuned with the volume low, and the loud VHF, which was not tuned to the common hailing frequency. Belowdecks Teller was listening to a radio he had brought with him. It covered all commercial radio frequencies: AM, FM, and shortwave. As he chopped vegetables he tuned in music stations. In the wheelhouse Priscilla kept jumping up to change channels and tune in to the ship-to-ship communications on the VHF. Fishermen and tugboat operators hailed each other on the VHF, then asked to go to other channels. They'd call out the names of their boats: the *Janice*

Lee, the *Ocean Cape*, the *Westerly*. I watched the shoreline. A kingfisher hovered above the elephant-colored rocks of low tide. It dropped a mussel on the rocks and dove on the splinters. Below, a Chopin nocturne mournfully strode up the scale. Chopin gave way to static and a cover of a Grand Funk Railroad tune, then Billie Holiday, then a news report of mass killings in Bosnia. Jane Marie begged Teller to leave it on one channel but he said if he couldn't get drunk and shoot things he would at least have his way with his own radio, which I think had a scanning mechanism that sought out the strongest signal, but apparently all the signals were weak.

The sun was setting and the long breath of spring was expelled. The blue heron waded the shoreline cocking and bobbing its strangely hinged legs, hunting slowly in the shallows. Richard Thompson sang about crime and love with his cock-eyed lead guitar. The darker it became, the better the reception and the songs pressed in more vividly. Bill Monroe, U2, Billy Strayhorn, an ad for tires, Cher, Ali Farka Toure, Moving Hearts, Garth Brooks, a comic sketch as an ad for a boat repair shop, the Beach Boys, Roy Acuff. Suddenly the radio stopped on a solo piano playing a Brahms concerto. I watched a land otter scramble after the broken mussel shells, the kingfisher swooped and the otter rolled on its back, twisting and flailing, as perfectly flexible as a drop of water. The sad, Gypsy voice of the Brahms shattered into more static and Al Green surfaced, then Elvis Costello, then a call-in show on the mill closure in Sitka. Finally, it was almost purely dark and I was watching my reflection on the glass. Teller had switched to shortwave, Russian softly gave way to booming Spanish, then static and strange tripping rhythms of high-pitched squealing. Finally Teller settled on the operatic voice of an Italian tenor. I didn't know the title but the melody of the tenor voice looped out of the galley, sung at some time unknown, some thousands of miles away from our boat sitting at anchor. The voice soared around the chart table and followed Teller through the companionway as he carried the spaghetti and red wine into the wheelhouse. The heron squawked as it took flight and I could barely see its form as it passed the last of the light in the sky. Its entire body worked the air in long strokes as it disappeared.

"How's the headache?" He handed me my dinner.

"Much better." I teetered the plate on my knees and shook away his offer of the wine. "Good choice of tunes."

Priscilla had to move out of the way as Jane Marie came up from the galley with a pan full of green salad. We ate in silence. Teller kept filling his mug from the bottle of red wine. The VHF radio broke in through the opera with the names of hailing vessels.

Jane Marie pushed back her plate. She said, "After dishes you guys want to play a game?" Priscilla snorted and looked up at the radio, not even wanting to dignify that with a response.

In his drunkenness Teller's eyes rambled around the wheelhouse. "I'm not into games. Sorry."

"Not into games? You're a lawyer. How can that be?" Jane Marie spoke in mock amazement.

He smiled. "Hate the goddamn rules." A bit of tomato sauce flecked on his beard.

"We could design a game where we all agree on the rules."

"Would I be guaranteed to win?"

"That could be one of the rules."

"What fun would that be?"

Jane Marie picked at a carrot slice on her plate. "Well, the game could be between Priscilla and me on how best to let you win."

"No." Teller wiped his beard and stared at her. He was not smiling anymore. "That's just keeping secrets. I hate that, too." Then he looked at me and his eyes brightened. "Anyway, once you do a murder trial, regular games don't hold much interest," he said with a dismissive gesture.

"Murder trials are not games," Priscilla shot back, taking her eyes off the radio.

"Oh, that's just one-upmanship." Jane Marie nudged her sister. Then she looked at me for some sort of support but I was listening to the opera.

The wine bottle was empty. Teller poured more whiskey into his mug. I was smiling because I could hear a raven and the Italian tenor simultaneously.

"Let me ask you," Teller continued, trying to aim his unsteady gaze on Jane Marie. "In Priscilla's case, what do you want more: a full airing of the truth or her acquittal?"

She leaned forward. "I want both."

"What if she is going to be put in prison for the rest of her life? What if you had to make a choice between the truth and your sister?"

Jane Marie turned away from him suddenly and adjusted the gain on the radio. "I just want you to follow the rules. And use the truth."

As he tried to steady his big head he looked sullen and fierce. "The rules change. That's one of the rules. I always try cases on the truth. Look . . ." He leaned forward and his eyes began to glow with the fierce stare that even pills and whiskey would not diminish. "The cops arrested her and they are going to prove she is guilty as sin of"—he rapped his fist on the wooden table—"cracking open Wilfred Taylor's skull."

"What is the story of Priscilla's innocence?" I asked from my corner. Priscilla had her head buried in her hands, her shoulders hunched. The radio was silent.

Teller mumbled, "I haven't thought of it yet. But when I do, it will be a true story. . . ."

On the commercial radio in the galley the aria was over; there was the static of the long-distance radio transmission. The voice of an Eastern European reader came up from below. Then the sad melody of a Balkan folk song.

Teller leaned forward. He reached across the table and rubbed the knuckles of Jane Marie's right hand. "You don't need to be so afraid of me."

She pulled her hand away quickly and held her mug up to her lips. She looked at me to see if I had noticed. The VHF radio crackled the transmission from a boat called the *Rose*.

Priscilla heard the voice on the radio and walked onto the back deck without saying a word. Jane Marie's eyes lingered on the radio, then back to meet Teller's with an intensity of her own. She took a long swallow out of the mug, then banged it on the table. "I'm not afraid of you. I just don't like you much."

Teller shook his head.

The radio crackled, the *Rose* was on channel 68. The operator never said the name of the vessel he was calling. He only said, "This is the *Rose*, the *Rose*, the *Rose*, channel six eight," and the transmission went dead. Below, the folk song had ended and the voice of the reader gave us the news in a language we didn't understand.

Jane Marie turned to me. "You just stay here and rest, Cecil. We'll take care of the dishes below. I mean it. I don't want you going anywhere."

I looked at her evenly and nodded my understanding. Jane Marie stepped down into the galley.

Teller and I were alone. He stared down into his empty mug. His eyes were nearly closed. He was looking at his cup as if it were a high pair in a poker game that he needed to stay in. Finally, he got up and went down to the galley. He did not speak to me. He did not acknowledge my being there.

On the back deck Priscilla was unstrapping one of the short broad kayaks that were secured under the skiff. She grabbed the double-ended paddle out of the panga and lifted the kayak over the gunwales of the *Winning Hand*. She looked up and saw me watching her. She waved vaguely, more in a gesture to dismiss me than to say good-bye. She lowered the kayak into the dark water.

I looked down into the galley. Teller had plugged headphones into his radio and was listening to the world of transmissions as he was doing the dishes. I could see the bright blue socks on Jane Marie's feet as she lay on top of a sleeping bag on one of the bunks. I could see the lower corner of a chart she was studying. If I was careful I might take care of my chores without being heard.

I hadn't locked the safe. I had worried all during dinner that if the boat rocked its door would swing open. So I had stayed close by to keep my foot near the safe. Now I leaned down and took out the nine-millimeter, reinserted the clip and tucked it in my belt. Then I took one of the flashlights that hung on lanyards near the wheel and I opened the accordion file folder that had been inside the safe, shining the light on the papers.

There were real estate contracts for a house in Sitka. Jane Marie had purchased Priscilla's house. There were some financial records of trust-fund annuities set up for Young Bob. There were letters from a Native man who was writing to let Jane Marie know that she could have partial use of the island that he held in a long-term lease from the government. She could use it as a base for her whale research. I flipped through the papers hurriedly, listening for a footfall on the steps or the rustling of Jane Marie's chart. More financial records, an address list with my and Dickie's phone numbers and residences on it. I was almost ready to jam the accordion file back in the safe when I

came to the manila folder marked "Adoption." I put the flashlight in my mouth and used both hands to go through the
folder.

There were letters back and forth from the Sullivan family
to Jane Marie. The last sheaf of papers were on Harrison
Teller's letterhead. It was an agreement for Jane Marie to as-
sume custody of Young Bob. It had been signed by Robert Sullivan II and Jane Marie DeAngelo. Their signatures had been
notarized in different states on different days. There was a sig-
nature line for Priscilla DeAngelo Sullivan that was blank.
Clipped to the back of the last letter was a handwritten note
from Senator Taylor. It read: *Jane Marie, we've known each other
too well and for too long to try and bluff now. Please, this situation
with your sister has got to stop. Just get her to sign this. We can all
get moving with our lives. I know you accuse me of complicating the
situation, but believe me, all I want at this point is to simplify.
W.T.*

I placed the manila file back into the accordion file in as
neat an order as I could manage. I shut the safe quietly and
turned the dial. I went out on the deck and unstrapped the
other kayak and put it in the water. I didn't worry they would
find me missing. They weren't going to pull the anchor at night
and I doubted they were going to have time to put the skiff in
the water.

As I sat low in the water trying to find my balance in the
kayak the grips of Teller's gun cut into my waist. I almost cap-
sized, but once I was situated I shifted around to set the gun on
my lap.

It was a rare clear night. There was not a trace of the morning fog on the water. I could hear the breath of the slight swells against the shore. I could make out the outlines of the islands that seemed like the outlines of dark animals in the distance. As I paddled away from the light of the *Winning Hand* I felt as if I were being sucked up by the darkness. I heard the water and a distant stream. Somewhere perhaps a rustling in the woods. I heard the generator of another boat around the spit of the island to the north. I dipped the ends of the kayak paddle and watched as the blades stirred phosphorescence in my wake. I heard the wings of a large bird whispering by in the dark. The wind sizzled in the hemlock trees. The kayak rocked and I could faintly detect a light reflected on the water from another boat deeper back in the anchorage. I came too close to the point and bumped a rock. I hadn't seen it and it jarred me so I almost tipped again. I regained my seat and turned inland of the rock and slipped into the shallow water around the point where a fiberglass pleasure boat was drifting.

It was the *Rose*, what looked to be a twenty five-foot planning hull cabin cruiser. On her back deck was a superstructure the fishermen call a hayrack that held the inflatable dinghy. Hanging under that was a light. Priscilla was in her kayak, clinging to the stern of the *Rose* and looking up at the figure standing under the light. The cruiser's light was bone bright and spread out over the black water as if it were a rainbow of oil.

Young Bob was standing there crying in long heaving sobs, reaching out his arms as if he were pleading to be picked up. He was wearing a bulky old life preserver and a blue sweatshirt.

Priscilla leaned forward in the kayak, the paddle laid perpendicular to the hull. She leaned forward and spoke in low soothing tones, but Young Bob cried and cried, his sobs like breaking glass and sirens on a peaceful night.

A man in a wool stocking cap came out on the deck of the *Rose* and put his hand on Young Bob's shoulder. He pointed over Priscilla's shoulder toward me. Then he ducked his head back inside the wheelhouse and the engines blared awake. All I could hear above the mechanical grinding was Young Bob's whining cry and Priscilla's voice thumping out a percussion. "Wait . . . wait . . ."

The *Rose* swung back out of the anchorage and powered up onto a running step past me in the dark. As it rounded the point I saw the man pulling Young Bob back into the cabin of the boat. In seconds the *Rose* was gone. The silence moved back in with a chill. I braced myself against a rock and the wake of the big boat sloshed into the cockpit of the kayak. I rocked back and forth pivoting my weight against the end of my paddle to keep upright.

Without the light of the boat my eyes adjusted again to the dark. The stars reflected on the water as if they were pinpoints of white rain needling down. Priscilla sat motionless in her kayak, which rocked in the last of the wake of the *Rose*. I pushed a few times with the paddle and drifted close to her. She lifted her face up to the sky and I could see she was crying now. Tears glinted on her skin.

"They weren't going to give him to me anyway," she said. "They want money and I don't have it."

I nodded and watched her. We sat for a long time listening to the sounds of her sobs, the night birds in the trees and the whine of the *Rose* disappearing in the dark. Finally Priscilla looked up at me and said, "An old woman told me about this bay." She took a deep breath and wiped her nose. "When the people camped here there was a beaver who would bring them food. The beaver brought them everything they needed: fish, berries, deer, even halibut. It was such a good place the beaver had her baby here. One day the beaver went hunting and a hunter killed the baby and thoughtlessly skinned him out. He wasted the meat. The mother was so upset she turned the river upside down."

Priscilla turned on a flashlight and she shined it toward the shore. There was a cavern at the tide line and a stream running out. "I don't believe anything the lawyers say, Cecil. I don't trust Harrison Teller as far as I could throw him, but I know for a fact that old woman told me a true story."

I followed the beam of her flashlight to the black mouth of a cavern where the river ran into the bay. Priscilla's voice seemed to follow the light.

"I've been inside that cave. You can see shells embedded in the rock, sticks and river stones, everything from that time when the river was right side up."

She shined the flashlight onto the shore but all I could make out were the dim forms of stumps.

"If I can't have my boy I'm going to turn this world inside out. I know you don't believe that, Cecil, but I swear it's true.

It's as true as the story about my being innocent." She turned
off the light and tucked it into her kayak.

"Do you think I'm innocent, Cecil?"

"Hell, Cilla, I think everybody's innocent."

"Well, they're not," she said as she paddled past me, floating in the swirl of phosphorescence and stars.

7

The next morning I woke up to the vibration of the engine, then the anchor chain rattling across the deck. I smelled the familiar mixture of diesel fuel, mildew, and coffee. Music was coming from the radio: a thumping rap song about guns and cops. As I pulled my damp pant legs on I felt the *Winning Hand* move away from its anchorage and I heard the water lapping under the planking of the hull.

Teller was in the galley bobbing his head to the rhythm and spooning thick oatmeal with raisins into mugs.

"Hey! How's the head?"

"Good. Good." I took some coffee. "Where are we headed?"

He looked up to the wheelhouse and nodded. "Ask the skipper. She's been quiet with me this morning." He handed me a mug of oatmeal. "I should know better than to try and flirt with a scientist. Why not take this up to her?"

I climbed the steep stairs to where Jane Marie stood at the

wheel. She didn't look down at me as I came in. She was watching the mouth of the cove.

"There are rocks just south of the middle of the entrance. They are wrong on the charts. I have to pay some attention here."

She waved for me to put the mug down and I set it on the chart. She scowled at me, then moved the mug to the flat shelf behind the wheel. The sky was purely blue this morning. There was no trace of yesterday's fog. To the east, the mountains of the mainland had fresh snow near the tree line. The granite peaks were vivid in the sunlight. The water showed only the slight riffle of wind from the north. On one of the near islands, six sea lions rested on the black slabs of stone. As the *Winning Hand* passed to the south they slipped into the water, jutting their sleek heads back out on the surface, blasting air through their nostrils, and lifting their heads to watch us pass. They curled underwater and their hides were slick in the sun. Then they were gone.

She scanned the waterway with her binoculars.

"I've been thinking. I could drop you in Tenakee. You don't have to be a part of this."

"That's true." I sipped my coffee. The engine droned, shouldering away at the silence between us. I carefully put my cup down away from the charts. I said, "I'd like to stay. If that's all right."

She studied her course, scanning the distance, her hands making slight course corrections on the wheel. Because she wasn't going to speak, I continued, "If they kidnapped him and you know who they are, the boy is in a lot of danger. Is that what you want?"

She turned her head. "No," she said. Her voice wasn't ironic but merely tired. The boat heeled slightly to port as we rounded the point of the anchorage. To the north there were streaks of low clouds near the surface. In the distance gulls circled like a broken mobile.

"Where are we going?" I asked over the engine noise.

"Right now? To whale camp."

"You don't have to tell me if you don't want."

"No, really, Cecil. I've got a camp north of here. It's an old mining site. I use it as a base for my research. I sometimes use it as a base when the humpbacks are feeding in Icy Strait and northern Chatham Strait. I'm going to meet an engineer there. He's coming out to clean the cabin up the hill from my camp. The Forest Service wouldn't let me use the site unless I cleaned up the camp." She read her compass heading and set the automatic pilot. Then she stood back from the wheel.

"You need an engineer to clean a cabin?" I asked her.

"Last summer we found some old dynamite cached there. The wrappers were rotten and you could see the nitro sweating on the outside of the sticks. Very dangerous stuff. The Forest Service is making me get an engineer's report. A blaster is going to fly out and take care of it for us. I didn't have to, but I decided to meet him there."

"Are we going to meet the *Rose* there too?"

She shook her head, saying nothing. She touched the tip of my finger. "Cecil, I'm going to drop you in Tenakee. You can

soak in the baths, then take the ferry back to Sitka. Really, I'm
sorry I got you into this."

"I don't want to get off in Tenakee."

She let out a long breath and scanned the water. We
didn't speak for several minutes. Behind us I could faintly see
the heads of three sea lions moving through the water. Jane
Marie absently tapped her compass. "This is such a mess," she
said softly.

I nodded in agreement but I don't know if she saw me.
She went on. "Look, I really don't know much more than you
do. Some of what I know makes logical sense but most of it
doesn't."

"That's what my whole life is like," I told her.

She grinned and dialed a course correction into the automatic pilot. "You know what I really want, Cecil?" She turned
back to her course heading. "I'd like to be free from all this
crap. I'd like to get back to doing my work." The momentum in
her voice built. "I'd like to have a decent conversation with you
but mostly, I'd like to clear my head of all this . . . fuzziness."
She adjusted the throttle. The engine noise reduced in pitch.
The boat seemed to relax.

"Cecil, all I've ever wanted is to be a scientist. I thought
science had the answers. I thought it was a perfect cooperative
and self-correcting language." She again reset the automatic
pilot, saying the new course heading softly under her breath.
"But it can't overcome the problem."

"The problem?" I asked tentatively.

She smiled to herself. The *Winning Hand* was approaching

the wheeling gulls. Jane Marie picked up the binoculars and spoke absently. "The problem is how to make sense of things. How can I understand the rules when I don't know what the game is?" She set down the binoculars. She was biting her lip. Her hands gripped the wheel tightly. "My handicap . . . ," she said almost inaudibly, ". . . my family's handicap is a low tolerance for unhappiness."

I thought about her family's problem. Below us Teller's radio started to boom out some African dance music. His voice rose above the din. It sounded as if he were lecturing Priscilla but I couldn't make out the words above the music and the engine noise.

I wanted to ask another question, but I kept my peace. Jane Marie ate her oatmeal, but as she ate she kept watching where the gulls were circling nearer and nearer. Then she stopped scanning and watched the surface of the water near the gulls, as if she were taking aim. "I wish I could explain it better but . . ." She paused. Finally she lifted her arm and pointed. "There!"

Off the port side of the *Winning Hand* a spume of vapor hung in the air. Three whales were feeding to the northeast. One, closer in, was at rest. Jane Marie glanced at her watch, then slowed the engines, flipped off the autopilot, and turned the boat away from the resting whale.

Two hundred yards off, a humpback lay still in the water. Beyond three more moved in slow even breaths. The whales rose in the water showing only the high ridges of their curved backs with the triangular dorsal fins on top. In the sunlight you could see the water sheeting down their slick rubbery hides. One dove and at the end of the dive lifted its flukes out of the water. Behind them round flat spots of water were forced to the surface by their dive.

Jane Marie grabbed my hand. Her eyes sparkled with adrenaline. "Come on, I'll show you." For some reason I didn't like the sound of her voice, but there was something in her expression, the way she physically urged me, that unplugged my better judgment.

I don't really remember now how we ended up in the water swimming near the whales. Any of the preparation has been crowded out of my memory by the animals I saw flying beneath me. I've felt small before, like when I was a child holding my father's hand and we walked under the hull of a battleship in dry dock. And I've felt uncomfortably big, like the time I visited my old kindergarten classroom and tried to sit at a desk. But I've never felt such a swirl of disorientation as that first moment when Jane Marie helped me over the edge of the skiff into the water with the warm-blooded creatures feeding on the clouds of little silvery fish. I had never been so close to an animal the size of a Continental Trailways bus, and I wouldn't have then if I hadn't been caught in the stupid push/pull of fear and exhilaration. All I could see of the sleeping whale was its back near the sharklike dorsal fin. I knew from watching TV that it had other parts. I could imagine the wings of its pectoral fins and the head that looks mostly like snout. I had watched most of a documentary about whales. I had seen pictures of them circling their prey and blowing rings of bubbles to corral them against the surface, then lunging underneath and trapping them in their pleated throats. But this was uncomfortably different from TV. I was in a wet suit hanging on to the side of the skiff. I was sure I felt the humpback's pulse vibrating against the hull of the skiff, which was beginning to feel like the size of a walnut shell. The cold water sliced down my backbone. We were about thirty feet away from the whale but I felt like I was standing on its back.

"Do you trust me?" I remember Jane Marie asking.

"No."

She smiled. "Okay, but do you trust her?" She pointed to the nearest whale.

"No. Not in the least. I mean, she looks kind of clumsy, to tell the truth. What if we wake her up and she . . . rolls over or something? I mean, she might have a nice disposition but so do golden retrievers and I wouldn't walk up to a forty-ton golden retriever when it was asleep."

"Oh, come on."

That was all the argument it took, "Oh, come on," and suddenly I'm risking my life pulling a tiny skiff through the water toward a snoozing mammal larger than an earthmover.

Jane Marie strapped the weight belt on, then moved closer to my head and jerked my hood away from my ear. She whispered, "Try not to splash when you swim close to her. I don't want to wake her up." I started to offer to get back in the boat. But she interrupted me. "And don't try to make sense of it. That just gets in the way of your observations." Then she stuck the snorkel in my mouth and pushed away. I watched her for a second and she turned back suddenly, then her face reappeared in front of mine. She spit out her snorkel.

"And Cecil, you shouldn't have read those papers in my safe." She pushed off from the side of the skiff and swam away.

The cold water crawled up my shoulders like fire ants. I wished I had drunk more coffee so I could have peed to warm up. I lowered my face mask below the surface. In every direction was the green curtain and the sunlight forming a single halo everywhere I looked. This was my worst fear of flying. I was suspended a thousand feet above the muddy bottom. I put my head above the water trying to orient myself. I looked back up to the impossibly high sides of the skiff. The *Winning Hand* sat two hundred yards off, as distant as a tropical island. As the water numbed my face and forehead around the rim of my mask I knew I wanted to be back on board the boat standing next to the warm stove. But Jane Marie had disappeared, the skiff was drifting away. I was there, flying in a thousand feet of water. The panic was a mild nausea until I turned my head and saw the whale. Then panic became a sparkler burning in my chest.

From this angle the whale was a breathing ridge of warm-blooded animal engulfing the horizon. I put my face back in the water but I could see nothing. Just the green infinity. I paddled quickly after Jane Marie until I could see her flippers churning. I looked up out of the water; the sleeping whale was so close I had to turn my head to be able to take in what was showing above the surface. With my head above the water I heard the explosion of her breath as pressure against my body rather than sound. I looked under the water and again, nothing but the green halo.

Suddenly a low grunt almost lifted my body out of the water. Then a high prolonged creaking, dipping down into a hiccupping chattering sound, reminiscent of a forty-ton monkey. The three whales that had moved to the northeast were returning. I couldn't see them. I could only hear the barking that built from the impossibly low vibration, echoing against thousands of feet of water. Voices echoed in an immense space. Floating there, I felt like a wren trapped in a cathedral.

The sleeping whale grunted again. I felt the water stir. I heard the movement of water like the rush of a winter river. Rubbery white fins flashed in front of me. The shadow of something trailing bubbles the size of cantaloupes. The shadow moved slowly but with inexorable force, like a school bus rolling off a cliff. I could never see its entire length in this murky water, but only dim parts of the whole: a shifting of enormous curve and shadow.

Then the flukes were there. They were as wide as a blade of a bulldozer about to roll over me. As the flukes swept past, the push of water threw me back. Water rushed down my snorkel. Icy pain burned up my nose and around my sinuses. "I've got to get out of here!" my inner, most sensible, voice began to shriek like a spoiled child.

Below the surface of the water, the greenness began to shimmer with silver. These were herring. I had watched enough TV to know the whales were beginning the next step in consolidating the feed. Like the aurora borealis, herring curled and roiled beneath me. The water felt hot with the possibility of whales. Then the grunts came louder by a factor of ten: the echoing bellow of huge lungs, and a curtain of bubbles started to rise up all around me. Panicked herring swirled around me.

I jutted my head out of water, spit my mouthpiece out and sputtered for air. Jane Marie bobbed next to me. She grabbed my shoulders and spoke slowly and evenly.

"Just. Swim. For the skiff. Splash as much as you can. Swim."

Underneath us, storms of fish geysered up toward the surface. Trillions of flashing strips like rain caught in the light: eyes, tails, black mouths gaping, and disappearing. I worked the water with my legs. Arms struggling, I tried to make my awkward walking body slice through water. The grunts grew louder. Wings of white fins cut the green.

Suddenly a sea lion was poised right in front of my face. A five-hundred-pound creature clear and perfectly defined as if it were floating in a dream. The sea lion paused and considered me, the light in its dark eyes sympathetic and uncomfortably human. Then it was gone in the murk. Herring brushed my wet suit. The skiff hull floated just yards ahead. Underneath and just behind me the whales like buildings rose up out of the ocean: rubbery forms of immense curved space jutting up with maws wide. I looked at the hull of the skiff and I pushed hard.

We reached the skiff as the four humpback whales broke the surface ten yards behind us. Gulls had gathered to dive into the slurry of fish concentrated by the net of bubbles. Sea lions curled in and around, feeding on the herring. Everything was in the foreground of the lead-colored behemoths with knobby snouts and pleated throats distended with water. The humpbacks spilled out onto the flat plane of the horizon and rolled side to side gulping at the stunned fish and forcing water past their baleens. The gulls dove and the sea lions cut in and out between the whales. It was silent underwater but the air above was a clatter of wheezing blows, birdcalls, roiling water.

I clung to a line that was tied from the stern of the skiff. Jane Marie took the line and clipped her weight belt to it, then undid the belt from her waist. She helped me do the same. By then the whales were swimming idly fifty yards off, peaceful, and orderly. The raucous gulls were circling far from the scene. I heaved myself into the skiff.

I lay in the bottom of the boat looking up at her. She pulled off her mask.

"What . . . was that?" I asked, trying to catch my breath.

"Whales. Feeding on herring." She sat down on the transom and turned to start the motor. "That's what I was trying to tell you. That's what I want." She looked at me steadily.

"What? To see yourself as whale food?"

"Aw . . . come on. I just want animals to shake me up every once in a while. Clears the head," she said. Then she pulled on the starter cord.

"You weren't trying to get me killed, were you?" I shouted my question above the skiff's outboard.

"Naw." She pulled her diving mitt off with her teeth and dropped it on the floor of the skiff. "I just thought you would want to see something before I put you ashore in Tenakee."

Then she pulled her hood off and shook the water out of her hair, and gunned the engine steering back to the *Winning Hand*.

Teller steered the *Winning Hand* most of the way up the inlet to Tenakee. Priscilla kept sending out radio transmissions to the *Rose*, but received no reply. Jane Marie and I worked on the gear. We were standing in the wet lab that she had built in the old fish hold of the boat. We rinsed and dried her equipment. She gave her cameras a wipe-down. I picked up a three-ring binder full of playing-card-size black-and-white photographs of tail flukes.

"Listen Cecil . . . I want to tell you what is going on but . . . ," she stammered, then stopped, and looked at me challengingly. I knew better than to try and ask the wrong question.

She turned away and started flipping through her photographs of flukes. "The black-and-white pattern on the tail flukes is specific to an individual. Each photograph is marked with the date and code for its location. I can share these photos with other researchers and get an idea where these whales travel to feed and mate. I can make family associations and keep records of mother-and-calf relationships."

The engine was loud enough that if we stood apart we had to yell to be heard. Jane Marie stood so close to me her lips brushed my ear. Our hips touched as we flipped through her book. Her voice was soft.

"When Young Bob was born, something changed in Priscilla. She wants to be loving . . . but mostly what she finds when she digs down inside is anger."

"So you are going to get custody of Young Bob to protect him from Priscilla's anger?"

She kept looking at the photographs as she spoke. "I decided quite a while ago I didn't want to have kids of my own. I mean, look at this. I don't have room for a kid. I don't want to be a mom. It might mean . . . I don't know . . . I might have to buy a station wagon or something."

She moved away from me and flipped the page in the book of photos. Her voice changed pitch back to a formal tone. "The females usually have a calf every two or three years. Sometimes sooner, sometimes later. I'm not sure where they give birth but the females often show up on the breeding grounds with calves in tow. On the mating grounds the males range around and batter each other and sing to get the attention of the females."

"Do the songs the males sing have lyrics?" I asked the photographs.

"I don't know. Just now, in the water, some of those sounds we heard were just a by-product of the work they were doing: the blows and the grunts. But some of those noises did seem to carry some intention, didn't they?"

I nodded stupidly.

"Cecil—people put a lot of stock in logical intelligence. But I think it all starts in the imagination. Look, I'll never know how a whale thinks, what its intentions are, but if I observe them closely enough and long enough, I can imagine a story about their behavior. I put that story into words and I test it with science. My story will be judged by a jury of my peers. If I'm lucky I might discover one little thing and that discovery will start with experience, vigilance, and imagination, not logic."

She took down some padded headphones and plugged them into the tape machine. Then she turned on the tape player. Through the headphones I heard a chorus of sounds: squealing, creaking, and broad sweeping moans. "This tape was made during late fall in Sitka Sound," Jane Marie told me. "Some say it's a mating song. Others say it's just noise. What do you think?"

I shook my head. "I don't know. It's eerie, and beautiful. I don't know."

"I don't know either. But the humpbacks repeat pieces of that sound. It is consistent with the sounds recorded in Hawaii and in Alaska. I need to know more about it, Cecil. That's why I mortgaged my house. That's why I sell games to put gas in this boat. Maybe they have more than language. Maybe they can transmit emotion and intention directly through sound. Maybe their language is a combination of gestures including sound and movement. I don't know. I don't know."

She rocked her head from side to side. Then she spoke.

"What I love about them is they make everything else in my life so small." The engine noise filled the silence between us.

"I'm not trying to steal her child away from her," she blurted out. "She's my own sister, for God's sake." Her hands above her photographs were shaking now. "I don't want him forever. Just for a little while. Just while all this . . . stuff with lawyers . . . is going on, just until Priscilla and Robert calm down a little."

She slammed the pages of the catalogue shut. "When I look at that little boy when he is smiling, *especially* when he's smiling, he looks like my brother. I'm not going to let him go. I'm not going to let them hurt him anymore. I know that doesn't make sense." She leaned close, and reached out for me. Her hands were rough, the skin callused, and deeply scarred around the knuckles. She leaned closer.

"Most of my family is dead. There is nothing to do about that." Her grip tightened around my hand and her breath warmed. "And there is no logical way to rethink or solve that problem." Her shoulder was trembling against mine. "I just want a little more time with this boy. I want him to know that there is more to this family . . . to life . . . than all this"— she waved her hands vaguely around her head as if swatting flies—"grief."

She pressed her hands down on my shoulders. I held her and closed my eyes. Her grip was fierce, as if she were pulling me inside her skin. "Help me with this," she said.

I thought about all the water surrounding us and about

the whales flying through the ocean water and singing somewhere beyond the thin hull of the boat. I stroked her shining
hair and touched the white skin of her cheek. I was trying to
think of something to say when the engine slowed to an idle
and Teller yelled down that we were approaching the dock.

JOHN STRALEY

8

The *Rose* was tied at the end of the float. Jane Marie scanned the dock and the boardwalk running north to town. She looked agitated as she climbed the ladder to the flying bridge and took the controls from Teller.

Jane Marie eased the *Winning Hand* into the moorage next to the *Rose*. There was no one on board the cabin cruiser. As soon as the *Winning Hand* bumped the float Priscilla jumped from the boat and ran up the dock. Teller hopped off the bow trailing a line and I did the same at the stern. We secured the lines and stood facing each other.

Teller turned from me dismissively and spoke to Jane Marie. "They must have wanted a more public meeting. I guess I don't blame them." He looked around, still ignoring me, until his eyes found Priscilla running up the ramp from the floating dock to the path. "I imagine they're up in the bar."

He patted his coat to make sure he had his wallet. Then

he unexpectedly smiled at me. "Well, you're here, you might as well come along." He turned and walked up the ramp.

"Robert Sullivan and his friend will be there," Jane Marie told me. "I know you've figured that out already. Listen, Cecil. They don't want you to come. Robert doesn't know how much you're involved." She spoke over her shoulder as she climbed down from the flying bridge.

"That makes two of us," I said as I put on a brown canvas jacket and stepped back onto the deck.

"Robert Sullivan knows you from that parking-lot incident down in Seattle but he doesn't know anything more." She was on the dock now.

"Whose side is Teller on?" I asked her.

Jane Marie pulled her ball cap over her close-cropped hair and stepped off her boat. "Mr. Teller works for me." She checked the mooring lines, then added, "At least, I'm paying him."

"Let me grab my stuff and I'll head up to the bar with you."

"I really don't think that's a good idea."

As I went through the companion way I could hear her arguing with me but couldn't make out the words.

I found my wallet and microcassette tape machine. Both had taken a soaking in my jacket but the tape machine seemed to work. I put it in the inside pocket of my canvas coat. Just before I turned out the door I reached under the pad on my bunk and found the nine-millimeter and clip. I snapped the clip into the grips, made sure the safety was on, and then put it in

my coat pocket. I figured if things went bad I could crawl down
the barrel and hide.

Tenakee is a village built on a boardwalk on both sides of a
hot spring. The main thoroughfare is a trail wide enough for
four-wheelers and handcarts. There are no cars in Tenakee, although a fuel truck used to deliver to homes along the half mile
of trail. Down by the boat harbor the trail is surrounded by
salmonberry bushes. Jane Marie had given up on trying to talk
me out of coming but she was silent as we walked the path to
the bar where Robert Sullivan waited. Not wanting to talk either, I opened my eyes and looked around. The bushes were
stems that had few leaves but some green sticky buds. The
alders were more leafed out than they were in Sitka, but still
the limbs seemed spare, like thin bones clicking together. I
could hear a thrush back up in the cover of the rainforest. A
junco flitted in and around the stems of berry bushes. In summer this path would be crowned with berries and the air would
be dense with the breeze from the salmon spawn in the river.
As we got closer to the springs there were a few cabins built on
each side. Some of the buildings were from the twenties and
thirties; the roofs were green with moss and the siding black-
ened from decades of rain. There are newer cabins built out on
pilings over the tide flat, some with picture windows and satel-
lite dishes. Almost all the houses had flower boxes that were
now covered with plastic, protecting the soil from the possibility of frost.

We walked past the two-story general store and the ferry
dock, then went into the bar where the ceiling was low and the

light was dusky and the room smelled like wood chips and sour beer.

The floor was uneven, the doorjambs were out of square and the entire room had that off-kilter feel of a comfortable place to get drunk. Harrison Teller sprawled at a small round table near the window. Priscilla was sitting in a chair in the corner with Young Bob on her lap. The dark-eyed little boy was playing with a plastic figure of a superhero I didn't recognize. The boy was dancing it in the sunlight coming in through the dirty window and darting it toward his mother's face.

Sitting across from Teller was Robert Sullivan, dressed in slacks and a new-looking sweater. His black hair was neatly combed and he had a strained but bemused expression as he listened to the man sitting on his right who had his index finger in Harrison Teller's chest.

If the pointing man had been lying down he would have been about the bulk of a good-sized family sofa and about as soft, until you got to the iron frame. He wore a black leather vest that had dirty patches sewn on the front and back. His bare right arm looked about the size of a hindquarter of beef and had a detailed tattoo of a naked woman riding a wolf. His greasy brown hair was slicked back. He was speaking quite softly but punctuating each word with a thump of his clawlike finger.

"You didn't tell me this was a felony, man," he was hissing. "And then a fucking *murder*. I don't need this *shit*." The last five syllables he tapped out on the wobbly table, rattling the overflowing ashtrays.

The barmaid squeezed around the end of the bar and brought drinks to the table. Two cans of beer, one glass of brandy, and one soda pop with three cherries speared on a plastic sword in it. Teller slapped the table and picked up the soda pop and turned around to give it to Young Bob.

"When you're done with that we'll have another. So don't hold back now, son," Teller said cheerfully. Then he seemed to see me. "Cecil!" He spread his big arms wide. "I believe you know Robert Sullivan?" He pointed across the table where Sullivan nodded as he reached for his beer.

"And this is Gunk." Teller gestured as if he were unveiling the new fall fashions.

Gunk was the guy in the leather vest and the tattoo. He looked at me with an expression of hatred and amusement as if I were an IRS agent covered in shit. He didn't say anything and we didn't shake hands as I sat next to Teller.

Teller turned to me and started talking with quite some animation as if he were catching me up on the first half of the movie. "A couple of weeks ago I hired Gunk here to ask"—he flashed a look at Sullivan, who was brooding across the table, then continued—"I did say *ask* Mr. Sullivan if he would bring Young Bob up to Juneau so we could have a meeting. Mr. Sullivan agreed, but on the way up he gets Gunk here all worked up about the possibility that we were all involved in some sort of extortion and kidnapping. Silly stuff really. But now Mr. Gunk wants more money. I guess you'd call it combat pay."

Jane Marie took a chair from another table, which no one minded because we were the only people in the place besides a logger who was drinking coffee and playing cribbage with the barmaid. Jane Marie walked to the corner where the only two chairs were occupied by her sister and her nephew. Young Bob was pulling the cherries off the plastic sword in the drink.

"Hello," Jane Marie said softly and kissed the top of the boy's head. "I was hoping I'd see you here."

Young Bob looked up at her briefly, then held the cherries up to her nose.

"Look. Rubies." And he dangled them from his fingers.

Gunk began thumping me in the chest, his great bulk moving closer. He smelled faintly like eggs fried in motor oil. His finger hit like hammer blows as he hissed into my face.

"I bring this fuckin' kid and his pencil-necked old man up to Juneau. We're supposed to have a meeting where I get my money." He pointed to Priscilla in the corner. "Then she fuckin' kills this politician guy. Right before the meeting's about to happen. I'm in the fuckin' building." He leans back in his chair, nodding his head with an expression like we're sharing secrets now. "We're talking heat. We're talking serious downtime if I have to get some fuckin' Public Defender here in the fuckin' state of Alaska."

Young Bob flicked a cherry with the tip of his plastic sword. "That's not a nice word," he said softly, and he flipped a second cherry off the table onto the sawdust floor.

"Sorry," Gunk mumbled.

Jane Marie spoke up and as she did, I noticed she was covering the little boy's ears. "Why on earth did you have to break into my house like that? And why did you hurt Mr. Meegles?'' She spit out her words toward Gunk.

Gunk spread his arms wide and leaned back. "Hey! Take it easy. The break-in was his idea.'' He pointed to Robert Sullivan who shifted uneasily in his chair. "And besides,'' Gunk continued, "I never touched that old man. That was Superman here, too.'' Sullivan twisted his napkin and avoided looking at Jane Marie.

Then Sullivan sat up, straightened his sweater and spoke slowly to Teller. "Well, regardless of your problems with my methods''—he flickered a look at Gunk's hands around the beer can—"our original deal is off. I was going to agree to giving temporary custody to Jane Marie and let Bob stay in Juneau, but not now. Not with the killing and everything that will happen in the press. I grew up in Juneau, Teller. I know what it would be like for him. I'm taking Bob back. I want that agreement back. I don't care what our deal may have been.''

Young Bob was starting to dive under the table to retrieve his cherry when Jane Marie scooted him back into his chair and held the soda up for him to drink. Priscilla pushed back her chair and stood up.

"You are taking him nowhere.''

Jane Marie was covering Young Bob's ears and kissing the top of his head. "Let's just stay calm now, Cilla. Tomorrow we can all sit down and I'm sure we can work out some compromise. Let's not get . . . ugly.''

Robert Sullivan told Jane Marie, "You are not involved anymore.''

Priscilla turned on Jane Marie. Her face was twisted in an ugly kind of rage. Young Bob recoiled at seeing her face.

"That's right!" Priscilla spit out. "You just want him for yourself. My son and I are getting on the next ferry out of this place. I'm not agreeing to anything. But"—she stabbed her finger toward Robert—"if you try any more shit I just might sign it. I'd rather Janie had him than you."

Gunk's fist crashed down on the table. The brandy glass rolled off onto the floor and broke. Young Bob looked up in silent awe as if he had just seen a cannon go off. Gunk's voice was low and even. "Excuse me. Excuse me, please, but I want my fuckin' money or nobody is going anywhere. I want ten thousand dollars and a plane ticket, or Young Bob here stays with Uncle Gunk."

Young Bob was starting to sing "Itsy Bitsy Spider" loudly to himself. His brow was knitted. He sang and his eyes were distant as if he were willing himself away from the table.

" 'The itsy bitsy spider crawled up the water spout . . .' "

Jane Marie tried to hug the child tightly but he wriggled free and ducked under the table. He walked his toy superhero on the sawdust-covered floor.

"Will you sit up and behave!" Robert Sullivan snapped.

" 'Down came the rain and washed the spider out . . .' " Young Bob crawled along the floor and picked up the cherry that was dusted now with chips and cigarette ash. He started to blow on it to clean it up.

"Don't you talk to him that way!" Priscilla said with venom. Then she turned and ducked her head under the table.

"Sit up here!" Young Bob cowered. "Young man, you get up here right *now*!" Young Bob started to comply and as his hand came to the top of the table it knocked against the soda glass and spilled it across the table.

" 'Up came the sun and dried up all the . . .' "

Robert reached across and slapped the boy on the shoulder. "You sit down and behave yourself. You want to go back to the boat?"

Priscilla's arm was going back to slap her ex-husband. Young Bob hunched his shoulders and sank back under the table. He bit his lower lip and cowered beside Jane Marie's knees.

Priscilla started slapping Robert, and Robert began to gather himself in his chair. Gunk stood up. He lifted Priscilla by the collar of her coat and walked her back away from the table. She was screeching like a weasel in a trap. The logger and barmaid looked up with some interest from their card game. Harrison Teller was scanning all four corners of the room and Jane Marie held her arms tightly around the boy. I was thinking of going for a walk.

Gunk dumped Priscilla back in the corner. He held his finger up to her face. "Now shut the fuck up."

Priscilla stared up at him and was about to speak but abruptly turned her glare on Robert instead. "You'll never be his real father."

Robert Sullivan's face was white. "He's mine. I am his fucking father."

"That's not a nice word," Young Bob said, almost to himself, peeping from under the table. Robert cocked his arm back. His hand was open. Young Bob shut his eyes tight, and ducked his head toward the floor.

For some reason I grabbed Robert Sullivan's wrist just below his gold watchband. He stood up quickly, pushing his chair across the floor. Gunk came walking toward us breathing a frustrated sigh.

Most bar fights are one-punch affairs. Almost always it's the first punch that ends it; the rest is wrestling, swearing, and big-voiced threats. It's not the punch that is most important because it takes very little to reach across a table and break a man's nose, but it's the willingness to do it. Being a person with a heightened power of rationalization and a long-range view of almost everything, I knew I wasn't going to hit Robert Sullivan. I'm sure he knew it too. But I was not going to let him slap that little boy even if he had to punch me instead.

He thrust his chest and his belly at me. I took one step back. He put his face an inch from my nose, forcing his words through tight lips. "You lousy bastard. You nose around in my business one more time and I'll crush your skull for good." He shoved me again and his belly pushed against the hard angles of the French-made automatic in my coat. His expression changed, as suddenly he had a new concern.

"What the fuck is that?" Robert Sullivan had his right hand on the grips of the gun. He pulled it out. Priscilla and Jane Marie froze. Gunk stopped walking forward and stood still, appraising the situation.

Teller stood up slowly from his chair and walked between

us. Teller was much taller than the aggrieved father, a fact that dawned on Robert Sullivan as he backed slowly away from the wall of Teller's back.

"You've got my gun, Younger? How'd you get my gun?" Teller looked down on Robert, speaking to him in a jocular tone. "Can you believe this guy? He's got my automatic. I mean, he's a thief, besides being a meddler." He held his plate-sized palm out to Sullivan wriggling his fingers. "Come on. Give it over now." He smiled down at Robert and kept talking in a singsong voice. "I'm really going to have to do something about this. I'm sorry, I'll just be a minute."

Teller turned and spoke to the women in the corner. "Jane Marie, why don't you get another soda to go?" And smiling down to Young Bob he said, "I'll bring you out some more rubies, okay, buddy boy?"

Young Bob ducked under the table again and started skipping out the door into the sunlight flying his superhero over his head. Jane Marie grabbed her coat up and quickly followed him out. Priscilla sat for a moment looking as if she were calculating the odds on how to get her hands on the gun. Teller motioned to her.

"Priscilla, you've got enough trouble. Go on outside. Please. I'll meet up with you later."

Priscilla stood and after a moment left. I could hear Young Bob just beyond the open door.

" '. . . and dried up all the rain, then the itsy bitsy spider crawled up the spout again. . . .' "

Sullivan handed the gun to Teller. Teller pointed it toward

the floor, snapped the action back, flipped the safety down. Then he grabbed Robert Sullivan's sweater and pushed the muzzle into his nose. Teller's voice was no longer singsong. Now it was deadly flat and urgent.

"Now, leave the boy. Walk down to your boat and go. I think you know our deal is still under effect. You signed a legal document, and you're going to stick to it, aren't you? Nod your head yes, or I'm going to paint the walls with your brains."

The barmaid and the logger stopped in mid-deal, but they didn't look at us or the gun. Their eyes were looking straight down at their feet. Robert watched Teller's face, and he made a very wise, and very important decision. Because even the most amateur bar fighter could look up into those eyes and know that Teller knew the consequences and was willing to pull the trigger. Robert shook his head up and down.

Teller let go of Robert's sweater. He stepped backward. Then he put the gun in his pocket, took a deep breath and spread his arms wide.

"Good! Now have a great trip," and he gave Robert a big hug. Robert's eyes were somewhat glazed but his face was flushed as he backed out the door. Teller looked over at Gunk.

"Gunk. I'll take care of it. I'll make it right with you, man. All right? Don't worry about this kidnapping bullshit. Won't happen. Even if the worst comes down you won't have to have the Public Defender."

Gunk spread his arms wide. "Listen, man, I just want my money. I want out of this shit. I'm no fucking baby-sitter. I can't take this swapping the kid back and forth. I mean, fuck, shouldn't he be in school or something?''

Teller smiled and took a step toward Gunk and slapped his hand on Gunk's back. "See. You got a heart of gold. Gunk, man, I'll take care of you. Come down to the boat later. Make sure this guy leaves here without the kid.''

"Just get me my money, man.'' Gunk shrugged his shoulders. "You know I hate cops but even cops are better than this shit.'' He fixed Teller with a dead stare for a long moment. Teller nodded that he understood Gunk's meaning. Gunk moved through the door, momentarily blocking the sunlight coming in.

Teller sighed. He slapped a one-hundred-dollar bill on the bar and looked at the crib players' cards.

"Hey, I'm sorry. It's family stuff. You know, we're trying to open up and communicate.'' He reached into the bar well, grabbed a handful of the evil-looking red cherries, and wadded them into a napkin.

"All right then. Good luck.'' He waved over his shoulder. The barmaid nodded and then took a drag on her cigarette which was trembling in her hand.

Outside the door I squinted into the spring sunshine. Teller and I leaned against the damp wooden siding of the bar. We watched Young Bob and Jane Marie drawing figures in the dirt near the general store as Gunk's big leather-clad shoulders trundled down the trail. Priscilla was in the general store. Through the big plate windows I could see her talking to a

clerk, her hands circling in animated gestures. Teller took a pill
bottle from his wool coat, opened it, spilled some pills into his
palm and gave me two. He patted himself down and found a
silver flask, washed the pills down, then handed the flask to me.
"That guy spilled my drink," he muttered. I palmed the pills
and declined the drink.

Teller was still muttering. "Parenthood, Younger. Stay
away from it. Reasonable people—smart, responsible citizens—
can justify anything in the name of their kids. You don't think
that when they're born. I mean, in the hospital, you hold one of
those slippery little piglets in your arms, and you figure you've
found the source of life. It feels like the fountain of love. . . ."

Teller's mad blue eyes were staring out at his past. Tears
tracked into his beard. Young Bob came running over and
reached up his hand. Teller took the soggy napkin out of his
pocket and gave him the cherries. Young Bob's eyes were wide,
and he whispered, "Cool! Thanks!" Then he started skipping
over to Jane Marie but he stopped and looked back at Teller.
His face was very serious. He said, "Who am I going to live
with?"

"Don't know, buddy boy, but you can stay tonight on our
boat and then we'll see what you really want to do."

Young Bob thought for a moment, then looked down at
the cherries in his hand. "Can I eat all these right now?"

"You can eat them or wear them in your crown, buddy
boy." Teller took another drink from his pocket flask. As Young
Bob cantered away into Jane Marie's arms, Teller's eyes were
brimming and wet. "But I guess I don't really think kids are the

fountain of love, Younger. They're just the most important thing to act stupid about."

The sun rolled down from behind the trees and warmed the weathered siding of the bar. Someone had put a Willie Nelson song on the jukebox. Teller rested his head back and smiled up at the sun.

"Man, aren't these antidepressants great?" His eyes were sad but charged with the blue of a summer storm. Then he gathered up the entire front of my shirt in his fist. "And speaking of stupid, how'd you get my gun? Did Jane Marie give it to you? I mean, what the hell did you think you were going to do with it?"

I thrust my two pills into his free hand. I pushed away from him. "I was going to give it to you in case you had to shoot somebody."

"What are you still doing here, Younger? There's bound to be a ferry back to Sitka sometime. Hell, why don't you get on it?"

"I guess I still want to help out."

"I got too much help, Younger. That fucking Gunk is going to have to be paid."

"You hired Gunk to pressure Sullivan to give Young Bob to Jane Marie?" I tucked in my shirt.

"That's all there is, Younger. No big mystery. Only we had a little accident on the steps outside the Senator's office before the transfer meeting. The Senator was going to act as our referee. I guess he owed Jane Marie a favor. Now Gunk's got his tit in a wringer. He and Robert do the storm-trooper thing at Jane Marie's house, grab the kid, then arrange a meeting. It was supposed to be last night but they wanted to avoid you. Then I guess they changed their mind."

"What about Priscilla? At least let me help you on her case."

"Younger, Priscilla's going to be all right. I'm going to sit next to that young fella, the Public Defender. What's his name? He's about ready to shit himself he's got such a good defense case. They haven't even convened the grand jury yet. Priscilla's got nothing to worry about."

A raven landed on the bench across the path from us. It had a long strand of fish guts hanging from its bill. The raven gulped it, then stood cocking its head one way, then another, as if trying to formulate a question.

"Then why don't you let Priscilla stay in town with her lawyer?" I asked.

"Younger, what type of evidence sinks a defendant nine times out of ten?"

"Their own statements."

"Absolutely. The dumb bastards think they can talk their way out of it. But they don't realize there are no right answers. Priscilla would love to try and explain her way out of this. I had to get her out of Juneau. I wanted her to calm down." Teller nodded down the path toward the boat harbor. The raven hopped down and strutted near the tips of our shoes. "I don't want her talking to anyone. No one. Leave her alone. Leaving her alone is the only thing that is going to help her, Younger."

Priscilla came walking out of the store. She had a ferry schedule in her hand.

"Who are you working for, Mr. Teller?" I asked my shoes as the raven hopped closer.

Teller grimaced. "That's complicated." Then he added, "I work for the family interests."

The raven pecked my toe. "What about Jane Marie?" I nodded to where Jane Marie and Young Bob were playing a game of jacks with bottle caps and a rubber ball.

"She wants that kid."

"Is she going to get him?"

Teller pushed a ridge of dirt with his toe. The raven pecked at something uncovered in the dirt, then took two quick hops and flew to the rail near the ferry dock.

"That hasn't been decided," he said.

Then he walked away from me, lifted Young Bob over his head, and plopped him on top of his shoulders. The boy rode Teller's shoulders, laughing and squealing down the narrow path.

That night the four of us made hot dogs baked in biscuit dough and washed them down with some noxious red juice. Priscilla was pouting up in the wheelhouse. She was angry because the ferry that could take her and Young Bob to Sitka wouldn't arrive for two days. She tried to keep Young Bob away from us but the radio played and he whined and struggled to join the party so finally she let him come down to dance.

Teller kept pouring brandy into his juice and dancing

around the table to the rhythm of the music on the radio. He happily ate the hot dogs and the crumbs flecked down his beard. Once, in the lull between Al Green's "Take Me to the River" and the Bangles' "Walk Like an Egyptian," I was wedged into the corner near the cookstove and Jane Marie backed into me to make room for Young Bob who was playing some kind of bullfight game with Teller.

"I can't believe you broke into my safe, Cecil," she whispered.

"I didn't, strictly speaking, break into your safe."

"Why have a safe if your friends are going to root around through your secrets?"

I put my arms around her waist. "Why have secrets?"

She looked over at Teller, who was dancing in the tight corner of the galley with one arm cocked over his head and the other trailing in an odd Egyptian dance. Young Bob was trying to get a roll of toilet paper out of the cupboard to wrap him up like a mummy. Jane Marie leaned close to my ear and whispered, "I don't want to talk about it now. Why not come up to the bathhouse a little later? I'm taking Young Bob at the end of women's hours to give him a bath. Mary, up at the hotel, says there aren't many people in town and she doesn't think many of the locals will be in the tubs tonight. There's a basketball tournament in Juneau. Lots of people went over for that. Come tonight and maybe we can find a place to have that decent conversation."

She moved away from me and grabbed the toilet paper away from Young Bob, who looked up at her with disappointment until Jane Marie started to show him how to wrap Teller by starting at the mouth.

The bathhouse in Tenakee is across from the general store at the end of the main dock. The main bathhouse is a concrete bunker with a skylight covered with fiberglass roofing. The changing room is a wooden room with benches and hooks on the walls. Like most of the old buildings in Tenakee, the bathhouse sags a little. The doorjambs are out of square. The floor has been chewed by thousands of work boots. Fishermen off the grounds and loggers from the camps come to bathe here. So do the residents of Tenakee, many of whom came to the village for the waters. The inside of the bunker is perhaps fifteen by twenty, built around a spring that bubbles up in a sunken pool in the middle of the concrete floor. The lighting is dim and the gray walls are streaked with mineral tracings. If tourists are expecting a Marin County hot tub experience, they are set back when they walk through the door into a cave of eggy smells to find two old fishermen with white lumpy bodies scrubbing their butts and talking about Rush Limbaugh.

Later that night I stood in the dressing room. I saw four piles of shoes and small T-shirts lying around on the floor. I heard suspicious squealing from the bathhouse. I knocked and heard Jane Marie's voice amid the splashing and squeals telling me it was okay to come on in.

There is a landing inside and several steps down to the floor of the bath. From the landing I saw Jane Marie squatting naked next to Young Bob who was hunched over in the pool having water poured over his head.

THE MUSIC OF WHAT HAPPENS

"Remember now, you can't put soap in the pool so you soap up and rinse here," Jane Marie was explaining. Young Bob sputtered as the hot water dipped from the springs ran down his skin. He hopped from one leg to the other, then broke away to the other naked white children splashing and bobbing in the pool. Jane Marie looked up at me standing fully dressed in my red rubber boots and all.

"Young Bob invited some other kids." Jane Marie looked apologetic. "We met them on the path. I'll just be a few more minutes. You can come down and keep us company, Cecil. I don't think anybody will mind."

I walked down the stairs, turned over a plastic bucket and sat down. The little girls in the pool were about four or five. The pool is maybe ten feet by four feet and is too deep for even an adult to stand in. But there are rock ledges along the sides and the kids were walking around and around in some kind of game whose rules only they knew. Every once in a while one would jump into the hot water and come out sputtering and pink. The others would splash and sing. "You're a fish. You're a fish. Put you in a broken dish." Then the game would start over.

Young Bob climbed out of the water and stood in front of me. Water purled off his black hair onto his peach shoulders. He looked at me seriously. "Do I have to go now?"

"Not as far as I know." I held my hands palms up.

"Cool!" he said, and ran to the side of the sunken concrete tub.

The other kids had stopped playing the fish game. Young Bob eased back into the pool again. He made a funny face.

"Wow! This makes my penis feel goofy!"

The two girls squealed with delight. One said, "You don't have a penis. You have a wiener." Again, mass hysteria ensued. Young Bob starting covering his genitals, a little embarrassed but with an air of superiority. "My mom says it's a penis. You don't have one 'cause you're a girl."

The girls stood in the hot water and looked down at themselves quickly. One of the girls put her hands on her hips and spoke for her sex. "Yeah? Well, that's because we have vaginas, Mister Weenie."

Young Bob did the only reasonable thing under the circumstances. He did a cannonball into the pool.

A dark-haired woman poked her head into the room. "Okay, you girls, it's time to get going," whereupon all of them jumped into the pool.

The woman rolled her eyes and looked exasperated. "Say thank you to Jane Marie and Bob." The guests said thank you in a droning chorus. As they swam to the edge and pulled themselves out on the floor their skins glowed with the heat from the water. One of the girls lay still for a second and she looked like a seal sunning herself on the rocks.

"Come on, kids. Thanks, Jane Marie. Do you want me to walk Young Bob down to the boat? I can, if you want."

"That would be great, Nora. His mom's there and she'll put him to bed." Jane Marie was still sitting in the corner. She gestured with her chin toward the dressing room. "Does anybody else want to come in?"

"No. It looks pretty dead. I think you have the place to yourselves." Nora smiled at us and then patted the kids one by one as they scooted through the door.

The door shut and the silence clung to me like the sticky heat in the bathhouse. Jane Marie moved from the corner and eased her body into the pool.

"Come on, Cecil, you can get in. I promise I won't tease you about your tiny little wiener." She looked up at me from the pool, her long neck extended above the water. She floated away from the edge, every part of her buoyant.

"Hey, how'd you know about my wiener? Don't answer that. That's it. I'm definitely not getting naked in front of you."

In one strong motion she pulled herself from the pool. I stood up slowly. The damp tips of her nipples spotted my shirt. She started to undo the buttons.

"Come on, Younger. We're just going to take a bath. Relax."

She pulled off my shirt and I felt uncomfortable when she bent over for my boots.

"Why don't you like your body?" she asked.

"Listen, I don't know. You know, I just don't think it looks like it's supposed to."

"What's it supposed to look like?"

I pulled off my pants and hung my clothes over the rail of the stairs, then stepped quickly into the hot pool and lowered myself cautiously into the water. Jane Marie squatted near the edge, looking at me. Her thighs and hips were round but showed the pull of muscle up her legs and toward her back. Water beaded off her pubic hair. I knew I needed to start talking or I was going to get caught staring at her, which I understand is bad form in these circumstances.

"My body is supposed to look strong and limber from pulling in fish and picking ripe fruit"—I dunked my head under the near-scalding water and came up sputtering my words—"but it looks just like what it is, a body that sits in the back booth and orders rounds for the house."

"What happened here?" Her finger traced the indented scar on my shoulder.

"It's a gunshot wound."

"Gunshot? I didn't think you were a fighter."

"I'm not. I'm a target."

She slipped into the water. Her breasts lifted slightly as she reached out and laced her hands around my neck.

"And what happened here?" She had one hand on my shoulder and the other hand traced a crescent scar in my eyebrow.

"Seventh grade. Water fountain. I'm telling you, this body is not good reading."

"Well, I don't know." She moved around me. The warm water was making me weak as her hands worked over my belly and my chest. She kissed me on the ear and I held on to the edge of the pool. She held her cheek flat against the back of my neck. She reached around and roughly stroked my penis with her hand.

THE MUSIC OF WHAT HAPPENS

I turned around and faced her. "Listen," I forced myself to say while I brushed the wet spikes of hair from her eyes, "I would like to continue this. I would, but"—she moved away slowly and the water curled in a current between us—"you have got to tell me the truth about what is going on with you and Young Bob. No more background. I want to know what is really going on right now."

Her eyes narrowed in the hazy heat. In them I saw some bitterness. "You lied to Priscilla all the time, Cecil. All of your reports were lies."

"Priscilla didn't want to hear what I had to say. But I want to listen to you." I lifted myself out onto a ledge. "And by the way, I'd very much like to have sex with you," I told her. "I'd like to melt down and cover your skin like warm wax."

Jane Marie bit down hard on her lower lip. She crossed her arms in front of her chest. I went on.

". . . but if I started to let this goofy penis do what it wants"—she started to smile—"then later I found out you were just going along with it to avoid telling me the truth . . ." Her eyes snapped at me, sharp and focused. Then she splashed the water petulantly. I reached over and cupped her face in my hands.

"If that happened," I continued, "I think I'd go crazy. I've wanted to kiss you since the fourth grade, since the Warren Commission and the moon walk. Shit, most of the significant events of the twentieth century have occurred since I started wanting to kiss you, but please don't fuck me just to get that little boy away from Teller or it will ruin the whole last half of the 1900s for me." I wiped the perspiration from her forehead. "I was going to tell you all this the morning of our graduation but you cut me off." I kissed her lips and she laughed, filling my cheeks with her breath. We kissed three more times, laughing and filling each other's cheeks like balloons.

She leaned away from me but kept her arm draped across my scarred shoulder. "Hell, Cecil, I thought I just had to grab your crotch and you'd do anything I'd say."

"That's usually true. But Young Bob's right, the water's too hot."

She laughed and splashed the water again and lifted herself out of the water. Then she groaned.

"Okay," she sighed. "I hired Teller to broker an agreement between my sister and the Sullivans to get custody of Young Bob."

"Are you sure he works exclusively for you?"

"I have no idea," she said, and dipped hot water out of the pool, pouring it over her body. The water curled down her skin and splattered on the concrete. "Old Bob Sullivan suggested we negotiate through Teller. But I had no idea what I was getting into when I asked for his help."

I sat up on the stone ledge listening. Jane Marie draped her finger on my shoulder. I held on to it. "So?" I prompted her.

Jane Marie sighed again and went on. "Teller drew up an agreement and I signed it. Then apparently Gunk had Robert sign it. Wilfred Taylor arranged a meeting in Juneau at his office. The purpose of the meeting was to make sure they had a

solid front so they could convince Priscilla to accept the agreement. Wilfred was going to make sure Robert was on board so
all of us could work on Priscilla together."

"Why was Senator Taylor involved?" I asked.

She took a deep breath. "Wilfred Taylor is an old friend of
the Sullivan family. Young Bob's grandpa, Old Bob, has been in
business with the Senator for years. Everyone thought the Senator could referee the deal."

Her fingers drummed on my neck.

"Old Bob decided the whole situation with Priscilla was
way out of control. He was going to help me get temporary
custody and try to play the peacemaker. Will—the Senator—
had had his fill of Priscilla, too. She'd been pestering his office
for weeks and he kept trying to get me to calm her down."

"How well did you know Wilfred Taylor?"

"I knew him, Cecil." She stared down at me. "I wasn't
one of his conquests, if that's what you're asking, although I
don't think it would have taken much effort on my part. We
played bridge together and dominoes. Double twelves. He was
good with big numbers. He would squeeze my knee but that
didn't bother me. I saw it as another element of the game."

"What do you know about his death?"

Jane Marie shifted her position but never let go of my
shoulder. "Early that morning Gunk brought Young Bob to my
house. I suppose it was a show of faith. I was to take care of
Young Bob until after the meeting at the Senator's office. But
Priscilla showed up at my house unexpectedly. She said she
knew the Senator had been holding back important documents

that would prove he had bribed the custody judge. She said she was going down to the Senator's office to get them. Then she was going to take Young Bob away.''

"Did she threaten to hurt the Senator? Anything . . . any suggestions that she was planning to hurt him?''

"She was angry, Cecil. It sounded like she was going to storm the office and take the papers she wanted.''

"Was Gunk supposed to go to this meeting?''

"I assumed so. They were going to talk about the conditions of my temporary custody. Robert really didn't much care for the agreement. I suppose Gunk was there to keep the peace, kind of a sergeant at arms.''

"Didn't you tell Priscilla that?''

"Cecil, I couldn't. It sounded too much like a threat. Besides you know what my sister is like. She wouldn't listen. When I said the Sullivans had agreed that I would be temporary custodian, she went crazy. She accused me of being part of the conspiracy. She swore she was going to blow the whole thing out of the water.''

"Was Harrison Teller going to be at the meeting?''

"I don't think so, Cecil. Teller said that he couldn't stand the Senator. I think Teller feels this whole affair is . . . I don't know . . . beneath him.''

"Dickie has some theory that Bob Sullivan is a mobster in the witness protection program.''

She shook her head. "That sounds like one of Priscilla's theories. It's crazy. Old Bob moved from the Midwest years ago. I don't know anything about his past. He claims he's Black

Irish but that's all I know. People have always gossiped about his business dealings. But he's union, you know. There is always talk."

I rubbed my head and tried to calm this swirl of facts. "Tell me again, why did Robert and Gunk steal him?"

She leaned against me and I could feel her slick skin against mine. "After Priscilla killed . . . or, I don't know . . . after the Senator died, Robert wanted to back out of our agreement. He called early in the morning after her arrest and pleaded but I didn't agree. So that night, the night you stayed at my place, he came with Gunk and took the boy back."

I splashed the water idly, rolling this mess around in my mind. Jane Marie folded her arms around my neck. Her slick body flattened onto my back.

"Why don't we just take him, Cecil?"

"What?"

"Let's just take Young Bob out of here tonight. We can go to my camp. We can negotiate from there." Her voice was building with excitement. The muscles in her arms hardened around my throat, her breath in my ear.

"There are some serious problems with this plan." I tried to free myself.

"Like?" Her hand was hot on the side of my face.

I held my fingers up and started ticking the reasons off.

"Well . . . there's your sister. Then there's Robert and Teller, and let's not forget about Gunk. Gunk may be first in line."

She turned me around and held my face in her hands. She spread my wet hair off my forehead with her thumbs. Her glittering eyes were fixed, her strong body moved like a slow-moving fish.

"Once we get out to my camp," she said, "I can take care of everything."

She pulled me forward, kissing me with her wet mouth.

An old man poked his head in the door and then quickly averted his eyes.

"Men's hours started a few minutes ago. Do you think the young lady will be much longer?" he called in through the crack in the door.

We got right out and dressed hurriedly. The old man was wearing rubber slippers and heavy wool pants, suspenders, and his striped work shirt. He smiled as we came out.

"It's a heck of a night out here tonight. I hope I didn't rush you kids but I got to get my bath while the wife listens to her radio show. I got to get out of the house, can't stand that guy over in Sitka talking, talking. I don't know where in the heck they find these guys but they seem to have an opinion about everything."

He walked into the bathhouse. Jane Marie and I rolled up our wet towels in the changing room. I could have been mistaken but I think the old man kept talking, sitting alone in the bath.

We walked the trail in the dark. Above, the stars were out and she tried to show me the position of the constellations by

pointing her finger into the immense sky. But I was distracted
by what she had told me in the baths and the stars stayed a
confused jumble of lights.

The wind was a ripple from the southeast. Several of the
cabins along the path had music playing behind their windows.
The lights cast a milky shadow down on the tide flat past the
beach fringe. Jane Marie was carrying her towel rolled up in the
same way she carried it back from the pool in the sixth grade
and she shifted it under her arm as she kept trying to show me
the planets and the patterns of stars. I stared and stared and
tried to follow the trajectory of her finger but I kept trying to
make sense of the whole day.

Finally, she gave up on the constellations and spoke.
"Cecil, I'm sorry. Forget about what I said there in the tubs.
You're right. It's crazy. I'll just deal with my sister. And from
here on out, I won't try to seduce you."

"Let's not be too hasty. I mean, we're still a long way
from home. . . ."

We heard a sound and looked to the inlet. A quarter of a
mile off the beach, a humpback blew. All we could see was the
vapor of its breath hung in the starlight like a veil. In the salmonberry bushes the juncos flitted, and there was the steady hiss
of the waves lapping on the muddy flats. Down the inlet we
saw the running lights of a powerboat heading away to the
south. I put my arm around her shoulders and we walked without speaking for the rest of the way, until we heard the sound
of Priscilla's screams down on the float near the boats. I could
also hear the sound of slapping flesh.

JOHN STRALEY

The door to the wheelhouse on the *Winning Hand* was open. Teller's radio was turned up loud. We could hear it as we rounded the last turn in the path heading for the ramp to the float. The lights were on and some lines that had been coiled on the mast earlier were lying on top of the skiff. Robert was holding Priscilla by the hair and slapping her open-handed across the face. Priscilla lashed out with her fists, shrieking like a wild animal. Jane Marie pulled away from me and ran toward her boat.

I was so relaxed from soaking in the hot water that I had a hard time springing into action. But then again I've never really been one to run toward an ugly fight. Jane Marie jumped up onto the back deck of the *Winning Hand*. Robert and Priscilla broke their clinch and Robert ran into the wheelhouse. As I approached the boat Priscilla stood shrieking on the stern hatch cover.

"He's gone!" she cried in a tone of trembling rage.

I walked past her and into the wheelhouse. The charts that had been stowed flat on racks under the table were scattered everywhere. The tool kits were turned over and the contents spilled. Under one of the panels the wiring for the radar erupted in a snagged tangle. In the corner by the safe, tear-shaped streaks of blood spattered the white bulkhead. The radio was very loud. Robert Sullivan was in a wild fury, banging at the safe's locking mechanism with a hammer and yelling, "I'll get that fucking paper and I'll ram it down Teller's throat—"

"Enough!" Jane Marie said, grabbing the hammer from

Robert's hand before he could swing it again. Then she curved her finger, beckoning me to the galley.

I moved down the companionway steps to the galley. As I turned to my right I tripped on Teller's shoe.

He was handcuffed to the leg of the stove. He lay flat on the deck with a large pool of blood easing away from his head. His eyes were closed. His skin was very white.

From the radio speakers a DJ in Sitka talked about making a better life. Miles Davis was playing in the background. I glanced out the port and saw the vapor of the whale blow that followed the fading lights of a boat leaving the harbor.

9 Gunk, Young Bob, and the *Rose* were gone. Jane Marie found bolt cutters in the engine room. To cut Teller free she rolled him to his side and held the jaws on the chain between the cuffs and I applied pressure with my feet. When we turned him all the way over he sputtered; bubbles of saliva and blood trickled down into his beard. He coughed and a tooth fell out, hitting the floor like a dime.

We propped him up in a bunk. We checked his breathing, looked him over for broken bones, and washed off the cuts on his face. A large lump on his forehead disturbed the symmetry of his face. Jane Marie found a chemical cold pack and when she put it on the growing knot, his eyelids flickered. After ten minutes, two aspirin and two painkillers from his kit, he started to talk.

He started with moans, then some syllables. I was bent over him and I think he recognized me because he smiled a strange illuminated grin, like the Dalai Lama. He said, "Gunk is more than just a little peeved."

He patted my hand and continued. "I had tucked the kid in. I heard Mom and Dad start bickering. So what's new with that? Then I heard someone else rustling around. At first, I thought it was you two. I looked up and he hit me. I remember trying to make it back up. Then I don't remember much." He held up the cuffs that dangled several links of chain. He smiled at them. "Oh, he cuffed me!" he said in a voice of a preschool teacher praising the inventiveness of some naughty scamp. He put his wrists down into his lap as if he were too tired to hold them up any longer. "I do remember this. Gunk said he wanted his money. He said he needed some time, but he would meet us later at the camp. He said to have his money and a ticket." Teller smiled up at Jane Marie and me. His head wobbled above his bloody shirtfront. He spit out a fleck of blood and said, "I don't think Gunk would hurt this kid. Gunk isn't really a hard guy. Hell, I think he even owns a Jap bike." Teller spit more blood. "I really need to pick my friends better."

Jane Marie turned off the radio. Teller closed his eyes and tentatively reached his index finger into his mouth to do a survey of teeth. He swallowed hard and asked for water again, then drank from the glass that Jane Marie was already holding out for him.

"I remember thinking that he might turn over the stove. Or that if I struggled too hard, I might tip it over, open a fuel line and start a fire. I knew I didn't want that. Even as Gunk was working me over, I remember thinking it was better than being trapped in the hull of a burning boat."

"Where's your gun?" Jane Marie asked him.

Teller smiled sweetly and his eyebrows arched on his puffy face. "On top of your safe. I left it up above. I was going to abide by the rules. Let you lock it up when you got back."

Jane Marie patted his thigh, left the cup of water on the ledge beside him, went to the wheelhouse and started the engine.

She was grabbing the charts up as I made it to her. She was muttering in an angry voice.

"He took that damn gun and the charts I need the most. He knows where my camp is from looking at the charts."

I pointed to the broken radar and the mass of wires hanging in the wheelhouse. "This is going to take time. We don't have radar. We don't have the right charts. Are you planning on going somewhere?"

She continued to scoop up the tools and scattered charts. She did not look at me as she spoke. "Get ready to handle the dock lines, will you?"

"How are we going to navigate at night?"

"We'll do fine, Cecil. Just take care of the dock lines and let's get this place cleaned up a little."

The tone of her voice made it clear that arguing would only result in my standing on the dock waving good-bye to the *Winning Hand.* I stood by the dock lines. Priscilla and Robert Sullivan stepped up on the deck. Robert decided this was the right time to confront Jane Marie. "I want that letter of agreement. This is insanity. I—"

Jane Marie pointed down to the closed safe and spoke as if she were spitting broken glass. "You stupid asshole, you broke the safe. I can't give it to you."

Robert started to speak but before he could say a word Jane Marie stuck her index finger in his chest.

"We are. Going to. Find him." She reached into her coat pocket and handed Robert a fistful of change. "There is a pay phone at the end of this dock. Call anyone you can. I don't care how you do it but you arrange that money and a ticket."

Robert Sullivan stood still, sweat dripping off the tip of his nose. He was shaking. His features were contorted in anger and as he drew a deep breath to speak, Jane Marie cut him off again. "There will be no discussion about this. There will be no more fighting on this boat or I'll put you both ashore. Understand?"

Both Robert and Priscilla stepped back in surprise but they both nodded their heads. Jane Marie continued, "I want you two to travel in the stern, in my lab. Do not set foot in my wheelhouse. Do not set foot in my galley. We will not be able to catch up with Gunk but will meet him in seven or eight hours at my camp. These are the rules. This is not a discussion or a negotiation. If either of you don't like it you can find your own way."

Both Priscilla and Robert started to speak but both stopped. Priscilla turned and stomped back toward the stern. Robert started to follow but doubled back and spoke softly to

Jane Marie who was now standing in the wheelhouse with the door to the deck open.

"Ten thousand dollars?" was all he said.

Jane Marie looked down at Teller in his bunk. Teller nodded in the affirmative. Jane Marie looked at Robert Sullivan. "Ten thousand dollars plus the cost of a one-way plane ticket from Juneau to Seattle."

Sullivan played with the coins in his hand. "Who do I call?" he asked.

Teller yelled from down in the galley, "Call that little pissant of a lawyer. He should be good for something."

Robert heard Teller's voice and grimaced in disgust. "Which little pissant lawyer?"

"Whichever one you want." Jane Marie was crawling into the access hatch near the wheel to have a look at the wiring. She stuck a small flashlight in her mouth and waved Sullivan away. Both he and Priscilla walked quickly out the door and up the dock to use the phone.

Within fifteen minutes Robert and Priscilla returned and I uncleated the dock lines and we headed south out of the inlet.

Jane Marie stood at the wheel and looked at her watch, then back to the smooth water easing under the bow. "Okay. I'm going to need some help, Cecil. Maybe we can take watches at the helm. We're going to have a quarter moon up in about an hour. Landmarks should show up, and there are marker lights for all of our course but the very last. By then we'll be picking up daylight, I hope."

"I don't know how to navigate." I thought that this was a good time to start a total honesty program.

In the light that seeped in from belowdecks I could only see her silhouette. The windows in the wheelhouse were a curtain of shiny darkness. She said, "Okay. To navigate, you need to know just three things: where you are, where you're going, and all the obstacles in your way. The object is to get there without running into anything bigger or better connected to the earth than you are."

"Well, why didn't you say so? And I always thought it was complicated."

The rest of the night we took turns at the wheel. Mostly, I remember the drone of the engine, standing at the wheel steering between red and green marker lights, drinking coffee, and watching as Jane Marie periodically scanned the water with a spotlight attached to the top of the wheelhouse. We didn't sleep. Jane Marie rooted around in her storage lockers and found Forest Service topographical and trail maps that showed the territory we were crossing. She sat bent over them with a tiny reading light and sketched with pencil every light and hazard to navigation she could recall. I remember watching her. Part of her time was spent staring outward trying to bore a hole in the darkness and the rest of the time she spent searching her memory for every rock or reef that could be in our line. She murmured to herself, thinking of the times she had rounded a certain point. She listed the names of the rocks and anchorages but separated them with the names of people she had been with.

"Tenakee . . . Kadashan . . . Saltery Bay, Seal Bay, Long Bay, and Freshwater. Took the hooktender and his girl-friend to Freshwater when the water pump went out. Point Augusta—Cilla saw the orcas that time. Spasski, The Sisters, Point Adolphus." She drew with her pencil and muttered. She would sometimes walk over to the wheel and gently correct my course without speaking. She would check the fathometer, which was still working, then she would say the course heading. I watched the compass and steered.

As we rounded the point out of Tenakee Inlet and headed up Chatham Strait, Jane Marie opened the window and lis-tened to the water slipping under our hull. A swell was running from the south, large rolling waves, but they were smooth without any chop on top so the boat moved through them easily. I heard her voice in the dim light. "If Gunk has hurt that boy, you're going to have to kick his ass, Cecil."

I looked at her in stunned amazement. "I'm going to kick Gunk's ass? I don't think so."

She turned away from me. "Yeah. He probably won't hurt him anyway." She said this in an uncertain voice.

All I could see over the bow was a distant pinprick of light in the black curtain. I looked to the compass; I had drifted five degrees off. I steered the numbers to our heading.

"From what I've seen I think they like each other. He won't hurt him," I told her, and I hoped it was true.

The light seemed to rise out of the water at first. The shoulders of the islands began to step forward. Textured carpets of green appeared, rolling up the bluffs on both sides of the strait. Then briefly the ridgeline showed silver, exposing the sawtooth rim of the mountains. Within moments the light vented in from above, creating silver shafts through the damp air. The tips of the waves sparkled beneath them. The shoreline retreated in shadow and as Jane Marie opened the side port we could smell the morning air: the muck of the tide line, the spruce and hemlock hills, the icy breeze from up the valleys. Gulls cut the air in front of our bow, and Teller came from below holding a cup of coffee, and grinning through his swollen lips. He stepped out on deck and gently put the cup to his lips. He winced as he drank the hot liquid. The bow heaved as we worked into the swells coming through Icy Strait. Spray flew off the bow and spattered around him in the sunlight. He shook his head and gingerly rubbed his eyes.

Teller finished his coffee and walked back in the wheelhouse. "Nice day," he said to me.

It had taken us much longer than Jane Marie had originally estimated, partly because she kept cutting our speed in the areas where her memory was uncertain. So it was late afternoon by the time we rounded the last point. Clouds were gathering high in the atmosphere and they glowed with the slanting sunlight when we turned into the cove where the mine had operated. The anchorage was filled with two ancient spruce logs anchored in the bay. The spruce logs were connected to the beach by a wobbly ramp. The *Rose* was tied to the spruce logs. It sat quietly and no one appeared to be on board. Up on the beach fringe a small cabin sat back in the alders. A thin streamer of smoke came from the six-inch pipe running up the back wall. In front of the cabin was a bench made of rough-hewn timbers. There was a piece of paper nailed to the door.

As we slowed the engines, Robert and Priscilla appeared on the back deck. I went to the bow and took the bowline. Teller went to the stern. Jane Marie gently eased the seine boat into the anchored spruce logs. I hopped down onto the logs and tied the *Winning Hand* off to a chain on the end. Teller did the same at the stern. Priscilla, ignoring everything else, ran down the length of the logs to the ramp for the shore. As I was taking the second wrap on the chain I could see she was heading for the cabin and the note. Robert Sullivan was close behind her.

Jane Marie shut down the engines and set the batteries to run the pumps. As she swung down onto the logs we heard the sound of a small prop plane circling the anchorage. Teller stood on the back deck and watched as the float plane circled once and then flattened out for a landing. Teller spoke to us from the bulwarks. "You don't need me. I'll stay on the boat. Gunk and I aren't exactly on speaking terms." He waved us on and Jane Marie hurried to catch up with the rest.

The float plane was on the water with the engine off. The pilot stood on the floats paddling the plane in toward the log where Jane Marie and I were standing. In a few moments Dickie Stein was standing next to us. He was wearing a long raincoat and baggy shorts with his sneakers unlaced. He had a knapsack that was stuffed full of what I assumed to be Gunk's money. Dickie waved to the pilot who, after tying up the plane, was putting his seat back to take a nap. He told Dickie he would wait. Dickie turned to me.

"Teller on the boat?" he asked. I nodded and Dickie strained to look up into the ports of the *Winning Hand* hoping to either see Teller or be seen by him.

"What's up?" I asked him casually as Jane Marie started up to the beach where Priscilla and Robert had pulled the note off the door and were reading it.

"What do you mean, 'What's up?' Christ, Cecil, I was hoping you'd tell me. You're on the ground here, aren't you?"

"Not yet," I said, as I walked down the logs that led to the ramp up the beach.

The note read: *All I want is my money and a ticket. Then you can have the kid back. But I think he'd be better off with me. You guys are fucking nuts. Anyway we are going up the hill to have a look at the old dynamite and shit. I told the kid to be very careful around it because it is real dangerous. When I have the money you can have the kid.*

Robert Sullivan was standing alone near the corner of the cabin. He had his hands jammed down into his jacket pockets. He saw Dickie reading the note over my shoulder and ran up to him.

"Did my dad get hold of you?"

Dickie nodded and held out the knapsack. "Yeah, he did. He had someone drop this by my hotel. He even arranged the charter flight out here. Of course he didn't tell me much."

Robert Sullivan grabbed the pack and headed up into the trees where a trail took off up the hill. Priscilla, seeing Robert leaving with the money, took off after him.

"You're welcome," Dickie called out at their disappearing backs. Dickie started to laugh. "I love this." He looked at me and scratched the frowsy top of his dirty hair.

"What's to love about this?" I asked.

"Oh, Christ. All of it, Cecil. This is the real thing. This is gangster stuff. Not some divorce case or a bad contract on a house. How often do we get a chance to fly around with gangster money?"

Jane Marie looked at him quizzically and with a touch of fear as if Dickie were some sort of talking rat. "Are you a lawyer?" she asked.

"Oh, yeah. Hi." He held out his hand to her. "Richard Stein. I'm Priscilla's real lawyer. I know you. Jane Marie, right? How are ya?" Dickie was excited. In his shorts and long raincoat he could have been a barker in a freak show. He went on without letting us speak.

"According to what I've been able to find out, the late, lamented Senator Taylor was blackmailing a group of important businessmen." Jane Marie took a step backward and sat down on a stump.

Dickie turned to me with an expression of amazement and went on with a storytelling lilt to his voice. "This goes back quite a ways, Cecil. Back in the fifties on the East Coast, there were large-scale arrests of organized crime figures. This was the era of the Kefauver hearings. The feds took down dozens of crime bosses in Miami and Chicago. The FBI needed snitches to make their cases. So they recruited mob accountants, book-keepers, and some of the lower-level types to testify. In exchange, they put everyone who cooperated in the witness protection program."

I nodded. Now Jane Marie was skipping rocks. She had a good arm and her stones sailed over the water leaving a trail of concentric rings. A varied thrush was singing in the woods. I became so absorbed in watching the rings widen on the water I had to force myself to sit still to listen to Dickie's voice.

"Back then the feds figured that the Territory of Alaska was the end of the earth. So a bunch of these old mob guys got shipped up here and were given new identities and new jobs. Alaska was like a dumping ground for these crooks. This was a perfect setup: whole new lives in a country that was just beginning to grow. These guys worked their way into good jobs in the state bureaucracy and almost every aspect of the oil, shipping, and fishing businesses. They were kept apart. No one knew who they were and they didn't know each other. But one guy did know. One guy got hold of the list."

"Senator Wilfred Taylor," I said, still watching the rings on the water that Jane Marie's stones made.

Dickie was sitting up straight and in spite of the fact that he was trying to act nonchalant about this display of superior knowledge, his face was ruddy and he was beginning to talk faster.

"Exactly. From Taylor's connections in the federal prosecutor's office he got hold of the FBI list and he used it in all aspects of his political career. Remember, the witnesses were highly placed in business and the government. All Taylor had to do was apply polite pressure and they'd do whatever he needed done in his district."

"Did they ever put pressure back on him?"

"I expect so. After about twenty years they were out of the woods with their old friends in the mob, but they had such respected positions here they didn't dare risk blowing their cover. So they never pushed the Senator too hard."

"Old Bob Sullivan was one of these gangsters?" Jane Marie said to no one in particular as she threw another stone.

"I had a friend in Chicago check around in the records. I gave him Robert Sullivan Senior's Social Security number and date of birth and he found a hit. Not everywhere, but one old hit. Like it was a mistake when he first went into the program. I mean, it must be hard to remember a new Social Security number. It was a real estate contract for a man named Steven Profieta. With that, I was able to go back through and dig up more. All the records for Sullivan Senior start in fifty-six. All the records for Profieta end. Sullivan and Profieta are the same age, same height, and their handwriting looks the same. There is more to do but I'm certain—Old Sullivan is dirty and so was the Senator. I mean, come on. Some stranger arrives at my hotel and hands me a sack of money and tells me where to take it. This is not business as usual. I tell you, Old Sullivan is real-live gangster stuff." Dickie was grinning like a lottery winner holding a check the size of a bedsheet.

The thrush continued to sing and I heard the clicking of stones. Jane Marie was squatted down on the shore sorting through the stones looking for the best ones to throw.

"Supposing all of that is true. How does it help Priscilla?" she called out.

"Priscilla had asked for all the Senator's records. Everything. Now usually there is no problem in hiding stuff from people with FOIA requests but Senator Taylor had made lots of enemies over the years and there had been talk that he was involved in something dirty. All politicians make enemies and one of the Senator's enemies worked in the Attorney General's office. The Attorney General had ordered Taylor to turn over everything to Priscilla. Taylor wasn't going to do that but he was trying to figure out just what to give Priscilla so that she would be satisfied and just go away. Her accusations of conspiracy theories were bringing too much attention to him. Priscilla doesn't know any of this, she just shows up in Juneau. She arrives in his outer office and the Senator is there shredding papers. He refuses to give her any documents. They argue and the Senator tries to throw her out. They struggle on the stairs and"—Dickie slapped his palms together in front of his face— "he falls and cracks his head open on the banister post."

Dickie beamed at me as if he were done with a command performance. I turned to Jane Marie and said, "That is some story." Jane Marie nodded and didn't look at either Dickie or me.

Up the hill I could hear Robert Sullivan and Priscilla

squabbling as they labored up the switchbacked trail. They had been gone ten minutes but were not far up the steep-sided mountain. Jane Marie stood up and slapped her hands on the front of her pants. "We should get up the hill. It's going to be dark soon and I don't think Robert and Priscilla can turn this money over without making Gunk angry." She started to walk toward the trailhead.

I took Dickie by the elbow and followed in behind Jane Marie. "What are you doing in this?" I asked him.

"What are you talking about? All I want is to walk Priscilla out of this murder charge. What are *you* doing?"

I looked past him and saw Jane Marie walking steadily in strong even steps up the hill. "I don't know. I think I'm working for Teller."

Dickie smiled grimly and grunted, "Teller? He's out of this. He's nothing but a glorified bail bondsman."

"Who is putting up her bail?"

"My guess is the Sullivans. Old Bob Sullivan doesn't want any of his past coming out. He hired Teller to make it all go away. To make Priscilla go away. It all fits with everything else I know."

"What if everything you know is wrong?" I asked him.

"Man, you worry too much." The thrush sang again and a slight breeze rustled the spruce and hemlock boughs. "Besides, I'm not worried. If everything I know right now is wrong, I'll just correct it later." He slapped me on the back and watched Jane Marie disappear up into the overgrown trail.

"You go on," Dickie said. "I don't really have to go up there. This is just paying off the help." He squatted down and started to finger a flat stone himself. "In fact, the less I know about it the better." He waved me off.

I started up the trail by myself. Jane Marie was two dozen steps ahead of me and I was having a hard time catching up to her. I labored into each step and my lungs filled with the cool air. As I gained elevation the air began to warm. As we climbed I felt the first traces of a flavorful wind. It was as if we were all hiking into a new season.

I had read the newspaper stories about Jane Marie's mine site. The mine had been played out thirty years ago. In reality it never had produced enough gold to make it worth the investment. In 1920 some color had turned up in the pan of a prospector working the sand along the shore of the lake. He immediately patented it and brought in eastern investors by the dozens. The prospector used the investors' money to build the docks and the facilities up by the lake. He made the mine a comfortable place to live but he never got much more gold out of the sand. Rather than face up to his error the prospector followed a tried-and-true method of the era. He bought some gold dust and salted his claim. He brought up another likely investor, gave him twenty minutes out on the sand surrounding the lake and then offered to sell him the entire kit and caboodle for what it cost him. The prospector headed for the tall and uncut, leaving the mine to a series of unlucky investors.

Someone had built stone stairs into the hill and others

tried laying a wooden roadway made of logs crisscrossing the hillside. Another investor tried blasting a shaft in the bottom of the lake so he could lower the level of the water, exposing more of the sand. The old shed from this project held the remnants of the blasting material. This is where I suspected Gunk was keeping the boy.

I caught up to Jane Marie but we did not speak. Our chests were too busy working to fill our lungs. I worked harder than she did. We walked quickly up the steep stairs laboring our way back and forth up the hill. To the south I could hear the stream that was the outlet from the lake we were climbing to. The old puncheon road was a rotted skeleton that we had to climb over. A canopy of old-growth trees shaded the mossy floor. A few green buds spiked up through the duff. The wind hissed in the upper story of the trees and at eye level the branches of the blueberry bushes and the scrubby dwarf dogwood glinted in the sunlight.

It was straight uphill for almost a mile, then the trail contoured around the hillside to follow the steep-sided canyon of the creek. We caught up to Priscilla and Robert just as the trail came out from the trees into an alpine meadow that held the lake. Twenty yards in front of us was a plank cabin. Young Bob was sitting in a straight-back chair. His arms were behind him. There was a weathered wooden box under the chair. I could see a small antenna sticking out from inside the box. Gunk stepped out from behind a tree just to our left. He was holding a small plastic box with a button on it. He spoke casually. "Listen, I don't really mean to be a pain in the ass but I really need to have a straight answer about my money." Gunk held up the plastic box and waved it in front of his face.

"I don't want to blow this boy into tiny little bits but then"—Gunk looked over at Young Bob who sat quietly in the straight-back chair, then back at the group of us panting in the trail, "I wouldn't really be responsible if you didn't keep your end of the bargain, would I?"

Robert reared back and stood as straight as breathing would let him. "You are someone else's problem. After this I'm not dealing with you anymore." His voice was wheezing. "I'm taking my boy and heading out." He handed the knapsack to the smiling Gunk. As Robert began to push past him, Gunk put the plastic box in front of Robert's eyes.

"Now just wait a minute there, Dad." Inside the cabin I could see Young Bob watching us. Although his eyes were wide, there was something in his expression, an arch to the eyebrows, that I was having a hard time interpreting. Gunk handed the pack to me. He kept hold of the box.

"I told the kid and I'm telling you too. This old dynamite is very, very dangerous stuff. Some of this stuff up here is rotted and the rest has nitro sweating all over the outside. I hardly need this detonator or the caps. That kid wiggles on his chair, it's going to go." Gunk smiled at me and his voice was calm. He nodded down to the knapsack. "Open that up for me, would you, amigo?"

I unzipped the knapsack Dickie had flown up with and

showed Gunk the bundles of tens and twenties inside. He leaned back and took the nine-millimeter pistol out of his belt. When he smiled I could see two freshly made gaps from missing teeth. Without saying a word he stepped back from Robert, held the detonator high above his head, leaned away from the cabin and pushed the button.

Priscilla and I fell to the ground. Robert ducked behind a tree and Jane Marie stood flat-footed and did not move.

I crouched with my arms around Priscilla. I braced for the explosion. I even imagined that I felt the shock wave ahead of the blast, but several long seconds wore on. There was the wind slurring around in the trees and the skittering of a songbird somewhere. Finally there was Gunk's resonant laughter falling like dead fish out of the trees. I looked up and Gunk was pushing the button on the black plastic box. He was laughing at me and wiping the tears from his eyes. "My garage door must be flapping around like someone's laundry." He laughed and put the plastic door opener in his pocket. Young Bob ran up from the cabin hopping and cantering like a colt.

Jane Marie shook her head and smiled down at us on the ground.

"You didn't duck," I said to her.

"You need to play more poker, Cecil." She nodded toward Gunk, who was fanning himself with a bundle of money. "This guy was way too pleased with himself to be about to blow up a six-year-old. Besides, Young Bob's hands weren't even tied. He was giggling at us the whole time."

The boy ran up and Gunk peeled off a twenty-dollar bill and wadded it into Young Bob's tiny hand. "Here you go, little dude. Partners. Just like I told you."

Priscilla stood up and pushed me away from her. Cursing, Robert charged Gunk. Gunk kept laughing, but as Robert came closer he held out the pistol and eased it into Robert's chest, laughing all the time. "Relax, Dad. No harm done so far. Just a joke. I wasn't going to hurt that kid for the world."

Robert Sullivan was livid. He kept pushing against the gun and his arms started up as if he were going to reach for it. Gunk stopped laughing. He pulled back the hammer and spoke between clenched teeth. "But I would shoot you through the heart for nothing but the fun of it."

Robert backed away.

Young Bob pulled on his mother's hands. "Come on, Mom. There's all kinds of neat stuff to look at. Gunk showed me all this mining stuff. There's all kinds of cool things. Gunk said there was even some gold here we could look for."

Robert Sullivan brushed himself off and regained his dignity. "Come on, boy. We're going down the hill. We're going to take that plane back to town. I want to get you home."

Young Bob hung his head. Priscilla stepped toward Robert. Young Bob ran off to play and Jane Marie followed behind. Priscilla's face showed tired desperation. Her voice was almost pleading. "You're not going to take him now, are you?" Robert was watching where Young Bob had run. He was ignoring everyone. "I won't let you," Priscilla said, almost sobbing. Robert called out, "Boy, you get over here right now."

Over their shoulders I saw Jane Marie standing in the front of the cabin. The boy was playing in what looked like an old dump site off to the side of the old camp. I looked at Gunk who was squatted down counting his money. "Are there any old explosives up here?" I asked him.

Gunk kept counting and then paused, but he never took his eyes off the money. "Not that I saw," he said. "The cabin is pretty clean. I tell you, I was never going to hurt that kid. I'd never let him near that stuff if I knew it was around."

Priscilla regained some of her strength and was standing right next to her ex-husband pointing her tiny finger into his stomach. I'm sure they were arguing but I blocked out their voices as I watched what happened next.

I watched Young Bob empty out an old red coffee can onto the moss. He was running his fingers through the nuts and bolts and shiny bits of metal. I shut my eyes listening to the slurry of his parents bickering. Their voices made me tired, and I felt the knifing pain of a headache easing in.

Then I opened my eyes. I stopped hearing their voices. I couldn't hear the wind or the sound of the can Young Bob was tapping. I was focused on what was in his hand. "Stop. Oh, please, stop," I whispered.

Jane Marie saw what I saw, then started walking quickly toward Young Bob. My mind was running but I must have been walking toward him.

Even from twenty yards away I could see the blasting caps were split along their rusty seams. They looked like fat pen refills. There were several of them taped together. Young Bob was humming and tapping them against the edge of the can with one hand. He was running his fingers through the rusty hardware with the other.

Jane Marie cleared her throat. In a strained but cheery voice she said, "Hey, buddy boy . . . just put those things down on the moss, okay?"

"What in the sam-hell do you think you are doing anyway!" Robert's voice boomed over everything. He rushed toward his son, then stopped. He turned and yelled at Priscilla and Gunk. "Look! Look! Goddammit. Look what he's playing with. You said there was nothing here. You are supposed to be watching him!"

Jane Marie was down on her knees crawling toward the child. "Come on, baby," I heard her say, as I walked closer and closer. "Just put them down."

Priscilla rushed forward and now the adults were a triangle surrounding the child. Priscilla shrieked, "You put those down right this minute, young man!!"

Young Bob paused. He watched the red-faced adults surrounding him. He dropped the caps back in the empty can and scrambled to his feet. His mouth turned down as he started to cry.

"Bitch. Whadda you think you were doing?" Robert strode over and slapped Priscilla to the ground. Gunk got to his feet and scratched his head with the muzzle of the gun.

The next few moments have shattered in my memory. I'm fairly certain I remember Priscilla screaming and covering her face from the blows that she was expecting. I vaguely remember thinking that things were going very, very wrong as Young Bob bent down again to pick up the can. There is something about Jane Marie diving toward him. But I can remember with great clarity the dark-haired child's snarling expression as he heaved the rusty coffee can at his parents.

The next seconds were a haze of exploding red. Shards of metal whirred noisily past me, imbedding into the trees with a flat ticking sound. I was running toward the child and I had a hot itching in my chest. My own blood flecked down onto my pants as I ran toward him.

The can had exploded as it left Young Bob's right hand. The force of the blast had thrown him backward. He lay in the moss, his white skin flecked red. A tiny bit of his scalp was lifted off. The flecks of red were running blood. As I looked down at his body I had to look at his arm several times because I couldn't make sense of it.

There were no fingers, but a tiny fan of pure white bones where his palm should have been. His light blue jacket was in tatters around his chest and the sleeve and skin on his arm were completely gone, leaving the raw musculature exposed. The arm was vivid and red against the green of the moss. I could see every detail of his sinews, the tightly bundled muscles twitching for the first time in the air.

Jane Marie was saying Young Bob's name over and over. Her fingers were arched and shaking over his face, then over his arm. Her hands stayed suspended, trembling over the unconscious child, as if she couldn't bring herself to touch the boy's body. Robert Sullivan was staring. His expression was blank and pale. His mouth was open like he wanted to say something but couldn't. Priscilla crawled slowly over and touched Young Bob's toe with the tip of her finger. She was crying and the sound was like the air pinched from a balloon.

Gunk threw the pistol away in the brush. He looked around and for a moment I thought he was going to run down the hill, but he walked over, reached down and put his fingers to the boy's throat. He tilted the boy's head back and listened near his mouth. Then Gunk patted his hands down Young Bob's chest and remaining arm. He felt the good arm and looked at the remaining fingers. Gunk looked up at me, his expression now serious and scared.

"He's got a pulse. He's lucky. The explosion seared the blood vessels so he's not going to start bleeding real bad for a while."

I stared at him blankly, not able to comprehend how this was luck, my mind not ready to unspool into the future.

Gunk spoke to me. "We've got a chance at this. I've seen this kind of stuff. We can do something."

Jane Marie's face was streaked with blood. "Cecil, there is a handheld radio on the boat. Go to the boat. Call them." Priscilla was starting to whimper sitting at the feet of her boy. Robert was pacing back and forth talking to himself and running his fingers through his hair.

Gunk continued to look for other injuries. He lifted the closed eyelids and gently felt under the boy's back. "We've got to get pressure on these wounds. We've got to treat him for shock. We don't have a lot of time. But if you can get some communication going, we'll be ahead of the game. Can you do that?''

Finally, his words seeped into my understanding. I got up from my knees and saw I was bleeding from a tiny wound in my chest. Gunk left the boy and walked up to me. He looked me up and down and touched the part of my chest that was bleeding. He tenderly removed a piece of metal, then took out his wallet that was chained to his pants, flipping through his credit cards. He found one grimy Band-Aid. He put it on the cut. Then he buttoned my tattered shirt and coat.

"When there's time, you get that cleaned up. You okay? You seem kind of screwed up." Gunk looked in my eyes and held his hand to my forehead, then patted his hands down the rest of my body. "You want someone else to go?"

The light beside the lake was beginning to fade. I looked down to Young Bob. Jane Marie was spreading her own wool coat over the child. She gently lifted the seared stump. It was red meat and delicate porcelain of shattered bones. Near them, Robert Sullivan had his hands in his lap and he was staring into space. He was still breathing hard from the climb up the hill. Priscilla was clinging to his shoulder crying.

I walked to the trailhead. Gunk called behind me, "Now, hurry, but don't run. Don't be crazy, man. The most important thing is to get there and make the call. If you fall and break your leg that won't happen. Understand? Make the call, then bring us the radio, a first aid kit, a sleeping bag, and some flares if you can find them. We'll do what we can here. You sure you're okay?"

I nodded, and waved over my back as I kept on going down the trail.

It was twilight at the lake. The shade crept away from the edge of the trees and moved up into the sky that was a darkening blue. I stepped into the understory of timber. Here the trees were reduced to shadow against shadow. The path was where the darkest shadows were not. I could orient myself by the sound of the stream in the gully below. Where it had taken us fifteen minutes to cross earlier in the day it took me half an hour. As I followed the contour of the hill, the sound of the stream merged with the wind moving through the trees. Soon there was no direction to the whispering rush of noise. By then it was too dark to see. I paused, then held my arms out in front of me like a blindfolded child playing a party game.

The trees and the underbrush became vague forms. I was feeling giddy with panic. The wind blew through the trees in wide swaths. I could hear the wave of wind overtake me and then rush past. I wanted to go back to the lake. I wanted to be back with the others but when I looked up the hill there was nothing. Somewhere, downhill, was salt water. Somewhere in the water was the boat. Behind me Young Bob was starting to bleed. I couldn't go back. I stepped off the level area and fell.

My face hit first, then I cartwheeled and planted it again. I was plunging through a thicket, pitching, gaining speed, then suddenly I felt weightless, as if I were spilling out of myself. I landed with a grunt, wedged under something wet and mossy my hands told me was a fallen log. Sparks slowly rose up from my body and hovered in front of my eyes. I was trying to find a pattern in the sparks when I made out the lightness of some lichen in the rotted log. In the dark it could have been a column of steam or a broken bone. I heard a snap, then a thump. I wriggled to free myself. A sharp pain in my ribs scattered more sparks. A stone clattered down and there might have been a black hump waddling through the brush. The wind was filled with grunts and snuffling coughs. Shadows filled with sparking teeth, jaws snapping like rifle shots. I stood and tried to walk slowly, but stumbled, pitchpoling again, branches whipping my face. I reached out but everything disintegrated in my fingers. My head pounded against something hard. My body twisted down a clay bank. I tore at it with my fingertips, until I came to rest in the bottom of a ravine.

Here was pure darkness. I lay still. I could taste mud on my teeth. The air around me felt hollow with cold. I tried stretching my eyes wide but nothing would show light in my brain. I listened again for grunts but not even sound would take shape. I put my hands to my face, trembling as I touched my nose. I put my fingers into my mouth, biting them to reassure myself I hadn't been sucked up by the darkness. I had been sent for help. I had become a kitten fallen into a well.

Then something cut through the air that was so distinct I could almost taste it in my mouth. It was a cutting tone that sustained a pattern, changing slightly only to repeat a similar pattern. This sound was music. It was so improbable I started to laugh. Someone was singing "I Can't Give You Anything but Love." The song was coming from Teller's radio. Suddenly this sound switched to a Motown tune, then an Irish ballad. The sad narrative of the fiddle hung in the wind and was gone. Hootie and the Blowfish. The Mighty Clouds of Joy. Nirvana. An advertising jingle for gear lube. Bob Seger. A talk show guest over a bad phone connection. The Kingston Trio. They all clicked past Teller's scanner. The radio was patched through the loudspeaker on the *Winning Hand*. The loudspeaker system was for the crew to monitor radio transmissions while working the gear. Also the skipper could use it to hail other boats.

My body felt warmer suddenly and the bile of panic seemed to wash out through my skin. I stood. The music was coming from my left side. Even though it was counter to any intuition I had remaining, I went uphill. I scrambled out of the ravine that ran north away from the cove and joined the larger drainage from the lake. As I crested the ridge I saw the sparkle of light from the boat cutting through the trees. I picked my way toward it, climbing and cutting myself on the branches of fallen logs. Fifty yards short of the beach I could see the hull of the *Winning Hand*. The float plane was still tied at the dock. Chop came into the cove from the gusts out in the strait. The plane's wings tipped slightly back and forth and the floats creaked against their tie-up lines.

Teller and Dickie had been drinking brandy and working on the handcuffs with a hacksaw. Teller had the left one off and had a half-inch gouge in the right. When I stumbled in they immediately knew that there was work to be done. Dickie cut through the right cuff.

The pilot had been waiting for us to come down from the

hill. Dickie told him there would be a small boy flying back to Juneau, accompanied by an adult. Dickie didn't know who the adult would be. The pilot had grown tired of waiting and was about to take off when they heard the explosion up the hill. He decided to wait.

As I tried to explain the situation to Teller he reached into his gear and pulled out the first aid kit and his sleeping bag. Dickie started gathering up as many flashlights as he could find.

When Gunk had torn up the wheelhouse the night before he had shorted the fuse panel for everything but the CB radio. No one was in range. No one seemed to be monitoring any of the channels we could hit. Tucked back into a protected cove, the plane's radio and the handhelds were not powerful enough to reach the main Coast Guard base in Sitka. We could monitor the stronger commercial transmissions that were drifting around us, but we couldn't generate the signal that would get out of the cove.

The pilot was a tall skinny kid from Oklahoma. He nervously offered to taxi his plane out into the strait to see if he could raise a signal. The winds were gusting toward forty knots and the seas were building. He was taking a risk by moving out in the water in the dark, and by his tense expression I could see that he knew it.

Teller and I packed the gear. We had several lamps and flashlights. We would try the handhelds once we topped the ridge. I shouldered the pack and had started jogging toward the trailhead when I looked up and saw a burst of flame moving rapidly down the mountain. I ran back to the boat and found the binoculars. I frantically glassed the hillside. The flames were gone.

I started for the shore again and as I did I saw Gunk standing on the dock. Jane Marie, Priscilla, and Robert held torches that looked like they were made from soaking strips of cloth in oil. Robert's shirt was gone. Jane Marie was wearing cutoffs. I went outside on the dock.

Gunk held a bleeding bundle in his arms. Young Bob's shattered arm was wrapped in bright red rags. Beneath Gunk on the bleached decking of the dock I saw blood dripping like a heavy rain. He was breathing hard and his former professional calm had cracked into tears. "He's dying . . . ," he said, and a gust of wind pulled his words out over the water.

I turned to the pilot and said, "Let's go. We're flying him in."

He shook his head and spoke very slowly. "You know I'd like to. But I just can't do it. Crashing my plane will not help this child."

I stepped out onto the float. "All right," I said. "I'm going."

"Cecil, you don't know how to fly, do you?" Jane Marie's voice was a mixture of amazement and panic.

"I took ground school and I've had a couple of hours in the air. Someone said it would help my hysteria about flying. I'm not kidding about this. I'm going." I began to fumble with the levers and the weird-looking knobs.

Teller reached for me with his still-cuffed hand. Gently he grabbed my forearm. "Hold on, ace." He asked Gunk evenly, "Is he really going to die?"

Gunk's shrug shifted the boy in his arms. A tear of blood stained his boot. "Shock, loss of blood, this kid doesn't have a lot of time out here." He said this without taking his eyes off Teller.

Teller turned to the pilot. "Everything all right with your plane? The instruments work? No personal quirks?"

The pilot shook his head. "Yes sir, it just had a go-through. It works fine, but not . . ." He gestured to the wind and the chop on the water.

"How many minutes to Juneau?"

"Twenty, once you're in the air. If you've got a north wind, maybe less. But he's not going. I'm not letting him kill that boy even if he wants to look like a hero."

Teller stood close to the pilot who looked very slight next to Teller's bulk. Teller's voice was urgent with a gloss of friendliness. "Well now, son, just don't talk to me about who's killing that boy and who is a hero. I'm taking your plane. You can fill out a complaint in town." He turned to Gunk. "I need one passenger in the copilot seat, one in the back with Young Bob. Tuck all the survival gear and the first aid kit in the tail. We've got a quarter moon and it won't last all night." He grabbed Gunk's arm. "I'd really like you to come along just so I could kick your sorry ass out"—he walked away, and his voice sailed up over his shoulder—"but you're too damn heavy." Then Teller poked his head into the cockpit of the plane where I sat. "Cecil, you ride shotgun."

"You mean I can't fly? You've been drinking." But I climbed into the pilot's seat.

"Yeah, and you're an idiot." Teller smiled. "At least *I'll* sober up."

Jane Marie climbed into the back of the plane with us. She signaled Gunk to lift Young Bob in. The boy was bundled in everyone's coats. I could see the pale skin of his throat as they lifted him in.

Priscilla was standing next to Robert on the dock. Both their faces were smeared in blood. They held their hands up as if making supplication.

"We want to come," Priscilla said in a reedy voice.

Teller lifted himself into the pilot's place, grunted, and put the seat as far back in the tracks as it would go. I strapped myself next to him. He leaned across me and spoke to Young Bob's parents.

"No room. Gunk and Mr. Stein here can take the cruiser in. You should be in Juneau by morning."

Priscilla started to argue but dissolved into heaving sobs. Robert put his hand on her shoulder. Dickie waved to me and started walking to the *Rose*. Teller slammed the door of the plane. "I'd rather have rabid dogs in the plane than those two," he told me.

Teller settled into his seat. "I need you for balance, Younger. Just stay in the plane, okay? And don't touch anything." He patted my knee. "Hey, we'll be home for supper." There were two braces coming down near the windscreen. I gripped one with my left hand and clutched the bottom of my seat with the other as we pushed away from the float and the engine whined, then sputtered into a steady roar.

At the mouth of the cove the plane bobbed on the chop

and rocked in a yawing motion in the wind. The moonlight made white sparks on the water. I could see the outline of the mountains across the strait. Gusts hurled down the strait in a wall of spray. They curled and whipped off the tops of the waves in a billowing curtain of water. Teller had the aviation map on his lap and a penlight in his mouth. He scanned the map on both sides, then back to front. He threw it over his shoulder in frustration.

"These fucking things. It's that way, right?" He pointed to the southeast.

"Yeah."

"Okay, I'll get up there and I'm sure to see some lights or something."

Another gust came through and began to spin the plane on the water. He gunned the engine and pitched it heavily into the wind. He stared out to the churning strait.

"Now . . . the way you go about this is: try and time the next gust so you're coming off the top of a wave with enough airspeed so it lifts you up into the air"—he grinned at me, his smile showing a crazed gap in his teeth—"and not down, into the water."

I asked, "You've done this before, right?"

He was hunched over the yoke studying the water and counting in his head.

"Not actually . . . but I've always wanted to."

Young Bob groaned in the backseat. I turned around in my seat and could see Jane Marie awkwardly cradling the bleeding bundle of coats in her lap. Young Bob was slumped limply into her chest, the seat belt tight around his waist. Jane Marie looked fierce and not afraid.

"Get this thing in the air," she told Teller.

Teller gunned the engine again and the interior of the tiny cabin lurched and vibrated as if it were shaking apart. I clutched at the frame and my seat as we catapulted down the waves; at first lurching up and down each swell, then banging hard on each crest until the water was a washboard thumping on the floats. Ahead was the moving gust, like a cloud of steam rolling toward us. Teller eased back slightly on the throttle, pumped the flaps, then jammed the throttle forward as we hit the gust.

When I was nine years old my mother took me to visit relatives in eastern Washington. My cousins took me to a fair during the middle of August. I remember the fairgrounds were on a slow-moving river. The air was dry and had cottonwood bloom drifting on the cool air from upstream. There was a ride called the Elevator on which my chubby cousin and I rode three times each. We strapped into a narrow chamber and rocketed over backward on a huge hydraulic arm. Our whole beings were light with our hysterical laughter and the whirling momentum of fear. I remember looking at the ground far below with the red paper cups scattered in the dust. I remember the spiraling horizon and the giddy terror of having our coins fall out of our pockets.

This was the only experience that even remotely prepared me for the takeoff of the float plane. The gust scooped the plane up as if it were a kite abruptly released into the wind on a slack string. I felt the confusing gravitational forces pushing me down, then lifting me out. The aluminum frame of the seat creaked. The engine blared as the vibration and rocking jolts pulled at my bones. I opened my eyes. Teller's right hand was still cuffed and it rested on the control panel adjusting the throttle and mixture. The cuff clicked against the dials. His left was tightly curled on the steering yoke. He was wincing, sucking air between his teeth. I looked out the side window and saw the sawtooth of whitecaps on a shallow reef below. My stomach felt sick with the sideways slide and yaw of the plane. I heard Young Bob moan in the back. Jane Marie reached over the seat and gripped my shoulder.

Teller horsed the yoke in, then turned. For a moment the plane dipped crazily but as the front of the squall passed Teller leveled the wings and began a steady climb. Young Bob was shrieking as the plane lunged up and down, the wind shaking us like an angry parent. With each jolt his arm moved involuntarily and blood spattered on the floor of the plane. As Young Bob's voice rose I could feel a scream building in my own chest, but before I let it out the plane eased over a ridge of the island across the inlet and stopped rocking in the air. I could see the moonlight on snowfields that were dropping below us. In the distance was a cloud of light rising from the ground and the string of pearls that was Juneau's road system.

Teller got on the radio. He identified himself and told the

tower in Juneau that we were going to be landing in the airport pond and we needed an ambulance. Then he studied the bulk of Douglas Island that hid the airport and spoke over the engine noise. "You ever do a plane crash case, Younger?"

I remembered working for the family who had died flying up Lynn Canal on vacation. I started to think about the pictures from the case but stopped. Teller said, "Hitting the ground too hard is a common thread in most crashes. I'm going to get a little more altitude." He nosed the plane in a steep climb and the ride actually became smoother although the plane felt different as if it had a more tentative grip on the atmosphere. The snowfields sank behind and soon we could see the Mendenhall Valley where the airport lay. I could see flashing lights near the pond next to the runway.

"What'd you think of the takeoff?" Teller asked.

"Impressive, what I saw of it."

"Didn't scare you, did it?"

"Naw. Felt a little different than I'm used to, but not really scary." My hands were cramping from my grip on the seat and the supports.

"Man, these new drugs are great!" He opened the pill bottle with one hand and shook out some sedatives.

The takeoff had been so frightening I was beginning to think of the rest of my life as a gift. As we descended toward the pond outside Juneau twenty minutes later, the plane dipped its wing and nearly caught a tip but we were so relaxed by this time I almost laughed at the foolishness of the weather to think it could bring bad luck, but I didn't because I know that nature punishes arrogance, especially from the lips of fools. The pond rose toward us, Teller straightened out the wings and we banged the floats down on the water, then turned the plane to the dock.

The ambulance was there and the EMTs lifted Young Bob from Jane Marie's arms. She climbed down and then into the back of the ambulance as the woman in uniform uncoiled the IV. The ambulance doors shut and the gravel on the runway apron crunched as the vehicle drove away. Teller and I stood in icy moonlight and watched it go. The lights faded and the night settled in. A state trooper stepped out of his car and walked up to us.

"Mr. Teller, the District Attorney asked that I meet you here and bring you down to his office for a chat."

Teller nodded, spit on the ground and walked to the car. He didn't look at me.

I was alone by the pond and once again on foot. From where I stood I could look across the valley and see the light of the quarter moon dancing off the face of the glacier. There were no birds nearby to tell me where to go.

 **11** I walked around the apron of the runway over to the airport terminal and took a cab to the hospital. The driver took a look at my clothes and put it on a tab. I found Jane Marie in the meditation room. She was laying out a game of solitaire on the table. Her hands cast angular shadows.

"They won't tell me much of anything. They're still in the emergency room with him," she said without taking her attention off the cards.

She laid out the cards across the top row. She leaned into the light to see the cards.

"You ever play snirts, Cecil?" she asked in a tight voice.

"No." I walked over and put my hand on her shoulder.

"Some people up north in Wainwright taught it to me. It's basically a solitaire game but you play it with other people. Everyone starts with a full deck of their own but you lay out the aces in the middle, then you play those as common. It's a race to play all of your cards. It's fast. The people who taught it to me were really good. They were good solitaire players and when they got together they'd play this all night."

I began to massage her neck. Her lips were a tight line across her face. Her hands holding the cards were shaking.

"If I could get another deck I would teach you how to play." She looked up and I saw that her eyes brimmed with tears. I didn't say anything.

"It's a good game really." Her voice cracked. I held her in her chair as she wept.

We fell asleep in the meditation room. A doctor came in and gave us a blanket. I remember him saying something about Young Bob being out of the ER. I recall sitting up and having a very long and serious conversation with him but the only thing I remembered about it later was the phrase "out of the woods." Then I remember dreaming about thousands of snow geese flying out of a marsh, their feathers drifting down on people in hospital beds. When I woke up, my neck was cocked at an odd angle on the arm of the couch and my muscles ached. My arm was numb with the weight of Jane Marie's head cradled there. The light coming through the stained-glass window spread out on her face. I cupped her cheek in my palm; in her sleep she kissed my fingers. She opened her eyes.

"I was dreaming about flying," she said in a husky voice. "You weren't really going to fly that plane, were you?"

"No. I would have crashed it and we'd all be dead now."

"My hero." She closed her eyes again.

We had some of the awful coffee that is mandatory in

hospitals and waited as the family and then the police gathered. First Priscilla and Robert came. I saw them standing by the admitting office. Robert was leaning his face over the counter softly reciting names and numbers. He reached into his wallet for his insurance card. Priscilla stood behind him holding his hand. I elbowed Jane Marie to look. She heaved a sigh. "The honeymoon starts again. Now I suppose they're united against me." She began walking toward them.

I went in the other direction. I nearly tripped over Gunk's feet. He was in a chair with a ball cap pulled down low over his face. He looked up from under the brim. "Hey, how's the kid?"

"He lost the fingers but they might save his wrist. They say he's pretty weak."

Gunk smiled. "No shit. How was that flight?"

"Exhilarating. Did you bring the *Rose* in?"

"Yeah. We had a couple of exciting crossings. The wind knocked us around but we made it into the dock a couple of hours ago. We doubled up the lines on the *Winning Hand*, and locked up the cabin as best we could."

I offered him a cup of coffee and he winced.

Dickie Stein walked in like a gunfighter in a long duster-type coat. "Oh, God," I murmured. Behind him came a state trooper in full uniform.

Underneath Dickie's duster he was wearing the pants from a blue silk suit, five-hundred-dollar cowboy boots, and a T-shirt that read *Eat the Rich*.

He strode up to me and I could almost hear horse hooves

clattering to a stop. "How's he doing?" he demanded. As I explained to him what the doctors had said, I could see in his expression he wasn't listening to a thing I was saying but was eager to tell me his news. The state trooper walked around us and stood in front of Gunk. He made a beckoning gesture with his index finger and Gunk stood up stony-faced and angry, then walked toward the door with the trooper close behind. "It's over. We can go home," Dickie burst in. I had drifted off in my description of Young Bob's injuries and was watching Gunk get into the back of the trooper's car.

"Over?" I asked.

Dickie had the smile of a man with superior knowledge. "Over, I'm telling you. The DA offered to dismiss the charges against Priscilla."

"Dismiss? That's it? Dismiss?"

"I'm telling you, it's almost a done deal. All she has to do is testify at a new grand jury they're convening."

"Who is the target of the grand jury?"

Dickie shrugged his shoulders in an irritating gesture of nonchalance. "Who cares? I just know they promised if Priscilla cooperated she would not be the target. But"—he scanned the room and put his back to the window as he whispered—"my bet is this: They don't want the story of this witness protection list coming out. They'll fuss around and in the end everything is going to go away unless they have some patsy. Nobody will even remember Senator Taylor is dead."

I looked back out to the empty parking lot. The trooper's vehicle had disappeared.

"Where's Teller?"

"Gone. They questioned him last night and he made the first plane back to Fairbanks."

"What are you going to do?"

"Just what I said. I'm going home. I haven't talked to her yet but I'm sure she will cooperate. This is a 'Get out of jail free' card. The fix is in, Cecil. I'm telling you, the feds aren't going to let the state take this to trial. They've got to protect the identities on that list."

"So they're going to let the person who murdered a state senator just walk out the door?"

"She can always fall back on the accident defense, Cecil!" He spoke slowly and clearly as if I were either hard of hearing or purely simpleminded. "They were having an argument on the stairs. He hit her; she struggled with him; he slipped and hit his head. Priscilla was hysterical when the cops came. She felt responsible for the accident but she was not confessing to a murder."

"It would have been a hell of a final argument."

"Cecil, don't worry about it. I've taken care of it. We can get on with things."

I looked over by the nursing station. I saw Jane Marie, Priscilla, and Robert in a huddle with the doctor. The doctor was talking and pointing to his own hand, drawing a line across his palm with a ballpoint pen. The others nodded with the rhythm of his voice.

I picked up my jacket and headed for the door, then doubled back to speak with Jane Marie.

"You wanna meet me at the airport tonight at six o'clock?"

She looked back at the doctor leading Priscilla and Robert to Young Bob's room. She watched them turn the corner at the end of the hall. Dickie stood silently at the door next to me.

"Yes," she said. "I want to meet you. Where are we going?"

"I'm not really sure, but pack for cold weather."

She looked at me with a confused stare but then flattened her expression into one of tentative trust.

"Okay, I'll meet you, Cecil. But can we make it tomorrow morning? I need to take care of some things and check in with Mr. Meegles."

I looked at my watch and then out the window. "Tomorrow will be good." I started out, then came back again. This time I kissed her before heading for the door.

Dickie grabbed my arm, trying to stop me. "What are you going to do?"

"I'm going to get on with things," I said over my shoulder as the door hissed shut behind me.

Robert Sullivan the First lived in a large house in the Mendenhall Valley. His street was as idyllic a scene of suburban tranquillity as any in America. A wiry terrier ran behind a towheaded boy on a bicycle. Four girls were playing jump rope in the turnaround of the cul-de-sac. They chanted a skipping rhyme as a girl in a blue jumper hopped over the whirling rope. Behind them I could see the glacier curling down between two tired mountains. The earth is new here behind the retreating ice, the trees are small, the ground is rocky and damp. But a pair of large alder trees bordering Sullivan's house must have been moved in by landscapers. They shaded his porch from the cold light of this spring afternoon.

Old Bob Sullivan was wearing a cardigan golf sweater and fuzzy slippers when he came to the door. His face showed a man over sixty but he was slender and strong. He walked upright with a lift in each step. I introduced myself as a private investigator who used to work for Priscilla DeAngelo. He smiled at this and held his arms apart in a questioning gesture.

"How can I help you?"

"You don't have to talk to me, Mr. Sullivan, but I'd like to ask you about Wilfred Taylor. I've heard a lot of stuff over the last few days and you would be the one to set me straight."

Old Bob looked at me carefully, taking me in: up and down my wrinkled and dirty clothes, at my face that had not been shaved in several days, and my hair stiff with blood that still had the kink of the hospital couch in it. He smiled.

"You look like you've put on some miles. Would you like something to eat?" He stepped back and led me to his kitchen.

When he walked in, he chased some kids out of the refrigerator where they were bickering about an ice-cream sandwich. It registered on me for the first time that it must be a weekend, for the kids were out of school.

"Grandkids," he explained. "I'm sorry. Here . . . sit." He pulled out a chair, then turned and took a ham out of the refrigerator and started cutting.

I sat awkwardly on a wooden kitchen stool with a padded

leather seat, fingering an apple resting in a basket. He motioned with the tip of his knife to "Go ahead, have one if you like," and stupidly I took a bite and started talking.

"Since Senator Taylor died last week, I've heard several theories that say you were involved in the events surrounding his death."

"How so?" He placed a thick pink slab of ham in a frying pan and set the frying pan on the stove.

I put the apple down. "They say you had been blackmailed by Taylor over the years. They say you were involved in trying to pressure him in order to keep your grandson in your family's custody. They say you were in the Mafia and are now in the witness protection program."

Bob Sullivan turned to me with a stern look, then looked down into the open drawer in front of him. "You like wheat bread?"

"Yes, that would be fine."

"Scrambled eggs okay? They're fresh."

"Perfect."

He took out the carton of eggs and began cracking them into a red glass bowl.

"Let's see. How can I help you? Yes, I had asked the Senator if he could help Robert keep custody of Young Bob. This was early on. Then I changed my mind." Here he made a comical expression and moved the fork in the air in a circular motion indicating some confusion. "I saw that it was useless to meddle because it just kept compounding the problem. But"— he began beating the eggs again—"no, I am not in the witness protection program. But yes, I was associated with organized crime. Years ago I was an accountant for a family that ran what I thought was a large dry-cleaning business. Eventually, I found out that it was not. I was arrested. I testified against some of my employers but I still went to jail. When I got out of jail I moved to Alaska. This was as far away as I could imagine. I changed my name to Sullivan here in Juneau. I claimed to be Irish. You can check the court records on my old life. It is listed under Profieta."

He took the spatula down from the rack above the stove and flipped the eggs. With his free hand he poured me a glass of juice. "If I had been in the program, you wouldn't find any records. The government has never given me any protection, Mr. Younger. If they were discreet about my past it was to protect themselves in whatever dealings they had with me."

"Did the Senator know about your past?"

He nodded down into the eggs. "Yes, he did. Wilfred learned about it as a federal prosecutor. Law enforcement always kept track of me. But I've been straight all my time here in Alaska. As for blackmailing me: no, not in the strictest sense. I could always say no to his propositions. Wilfred was a persuasive man, but in the end it was always more advantageous for me to help him out than it was to fight him. He was powerful. He could make things happen for me, in the union, in any other business I got involved in. It is not all that sinister for businesspeople to develop friendships with politicians. Well, maybe it is sometimes sinister, but I suppose that depends on your viewpoint. Wilfred was not a heavy player. No matter what the gossip was about him. There are many out there who are much worse."

"Was the Senator blackmailing any other important businessmen?"

He set the plate in front of me: Eggs, toast, and ham. He had even cut the apple into slices and flecked them with cinnamon. "No worse than what is the standard practice. I'm telling you the truth, Mr. Younger. He wasn't a gangster. I've met some in my time and he didn't have the temperament."

"Then why the secrecy about his files? Why shred the papers after his death?" I raised the first forkful to my mouth.

"Do you know what it really is?"

I paused and shook my head, waiting.

"Sex. Wilfred Taylor had been sleeping with everybody in the capital. His wife Barbara was frantic everything was going to come out."

The eggs were wonderful, as if I could taste the flavor of summer, finally. I sipped the orange juice and thought of the cabdriver who reminded me that this case was about sex.

"But surely he wouldn't have had to turn over anything about his romantic affairs in a Freedom of Information Act request?"

Old Bob Sullivan sat down opposite me. "I don't know if this holds true in your experience, Mr. Younger, but I've found that for many men sex makes them a little crazy. Wilfred was like that. He was a predator. In fact, when news of his death reached all of us we assumed it had to do with an affair. He scattered references to his love life everywhere in his writings.

He bragged about it in letters and memos. He invited women on all of his trips. They sat in the gallery, and met him in the gym. He worked with them, ate with them, flirted with them and slept with them. I don't think he had a relationship with a woman that wasn't in some way sexual. That's what he was hiding. That's what his people were trying to hide for him."

"But why would the feds be involved with shredding his papers? Getting involved in the investigation into his death?"

Sullivan smiled. "That is a funny part. You see, I've heard these rumors too. Those men in the suits. They weren't federal agents."

"Who were they?"

"They worked for Barbara Taylor. She hired members of their church."

"Their church? Come on."

"After Wilfred fell down those stairs Barbara took over. She didn't want his papers going anywhere. She arranged to have the church deacons come in. They showed up at the office. They wore their dark suits. They sat in on police interviews, particularly with female witnesses. They insisted no tapes be made but the cops didn't listen to them and made the tapes anyway. Most people assumed they were some type of federal officials. The Senator's top staff knew who they were but the people on the outside just went along thinking they were cops."

I ate for a while in silence. The juice was sweet and I added a touch more pepper to the eggs. Through the kitchen window I could hear the chant of the girls skipping rope. Robert Sullivan the First said, "Don't you think it's interesting, Mr. Younger, that when simple things happen in complex times everything looks sinister?"

I paused and looked at Old Bob. He was smiling broadly. I said to him, "I'll have to think about that. It's easier to believe in a conspiracy."

He sipped his coffee. "Conspiracies do exist, as you know. Groups of people do execute and cover up complex plans. This is largely how the government operates." He smiled and nodded at my empty plate. I shook my head no. He sighed.

"But all kidding aside, Mr. Younger, if this is a conspiracy, it is the most common kind. It is a conspiracy of flawed people following their most basic desires. This is nothing but a custody case. Priscilla and my son married young, for bad reasons. They compounded their mistakes through their child. People who loved them tried to intervene but failed. Just a custody case. It's that simple . . . and that complex."

He looked down at my empty plate. "If there is anything sinister . . . or complicating, it is that I never told the whole truth to my family." He got to his feet, took my plate and put it in the sink. "Robert was an infant when we moved here. I never told my son the whole truth. I never told him we were Italian, for instance. I think he always suspected. I don't think you can hide ancestry easily. I've always suspected my deception wasn't good for Robert. I think it made him a little . . . crazy. It may have been hard for him to be a father, probably because I wasn't . . ." His voice trailed off. We both listened to the music of children skipping rope. In the alder trees a varied thrush began to sing.

"Mr. Sullivan, will you tell me how the Senator died? Was it purely an accident?"

"Ask Harrison Teller. He was there that night."

"Teller was there? How do you know?"

"Barbara Taylor told me. She hired Teller in the first place."

"The Senator's wife hired Teller?"

"Sure. Barbara was terrified that this problem with Priscilla was going to expose the Senator's private affairs. She persuaded the Senator to hire Teller to fix the problem, to make Priscilla go away. Teller started in on that working with all the members of the family. And as you know it got very complex."

I nodded and tried to clear my mind.

"Wilfred Taylor called me in a panic several times the day he died. He wanted me to meet with Priscilla to get the heat off of him. Robert had apparently assaulted some private eye in Seattle. . . ." Old Bob stopped and pointed his index finger at me in surprise when he made the connection. Then he continued, "Anyway, Wilfred was afraid of Teller and this man he had hired to bring the boy up from Seattle. Wilfred was worried the whole mess was going to get into the papers. Priscilla was threatening to turn up any dirt she could find on him. Barbara was threatening to leave him. He wanted to appease them both. I knew better than to get directly involved. When he called I told him I'd meet with him and then I didn't go. I had already instructed Robert to go along with Teller and give Young Bob up to the sister, at least for a while. I called Wilfred's office about ten o'clock that night. Teller answered. I could hear Priscilla and Wilfred arguing in the background. I said I wasn't coming to the meeting. Teller said he would take care of it and he hung up.

"After Priscilla was arrested, Barbara and I both put up the money for her bond. Even though Barbara Taylor wanted everything about her husband's affairs kept quiet she didn't want to see that girl get saddled with the blame. She gave instructions to Teller."

Old Bob held his arms out wide in a gesture of exasperation. "Hell, when Robert called the other night from Tenakee and needed the money we didn't ask questions. I went to the bank early that morning and sent my grandson down to the hotel to give it to that young lawyer."

"You're both so sure Priscilla didn't kill him?"

Old Bob smiled. "Barbara said any woman who murdered Wilfred would have some compelling reason."

Bob Sullivan chuckled sadly. "I suppose you're going to want confirmation on my story," he said as we walked to the door. "Start with the court records, Mr. Younger. The old ones I think are on microfilm. My name change is there. Public record. Look carefully at my old records. I fooled around with my Social Security number a few times. People rarely check on those things. I thought it would muddy the water. I was hardly given a new secret identity. My criminal history is public record in New York, but they've probably lost those records by now, if I know New York. About the Senator, ask Teller; he knew. And if any of this doesn't pan out the way I've said, come back and talk to me. I'll answer any questions I can." We shook hands and kept shaking them as he added, "I suppose it's selfish, but I want you to believe me. I'm not happy about my past. I'd rather it wasn't common knowledge but it's better that it come out than have this full-blown conspiracy about me and Wilfred become lore."

He walked me to the door. In his driveway, a teenage boy leaned against the hood of a reconditioned red Impala. Bob Sullivan motioned to him. "Tom, take this gentleman downtown in that fancy chariot of yours. Then come right back. I'm going to go down to the hospital." The kid smiled and leapt to the driver's seat. Sullivan turned to me. "Robert called me. He told me about the accident." He shrugged his shoulders as a man does who has learned to accept fate. "You know, Mr. Younger, I think Robert does love that little boy."

"One last question. I'm sorry, but was Jane Marie trying to steal Young Bob away from Priscilla and Robert?"

He looked out toward the glacier. "No. We tried to make peace between Robert and his wife. Jane Marie tried, and I tried. But . . . peace was hard to find in that family. I knew the girls' father, you know. Albert DeAngelo was a good man. He loved fun and good talk. When his son died he almost went crazy. When the old man drowned, we accepted it. I don't know, but somehow Jane Marie accepted it. I think she has a lot of strength and . . . optimism. She'd be good for that little boy. I was the one who suggested that she have temporary custody."

Old Bob waved as the teenage boy backed the Impala slowly out the driveway. Once we were out of sight of the house, the kid slammed the tape player to nosebleed levels and accelerated the two miles to the first traffic light.

The next day I was still humming riffs from Green Day as I sat next to Jane Marie waiting to be let off the jet in Fairbanks.

Spring in Fairbanks brings a mania that cannot be countered by the most powerful drugs. When we stepped out of the terminal I was immediately bound by floating threads. The sky was a huge dome of blue. The air was dry and had the taste of ice and dirt. There were mounds of muddy snow in the parking lot leaking streams into puddles and lakes around the plugged gutters but rising above the snow were birch trees whose new leaves glinted like money. The air was sixty degrees and a lungful felt like my first breath. Compared to the interior, living in southeastern Alaska is like living underground. It may be twenty below tomorrow, but right now it is warm. I wanted to take off my clothes and lie on a rock. Jane Marie pulled me into the cab.

The day before, in Juneau, I had checked the court files and taken a shower in a judge's bathroom. The Profieta file was in the judge's chambers and I flipped through my copy while I used the judge's line that had an extension in the bathroom. I knew the judges were all in court and their clerks would never walk in on the sound of the shower.

I had walked down to the waterfront and asked about Gunk. He wasn't around. He wasn't in custody. He wasn't at the flophouses or the expected crash pads. The one trooper who would talk to me held his palms up and smiled as if he couldn't quite understand my words. "We don't have him, Cecil. He's free to go where he wants."

I had called my friend in Fairbanks who always dressed so well. She was now a grant writer for some arts organization and, yes, she did think that Harrison Teller would be at his usual riverside bar all afternoon. I was thinking about my friend's backless pumps as our taxi sprayed a curtain of muddy water on a pedestrian on the way toward the bar.

Teller was sitting at a table on the lowest deck near the Tanana River. There was a large pitcher of sangria and two glasses on the table. He sat next to a small wiry woman with gray-blond hair. Barbara Taylor was wearing cutoff shorts, an orange tank top, and mud boots. Her parka was draped over the back of her chair. Teller wore his long wool coat and was balancing his felt hat on the toe of his boot. He took off his Wayfarers as we came down the steps.

"Old home week," he said, and put the sunglasses back on.

We pulled up chairs and Teller pointed over to his companion.

"Did you ever meet Barbara? We've been talking about what to do with her husband's estate. I've advised her to buy a fishing lodge in Belize. What do you think?"

"Do it," I said.

THE MUSIC OF WHAT HAPPENS

Barbara Taylor took off her own glasses and considered the two of us with a distant and deeply stoned gaze. Jane Marie added, "I've heard the snorkeling is wonderful there. You might want to consider that for your guests."

Barbara stared at us as if we had fallen out of the sky and her pause let us listen to the chunks of ice colliding in the fast-moving current outside the bar railings.

"Thanks for the tip," she said. Then, working a wobbly stare on Teller she continued, "Listen, I'm going back to the office. I don't know, I might make some calls or something." She stood up and balanced her weight on Teller's shoulder. Her hand lingered on his cheek.

"Okay." Teller waved her hand away absently. "I'll be by later. Listen, you might want to cover up. You look a little pink."

Barbara Taylor poked at the skin on her chest. The impression of her finger lingered white on the angry red. She poured another glass of wine, gunned it down and wiped her mouth with the sleeve of her parka. "Yeah, it'll be fine." She walked away, tipping over her glass. A crow hopped off the rail of the bar and picked up the slice of orange sitting in the spilled ice cubes.

"She's a great client," Teller said. "But she drinks a bit too much." He poured himself another glass of the sweet wine.

Then he set his sunglasses on the table and leaned back in his chair. "Okay. What are you two sleuths up to? Didn't the DA's office dismiss?"

"He's getting close to it. You know why?"

He took a long drink, then said, "He had a dog-shit case."

I started to argue with him. "Priscilla confessed to the arresting officer. She had a long-standing hatred of the Senator. She publicly accused him of conspiring to steal her son. She had a claim of self-defense but not if she was attacking him in his own office. They've taken worse cases to trial, especially if there is a lot of press. I would really like to know what the DA told you."

Teller sat quietly and looked out on the Tanana River. In the distance, clouds were drifting over the plain and we could see their shadows moving over the hills. He rattled the ice in his glass. The crow bobbed his head on the nearby railing.

"It's not what the DA told me, Younger. It's what I told him."

"Which was?"

Teller watched the muddy river water slip by against the bank. "I told him Gunk did it."

A small riverboat came floating down the river. I could hear chunks of ice booming against its steel hull. Teller leaned forward toward the table speaking to the spilled wine.

"The DA was happy with that. That Gunk is so fucking ugly he'd indict himself."

I watched the figures approaching in the riverboat. Three men sitting on coolers. Another in the back driving and adjusting a blue tarp covering the stern.

I poured Teller another drink. "What happened?"

Teller took the glass and drank it down, then poured another from the pitcher. An ugly plum flopped into the glass and was lost in the bloody-looking wine.

"You know, Younger, I hate politicians. They are so impolite."

The crow kept bobbing on the rail, looking at the fruit in Teller's glass. The riverboat kept drifting down. Teller kept talking. "The Senator promised he would get me back in the Bar. I could practice law again. I could talk to a jury. I'd do anything. . . . This guy . . . this Senator . . . he was the worst kind of punk. He was always whining about his confidential materials. Jesus Christ, everybody knew he was an ass-grabber. No one would have given a thought to his goddamn papers, except his wife, I guess."

Teller flipped a piece of apple to the crow. "All I did was make some calls. Gunk owes me big-time. He used to ride with some of my old clients. He convinced Robert Sullivan to bring Young Bob back to Juneau. But before we got this all straightened out, Priscilla comes storming over to Juneau demanding to have the papers and screaming for the 'whole truth.' She is possessed. I try to explain that she's going to get her kid back. I'm saying anything just to get her to shut up. But that wasn't good enough. She wanted the evidence of a horrible conspiracy and she was not leaving without it. Wilfred whined at me to throw her out. When she wouldn't go, I started to walk away. I'm halfway down the stairs and I heard the ruckus."

Teller lifted his head up slightly and looked at me. He

took another drink and his eyes returned to the river. "He was beating her. Her arms were up over her face and she was cowering and screaming at him. He hits her with his open hand a few times, then she tries to bite him and he gets her with a fist in the eye. He yells at her that if she wants it this way he'll act like a gangster. She drops to the floor, covering her head, screaming. I step between them and try to lead him away. He is babbling about disrespect and 'you people' not appreciating his hard work and that kind of shit. Then he slaps me."

The crow hopped near his elbow and Teller smiled and held out another bit of the wine-soaked apple. "So I killed him," he said.

The crow gathered itself briefly, then flew from the deck over the muddy water. It labored with the apple for a few strokes of its wings but landed on the other bank. The riverboat was drifting past us. The man on the stern started to lift up the blue tarp. Teller held his palm up to shade eyes that looked red and suddenly tired.

"Did he slip and hit his head?" Jane Marie said softly, giving him the out.

Teller leaned back so his tired eyes could take her in. He was unsteady in his chair. "I'm a trial lawyer. I help people who have trouble. I mean, if this guy had robbed a liquor store and killed some kids I would have helped him. I would have. I would have listened to his whining then. But he didn't have trouble, he was just going to be embarrassed. Embarrassed, for chrissake. The law doesn't protect you from being embarrassed.

This guy was a bully but he didn't have the guts to be a real criminal. He needed a fixer. He treated me like his goddamn pet.''

He shook his head sadly and put the square sunglasses back on. Out of the corner of my eye I could see the figure of one of the men on the riverboat. He was dressed in black and was pointing at something.

Teller said, ''Taylor slapped me again and I threw him down the stairs. I threw him hard. I knew what I was doing. Gunk saw it all. His little play for money in Tenakee was just his way of putting the squeeze on me. Priscilla didn't see anything because she was still on the floor, covering her head, crying.''

Back inside the bar a waitress dropped a tray of glasses. Teller looked vaguely toward the crashing sound. ''But I don't think Priscilla was very sorry he was dead.'' He smiled to himself.

Jane Marie drank a glass of wine. The river ice clicked and skidded against the banks. The shadow of a cloud passed over. I was facing Teller, who was watching something behind my back. He stood up suddenly. He held his hands up as if waving. He looked as if he were going to laugh. I heard a pop and the pitcher of sangria sitting next to me exploded. I remember the rattling sound of shots as Jane Marie grabbed me and we rolled under the table. Red wine dripped down on our backs. I squirmed over decking covered in glass shards to see the riverboat speed out of sight. I could see a large white man wearing a black leather vest with a patch sewn across the back. He was putting a rifle back under the tarp.

People were yelling and I heard the sound of feet pounding on the deck. I pulled myself up and went to where Harrison Teller was lying backward over his broken chair. I rolled him over. His shirtfront was sticky with blood. His sunglasses were broken, the dark glass caught in his beard. His coat was stained with wine. He looked at me as if I were somewhere in the distance and his pale lips trembled.

"I need to get to court," he said and he closed his eyes.

THE MUSIC OF WHAT HAPPENS

12

Teller didn't die. He took a shot to the stomach and the bullet lodged in his spine. I have heard he was readmitted to the Bar and has outfitted his office in Fairbanks to accommodate his wheelchair.

Gunk may have gone to Belize with Mrs. Taylor, for all I know. He never turned up in Alaska. The Fairbanks police questioned some of the local bikers about the shooting at the riverside bar, but they never made any arrests. A biker shooting at Harrison Teller was hardly an infraction of the law in the eyes of the Fairbanks District Attorney, particularly because they didn't kill him.

The grand jury convened in the death of Senator Wilfred Taylor but they never returned an indictment. Several of the witnesses were unavailable, so there was no one to contradict Priscilla's sworn testimony that it was an accidental slip-and-fall.

Over the months that followed I heard all kinds of stories

about the case. I heard from a court clerk that Harrison Teller was having an affair with the Senator's wife and they had plotted to kill him together. I heard from an investigator for the Public Defender that Priscilla's family bought off the District Attorney.

Some of the stories were sillier than others. Some even had the heft of plausibility. But most weren't really stories at all, but more like gossip: the mind throwing out disjointed ideas in an attempt to make sense of the world.

I never took any more of the antidepressants. My psychiatrist has been telling me I probably never had any neurological damage. Although he still thinks I might be subject to weird brain shit, my biggest problems are an addictive personality and a florid imagination. He suggested I take up salmon fishing.

People still claim I'm a lousy investigator, and that could be accurate, but I always like hearing people talk and there is not one story I won't listen to. Every story, even the most calculated lie, has some phrase of music in it. So, that summer when I was building a whale-watching camp in Sitka Sound, Toddy asked me how I ever knew the truth about anything.

I was standing on a ladder; the wind freshening from the north was rare and warm with the smell of summer. Toddy was sitting reading an encyclopedia on the edge of the tent platform. The pup, Wendell, was chewing on the tip of Toddy's shoe when he asked his question and I started to say something clever about consistency and predictability but I stopped.

"I don't know," I said lamely.

Toddy looked up at me with his comical dazed expression,

his eyeballs enlarged and swimming behind his glasses. "What if there is no Heaven, Cecil?" His voice cracked and he suddenly looked frightened. I climbed down the ladder and sat next to my roommate.

"If there is no Heaven, Todd, then maybe this is Heaven."

I gestured to the small island we were standing on. I held my hands out to the hemlock trees sheltering the duff of moss and fallen needles down to the water. Toddy smiled but he wouldn't let me off the hook.

"How can this be Heaven? Where are all the dead people?"

I paused. I wanted to brush him off. I didn't want to talk about death on a beautiful day. But I couldn't brush Todd off because I love him so much.

"Listen," I said, starting to get angry, "I don't know. I don't know where all the dead people are."

The water lapped on the cobbles and wind blustered in the trees. A boat was running in the distance; the gulls were squabbling over our food scraps on the beach. We sat there for a while listening to the music of what happened, which was the only thing we could do under the circumstances.

"Are you mad at me, Cecil?"

"No," I said. "Are you mad at me for not knowing?" I asked stupidly.

Toddy smiled. Wendell had taken Todd's shoe off and was tearing around our campsite with it in his mouth. Todd punched me on the arm, dismissing me as if I were to be pitied.

"Naw," he said, slamming down his encyclopedia. "Actually, I'm glad you don't." And he ran off to retrieve Wendell and his shoe. He was humming as he chased his wild pet into the thicket.

It was late summer by the time we got the tent platform built on Mr. Tom's island in Sitka Sound. Mr. Tom was a Tlingit man and this island was his ancestral garden place. He was letting Jane Marie build a temporary camp as a base for when the humpbacks gathered in the fall. He wanted us to salvage the materials from the World War II bunkers and try to make something useful of them.

Robert and Priscilla's honeymoon didn't last and finally they agreed to let Jane Marie be the third-party custodian of their son while they kept working on the terms of their divorce. Young Bob was fitted with a prosthetic device but he fussed and fumbled with it, mostly because it itched on the places where the skin had been grafted on his arm. He became more and more comfortable with it as the summer wore on. He had spent several weeks on the island nosing around tide pools and staying up late watching the night sky.

I sat on the tent platform watching Todd chase after Wendell, and started to think of the stars two nights before. I had walked alone on the gravel beach. Jane Marie, Toddy and Young Bob were all asleep, Wendell was under the tent platform. The sun had set at ten o'clock but I had spent several more hours sharpening my tools and reading the books I had started in the winter. I looked up into the summer sky and in a strange moment I saw the stars as long strings of light funneling down in a great sheltering tent. In that moment I thought I saw their patterns: the ancient literature of stars, common to all people who share this night. I held up my hands to point. I wanted to show them to Toddy or Jane Marie. But then I heard the clang of a bell buoy in the distance and in that moment I lost it. When I looked up again I was alone in the randomness of starlight.

After Todd had disappeared in the brush I looked down to the narrow beach to where Young Bob was playing with a friend he had invited to stay the night. His friend Finn was a boy from town. He had light brown hair and flashing eyes that made me smile even when he was making mischief. I finished tacking down the plastic sheeting on the large funnel system that we would use to trap rain. I could hear them squabbling. Young Bob and his friend were playing with a pet mouse the boy had brought with him.

Young Bob called up to me, "Cecil, Finn says he is half human being and half mouse. Is that true?"

"It could be," I said. "What part of him is mouse?"

Finn looked up and scowled at me with impatience. "I said that I had a mouse personality. That's what I said."

Young Bob looked at him with healthy skepticism. His face was scarred, his arm was wrapped and laid against his side in a hospital sling. The sling had superheroes drawn along the edges.

I yelled down to them, "I think it could be true, buddy boy. He kind of acts like a mouse, don't you think?"

With that both boys got down on their knees and squeaked around in the sand, herding the actual mouse, the timid mouse, in front of them.

Jane Marie and Priscilla came in on the skiff. Jane Marie pulled the little boat up on the beach and walked to the tent platform near where I was getting off the ladder. Priscilla helped her. The two sisters had reached an agreement with Robert and with each other. Although Dickie had helped them write it up and the formal agreement was very detailed in its specifics, the main thrust of it was that both Jane Marie and Young Bob would stay in Sitka, Robert Sullivan would have certain visitation rights and all parties were to keep the craziness to a minimum. And on this beautiful, sunny day I was almost hopeful that it would work. Priscilla was pretty and relaxed, tripping up the beach after the two boys. Jane Marie came toward me.

"There's a mother and a calf out by Silver Bay. Have you seen anything pass by here?"

I shook my head no. She started to make a sandwich. I set my tools down and stood next to her in the tent. The air was a warm slurry of scents from the ocean and the drying rot of rain forest. The wind pumped the old canvas tent flaps with an easy popping sound.

"What a day," she said, and handed me a salmon sandwich. "Was it this nice last year?" I told her it was, but truthfully I didn't remember. Todd and Priscilla came up. Toddy cleared his throat.

"Cecil, I was considering mounting an expedition to explore the other side of the island. I wanted to see if there was anything new washed ashore that perhaps we could use in the construction.''

"I think that would be fine," I said. And in moments the arguing started, with Priscilla not wanting to go, but if she did go she wasn't going to go the way Todd wanted. Todd didn't think the pet mouse should come, but Young Bob and Finn were resisting all efforts to make him stay. After some negotiations the mouse stayed in his plastic container with the holes punched in the top and the entire entourage headed down the beach.

After a few moments I took Jane Marie's shirt off and she unzipped both sleeping bags on the cot. I kissed her and gently rubbed my hands down the skin of her belly, inhaling the wonderful smell of her mixed with the wind off the water that had blown unobstructed across the Gulf of Alaska. As we lay in the daylight touching and nipping at each other we could hear the others bickering off in the trees.

An hour later she looked up to see a whale surface a quarter mile past the cove. She started to get up for her binoculars but I pulled her back. We had been very lucky that day and we needed to harbor that luck if we were going to make Heaven perfect.

I told her this, and she laughed, but I think she believed me.